Until XOXO
invent whatever
you want
from here
if it
inspires
you

Drums
of the Winged Carrier 2020

Aryana

Cover design features
original artwork by Aryana

PUBLISH AMERICA

PublishAmerica
Baltimore

049

ISBN: 1-4241-3133-2
PUBLISHED BY PUBLISHAMERICA, LLLP
www.publishamerica.com
Baltimore

Printed in the United States of America

DEDICATION

For all who dream of a greater tomorrow

It will burn you at the start
As if to winds you were bare
Then fall deeply into your heart
Like a stone in the water's lair.

—*Wingmakers*

INTRODUCTION

Billions of people open their eyes and rise every morning to engage the labyrinth of life that they have often unconsciously crafted and move through till at day's end they return to their beds, close their eyes and sleep once more. Life unfolds this way for most engaged in work, family and observing the static world around them. Moments that break this silent, snail—like circular march occur when an original thought breaks these barriers to change and in a moment unfolds. Faces of friends appear different somehow as does the sky at dusk that is finally noticed as more relevant to life experience than reading one's e—mail inbox. The former likely provides greater inspiration to feed the little thought of originality that mysteriously appeared in one's day.

Commuting through cities I have noticed *the sky is falling* all around us as I wait for the traffic signal to change and turn off my air vents so as not to accentuate the odor of toxic chemicals moving into my breathing space. Faces of drivers in cars around me seem oblivious to what I have noticed or perhaps they have just accepted this as the normal state of affairs. I stopped reading the paper long ago because I began to withdraw from my own circular march that ended at the same point where it began; without meaningful progress. Most I read in the news represented a static world where problems are identified and highlighted creating anxiety, but no editorials of brilliant thought shone through the *facts* that would give hope to the readers consuming their daily dose of news. I had begun to insist on elongating my own moments of unique contemplations because I grew bored living a curved predictability. I began to awaken a child—like explorer within that questioned everything and wanted to grow up more meaningfully productive than my former self. Years passed that through my feeding of this new mind that I will term the divine intelligence within, many innovative ideas came forth from my being that changed the nature of my work and every aspect of my life. Exploration of consciousness afforded me personal experiences that some would term supernatural but to me are a normal expansion of mind and spirit in daily life.

I decided to craft the fruits of my journey into a story that would honor quiet, genius minds alive in pockets of simple people who embrace their individuality and creativity. I had met a few who knew what I know; that the mirror of reality all around us *is* our mind and what we think. This in turn affects the world around us that can be an astoundingly powerful force of change upon a static reality of Earth's problems if everyone knows the power of a greater mind. Progressive studies conducted by scientists in the way that the quantum field is engaged by the observer have already proven this. Solutions to a looming energy crisis are being born in the minds of a handful of scientists with ideas that often surpass current progress of their own area of science. This has made it difficult for them to have their concepts accepted by their peers and to raise funds that would allow beneficial, technological innovations to move forward. Unfortunately the "closed circuit" march has affected every area of our society including influential groups of people that make important decisions affecting everyone. In order to support change and the flow of new mind that can successfully improve life on our planet each person embracing his own moments of individual creativity is necessary. That would serve to change the model of our society from consuming what has already been accomplished to supporting a creative drive within everyone that adds genius and diversity to goods, services, political platforms, education and virtually all areas of life.

I have had the privilege as provided by the divine intelligence within me to remotely view a timeline where this has already occurred. The story you are about to read is a fictitious rendering of what I have seen and some of the phenomenon within the following pages I have personally experienced. Anything is possible within the quantum field of potentials and all have inherited the right to consciously create from it. As a collective, whatever our mind is on the most will ultimately become reflected in the way life unfolds on our planet. Each person has the opportunity to remember how influential his voice is when it breaks out in the song of personal expression applied to creating a meaningful destiny that is not determined by the stars.

A cast of eclectic characters awaits to take you on a journey into the future where time is not linear and the movement of spirit ascends within all to the drumbeat of hearts that never relinquish freedom.

ONE

Illuminated rain fell from lavender clouds onto a magenta ground electrified with blue and peacock hues. Slowly an enfolded, glowing form began to emerge from the earth. It became more solid and its back began to rise and fall with breath. Ethereal rain glistened on the female beings iridescent, rainbow colored skin. Larina sat up and opened shockingly beautiful, metallic colored eyes. Images flooded her mind of where she was to go. She knew it was a place very far away from her world that had evolved beyond limited consciousness and a tumultuous history.

Larina arose, tall and resplendent in dazzling color and extended her arm, pointing her aquamarine finger. Instantly a pool of brilliant plasma appeared in the air. As she focused her mind the mirage like portal continued to form, radiating from a complex geometric grid pattern. With lightning speed a set of coordinates flashed across the grid and she stepped through the portal which instantly closed and disappeared in a final flare of light.

Dawn in this place pierced the vibrant, swirling gaseous atmosphere with a violet sun. As it rose it washed over tepid pools of waters with a diamond reflection of spectral hues. A gnarled tree covered in snake smooth bark of turquoise and intermittent yellows reached up to the moving heavens. Another small tree next to it began to move and morphed into a male being. His copper eyes looked off in the direction where Larina had disappeared. He

11

closed his eyes and followed her presence with his mind, his silvery blue lips curving in a smile.

A red curl lay across a sleeping child's pale, freckled cheek gently moving with her rhythmic breath. She dreamed of orange skies on her home planet and lightning quick, sleek anatoas, a native creature, darting and morphing through treetops. Glistening waters carried her and her people deep through the underwater portals to indescribable worlds where they danced and changed shape in symphonic frequencies. Larina began to stir and slowly green eyes squinted at a sunlit window. For a moment she lay there snuggled in her covers and took in her surroundings on Earth. Her new body's DNA continued to respond to the code activated by the earth's electro magnetic field and adapted to the local environment. The year was now 2019 and her mind downloaded the remainder of the history and experiences of Earth from the grid. Thousands of places and life forms she had visited and become as an ancient being. Her race the Tribe of the Rainbow Light represented a genetic, living library of the multiverse. They could exist in any frequency an in any form down to the denser realities. Their DNA would respond to the vibrational signature of the location they arrived at and metamorphosis to genetically become the species of that particular world. In this seamless design they were virtually undetectable and indistinguishable form the local population they assisted.

Larina arose from her bed and went down the stairs to the little kitchen where John Willowby sat reading the paper and drinking his coffee. This ordinary looking man with perpetually disheveled hair was one of the most brilliant scientists on the planet. She noticed he looked rested. "Good morning John," She said softly.

"Good morning Jena," he replied with a warm smile referring to her earth name.

She had first appeared to John back in time in the nuclear winter of 2009 in Canada when the great cataclysms had begun. He had retreated to his log cabin in the woods and sustained himself there to the best of his ability but his food stores had run out and now he was living off whatever he could forage or kill. John was one of a handful of people who understood scalar electromagnetic weapons and their risks. He understood the technology, had anticipated its use and prepared.

When Jena appeared to him out of nowhere as a little girl of about ten years of age, wearing a hooded, silver parka, John had thought that he was hallucinating. She simply looked at him and said, "I lost my parents." He immediately took her in, gave her what little food he had to spare and at day's end he put her to bed in his little cabin on a simple cot. In the middle of the night he sat up and saw her looking at him. She approached, took his hand in hers and suddenly the walls of the cabin began to dissolve as an enormous surge of energy jolted through his brain and entire body. A rosy golden lit atmosphere began to absorb his reality and electrify his mind with a thousand fold sharpened awareness. Then he lost consciousness.

Aboard the great ship Lycos John's body floated in an emanation of electric blue matrix lines of light. A tall, beautiful man with a white beard and an elongated skull stood by the grid structure with Larina. "He has lost much weight and is malnourished." His words echoed inside her mind. Larina now wore her native form once more.

She looked at the being with her animated, metallic eyes and mentally replied, "we have some work to do here before we can send him forward."

John accepted that he had taken Jena in after the death of her parents and she stayed with him over the two months since he experienced the time shift from 2009 to 2019. He continued to develop his work but now enjoyed the fruits of his mind as it would have evolved in linear time by experiencing the technological breakthroughs he created.

Jena put some bread into the patisserie rond and watched as it turned silently and perfectly browned her toast in seconds. She inserted an orange into the opening on the side of it and flipped up the little window on the bottom front panel to reveal a glass of freshly squeezed juice.

John was vitally important because he had become a viable link to advanced technologies that the previous governments had successfully kept from the general population. He had been through a lot of turmoil and oppression before the time of the great cataclysms when all and any breakthrough in energy technology of a substantial nature was militarized and classified. Even though he had worked for the government before retiring they still routinely hassled and monitored him. Private industry fueled his only hope for getting vital technologies out with independent funding but the general suppressive program of the government against the release of such innovations made it an uphill climb to educate the public at large about the possibilities. People in the times before the cataclysms were a less enlightened society; much needed interest becoming involved with the development of eco friendly technologies did not exist. Such endeavors of mind and spirit were simply not contemplated by the general population but embraced by small pockets of innovative thinkers.

John stood up from the table, ran a hand through his unruly hair and kissed Jena on the forehead. "Well I had better get myself over to my meeting, you enjoy your day off school and I'll bring something special back for our supper," John said as he put on his coat to leave.

He was on his way to meet with Illuminated Members (IM's) from the Council of Illuminated Vision (CIV). He had been approached by the council to oversee sustainable technological development, application and policy in collaboration with other scientists. After suffering years of suppression in promoting his theories finally his contribution would be realized.

CIV Central officially functioned at the old Parliament building in Olympia, Washington. A devastating earthquake had badly damaged the White House and left the Pentagon in rubble. Other than some structural renovations and modifications the CIV Central building remained unchanged.

John drove his Avian 4X4 powered by hydrogen fuel cell technology. An light alloy made up the frame of the car reducing the load on the engine substantially. A moratorium on petrol products had been applied since part of the earth's magnetic field de—stabilization had been caused by excessive oil drilling and extraction. Truly innovative technologies emerged in a veritable boom of research and development of alternative energy sources. John's specialty, extracting energy from the vacuum, was what the CIV wanted to incorporate into new technologies for public use.

A soft hum issued from the Avian's quiet engine as John drove down the I—5 and approached Olympia. He took the turn off and arrived at CIV Central, parking his car and entering the building. The headquarters still emanated a timeless elegance and grandeur of its design. John entered the great hall, his footsteps echoed off the smooth marble floor to the vastly vaulted, domed ceiling. He announced himself at the reception area and took a seat. James Edwards, IM of Energy approached John and greeted him, shaking his hand. John followed him up the grand staircase through a long corridor to the oval shaped meeting room.

Since its inception the CIV operated as a radically progressive agency compared to any previous world government. It did not rule so much as it guided humanity and its progress. All decisions were approved by the people and full disclosure was given to the public of all visionary projects as dictated by their Mind Development Ranking (MDR). This meant that an MDR of one to four reflected each person's level of education, experience and contribution. The higher the personal ranking number the more access and input the citizen had in the CIV's vision and policy approval. Rather than having dated government elections after a term of experimental policy that often left much to be desired in its actual outcome and public satisfaction, disclosure was given to people. They had approval through a process that organized specific groups of people categorized by MDR. Citizens of the highest ranking reviewed more intricate issues, but ultimately everyone had a say.

Canada, the United States and Mexico had amalgamated into one nation and some of the IM's were former Canadians. North America became one of the new world sectors. Individual countries with borders were amalgamated into continental sectors. What had been the concept of the United Nations actually evolved into a unified world government, a grand Council of Illuminated Members that had branches extending across the different sectors but remained as a great unified tree of sovereign brotherhood. A golden plaque with an oak tree in the centre became the emblem of the World CIV. The words "A World United in Mind, Spirit and Vision" were embossed around the outside. The CIV had produced exact duplicates as gold coins that became collectable after gold ceased to be hoarded by the previous shadow organizations and governments.

Gold had always been plentiful on Earth and used extensively in the Egyptian culture for even for simple things like drinking cups. The illusion of its inflated value occurred with manipulation of this key resource. A super strong alloy had been blended to produce a newer, light weight version of coins in white, yellow and rose hues. In addition, everyone carried a round Sovereign Citizen Card (SCC card), valid in all world sectors, that had an embedded quantum chip. It combined personal identification with banking, shopping, vehicle licensing, MDR ranking, etc.

All branches of the World CIV met four times a year at the World CIV Centre in Vienna. This ensured the progress of all departments world wide and allowed for the integration of innovation from all sectors into the world policy platform. No borders existed that limited travel and trade between sectors. Goods and services now flowed freely and technology was globally released without restriction. Technologies that enhanced the development of mind, spirit and perfect ecological harmony boomed. Learning had drastically changed to support not only children but citizens of all ages. Through the innovation of a quantum brain chip which was injected into the base of the skull, knowledge could be downloaded into the mind and neurologically mapped. From basic skills like reading to understanding advanced physics or learning new languages, any information could be downloaded by the brain chips, sometimes through group electromagnetic programming, eliminating hours of traditional classroom learning. Children's schooling evolved into the experiential, conscious application of knowledge that was downloaded into the brain. In re—designing education all hoped for the effective creation of an enlightened population who had contributions of an exquisitely crafted mind to make to the world upon their graduation.

For the general public, updating one's knowledge and personal development garnered the reward of an elevation of MDR. The World CIV had made it a priority to make the brain chip technology and mind development accessible to all people. Effective elimination of poverty and drastic reduction of crime had resulted.

Two other IM's Richard Lonesbay, IM of Eco Sustainability and Samantha Rogers, IM of Health stood up to greet John and introduced themselves. "Please, John have a seat. We've really been looking forward to meeting you," Samantha said.

John took a seat at the round table. Samantha spoke, "we have a Scientific Advisory Group completed now and would like you to accept the head position. This is an unprecedented move to empower great minds that have brought us many gifts of scientific revelation and innovation to oversee and fine tune final vision and policy in the areas of eco sustainability, the application of energy, technological development, agriculture and health prior to releasing the packages to the public for vote.

Samantha handed John a hard copy of the Scientific Advisory Group project manual. "All the details of your proposed involvement and the function of the group are outlined in this document. If you can spare the time today, there is a quiet office at the end of the corridor where you can review this and then we can resume discussion."

"I would like that," said John.

Samantha rose and led John to the small office. "If you would like coffee or other refreshments just press three on the silver COM panel and someone will bring you a tray."

"Thank you," John replied and began going over the document.

TWO

Chantal Colombe loaded the holographic projector with the tiny laser diskette. The circular classroom of children chattered while they waited and finally the presentation began. It was a continuation of a documented record from the years leading up to the great cataclysms that had claimed many lives. The CIV of which Chantal was an Illuminated Member of Education and Cultural Evolution, had painstakingly compiled these records to inform future generations about what had occurred so that it would never be repeated again. Each week Chantal had visited the Rising Minds Centre for Learning and brought the next installment of the historical presentation. Today's segment was the last in the series.

"Quiet please," Chantal requested of the children and activated the hologram.

It came to life in the centre of the large, ivory classroom accompanied by surround sound.

"Last week we finished with viewing the events that had lead up to the destabilization of the earth's magnetic field through the abuse of the environment by the application of HAARP, and excessive drilling for oil. Today you are going to learn about the ecological and political instability that was caused by the world governments, the Illuminati and corporate power."

As Chantal spoke the holographic images that illustrated her words played out in the center of the room.

"Natural world resources continued to be depleted and the food chain suffered from ecologically unbalanced farming practices of crops and animals. Genetically engineered foods began to cause mutations in natural crops and upset nature's rhythms and processes. Toxicity in human beings and animals climbed and was augmented by improperly contained nanotechnology contaminating the environment and living organisms including humans causing increased illness and death. At the same time technologies that could have provided medical advancements and stabilized the environment were kept secret by world governments and developed for military application. The Illuminati that influenced governments and corporate business continued to believe that rationing natural resources which were becoming scarcer and controlling the money markets would avert global destabilization and Armageddon. With growing political corruption of world governing organizations and social unrest, secret weapons such as electromagnetic scalar technology and HAARP were used more frequently to cause earthquakes, and destabilization of the eco system resulted. Low frequencies used by the technology often resulted in mental disorientation. Depression, neurosis and crime rose to unprecedented levels in human history."

The holograph went blank as its photons whirled without purposeful display.

"To this day no one knows how our people moved forward six years but the earth's electromagnetic field was restabilized. Erratic weather patterns ceased and the gross mutations in agriculture were gone. Peace and a new way of life replaced the former more chaotic reality...." Chantal's voice trailed off and her last memory before she awakened to the restructured world haunted her.

She had been at a conference in Seattle when an almost deafening roar ripped through the air. The ground shook violently and the conference center's walls began to crack. Lights flickered, extinguished and the room came alive with panic. Something struck her head and she fell to her knees, her consciousness receded in a pinpoint to blackness.

In her next memory, which did not make sense in the linear sequence of events, she lay on a patch of grass outside the conference centre but it was no longer there. She watched as children now played in a park that spanned the area where the conference centre had stood. Cool hands gently rested on her temples and a high pitched sound droned behind her. The sun shone bright overhead and warmed her face. Someone was there with her but she could not see who. An electrical sensation surged through her brain and her lids fluttered as she watched images flashing through her mind at rapid speed.

Instantly she remembered what had happened.

A soft female voice spoke behind her as a blue, shimmering light filled Chantal's vision, "you are forward from these events now and living your new life with the rest. It is the year 2015. Not many of the others will know what you know."

The electrical surge overpowered her brain again and she saw her life from the perspective of no time and her role and life as an IM in the CIV as if she had always been this. She saw the dwelling where she lived, her acquaintances, and projects that she worked on with the CIV. An overwhelming wave of hope and renewal carried the population of the world in unprecedented achievement as a renaissance of mind and spirit unlike anything in the history of the earth rolled forward in full force. There were no other memories that connected what had happened from the time of the cataclysm to this reality as if she had literally jumped forward in time six years.

The soft voice continued, "one day you will your mind will open fully and understand this moment."

That event had occurred almost six years ago in linear time.

"Chantal," the child's voice broke her away from remembrance. "Is there more?"

Chantal stared at the blank hologram and inserted the next disk.

THREE

Julio Manderas stepped into Abraxas Tavern and took a window seat. He ordered a beer and gazed through the diagonally set window panes out at the gold colored, brick Sweet Shop across the street. An aroma that smelled like candied apples filled his nostrils. He knew he had arrived early for his lunch with Maya. Julio served as IM of Sector Building and Planning and had worked very closely with Maya Savanna, IM of Commerce and Trade over the past few years to conceptualize and build Evergreen Village. Creation of this magical place had been the dream of a handful of individuals since before the great cataclysms. Julio had moved to what used to be this small, unknown town to attend Initiates of the Sacred Rose mystery school. At the end of the twentieth century, it provided one of the only places of learning on Earth where a unique blend of science, philosophy and humanity's potential to become divinely powerful beings was taught.

Maya had become an adept master in her own right as had many of the initiates after years of unique training and study. These students had become some of the best minds in the world. While the rest of the population prioritized working long hours, raising children, taking vacation time and occasionally visiting the local church, the initiates learned how to become impeccable masters with brilliant, unlimited minds who did not search for their morality in religion. Though the intent of many religions was initially to honor the sacred aspects of life, most had succumbed to exerting power and suppression over people, especially women. No desire for an intermediary of any kind between the people and their God existed any longer.

Eighty graduates in total from Initiates of the Sacred Rose had become IM's. Six of them served the North American sector CIV: Chantal Colombe, Richard Lonesbay, Maya Savanna, Maya's husband Lorne Savanna and Julio. One of the first world wide efforts that had been implemented after the great cataclysms was the dismantling of world religions. All people approved and embraced this move. Through the implementation of the mass education quantum chip technology that stimulated certain brain and energetic centers, all had access to an opportunity given to the individual to develop a higher consciousness with greater potentials to connect to the divine intelligence within. The most popular and frequently consumed brain chip programs still featured content for inner exploration of the quantum field and a merging of mind and spirit through scientific understanding. This often facilitated the activation of dormant DNA as a result of exponential shifts in consciousness that the users of the programs experienced. Creative innovations from many enlightened souls added new material almost daily.

Every facet of life had been transformed and changed to reflect the blossoming consciousness on Earth. A new pride in creation had emerged that affected commerce and trade, building, the work force and agriculture. No area of society remained unaffected by this new renaissance.

Evergreen Village had become one of the most unique places on Earth. It blended an old style almost medieval, European architecture with the latest technological advances that allowed for a sustainable community. All of the buildings had been custom designed and built in the authentic tradition of European stone masonry. Influences from English, French and Austrian building styles resulted in a magical sprawl of uniquely paved roads, cobble stone walkways, cottage style commercial space and beautiful homes surrounded by lush gardens.

Innovative commerce exploded in the community as a direct result of so many fabulous, creative minds emerging from Initiates of Sacred Rose. World wide exports sustained a wealthy economy in the village. Products and services of all kinds bore the universal Evergreen Village emblem that had become highly prized among consumers. Tourists flocked to the little town to experience the magical atmosphere.

Maya walked into Abraxas Tavern and gave Julio a huge smile. Even in her fifty's she still radiated a peaches and cream complexion and an effervescent, girlish enthusiasm. The intense wisdom of her blue eyes intriguingly contrasted her youthful demeanor. A pair of baby pink, retro sunglasses hung off the collar of her cashmere sweater like a tribute to her eccentric humor.

Julio stood up and embraced her warmly, "Maya your radiance has eclipsed me as usual!" he said with his signature Spanish accent.

"Well I can still see you so it can't be that bad," she joked, purposely downplaying the compliment. They had known each other for many years and often played humorous gags on one another like mischievous children. Occasionally they ganged up on unsuspecting acquaintances with their antics who succumbed to inevitable peals of laughter.

"What would you like, my treat," he offered.

"Just lemonade," she replied.

"Chantal sent a gift," said Julio as he reached under the table to produce a most odd looking plant. "I can't remember what exotic, elaborate name this thing goes by but you *have* to smell it!"

Maya picked up the miniature orchid that displayed two small tube shaped flowers that were speckled with a smattering of Bordeaux colored dots. She held it to her nose and inhaled its scent. A tropical sea salt breeze mixed with lingering coconut was the only way to describe how the flowers smelled. "Mmmm, how unusual! This is so Chantal."

"Yes, she has been experimenting in her orchid nursery again. You should see her office. We've all been getting gifts of her creations. CIV Central is beginning to resemble the Amazon rain forest," Julio joked.

Maya and Lorne had taken some vacation time to spend away from the CIV. Lorne had been permitted to join her as an IM but with the changes he had implemented in Justice the past year he had been constantly traveling all over the North American sector. They had hardly seen each other all year. Maya planned to return to work on Monday and Julio had come by request of Chantal, who was completing her presentation at the Rising Minds Centre for Learning, to update Maya on the progress that had been made in the Global Communications project.

"Here is the disk with all the data on our progress in Global Communications at this past World CIV conference." Julio handed Maya the disk. "As you know the main hurdle is what to do with all the programming stations world wide now that everything is going to be centralized. Because of your exemplary commerce 'trouble shooting' record World CIV representatives agree that you're the best candidate to head this transition. They liked your idea of allowing the stations to submit programming implementation models that would ultimately collaboratively create the new outline for global program dispensation. They would like you to develop this project further and appoint a group of individuals to serve as a liaison to the world wide programming executives."

"So what is your schedule like, Julio?" Maya said with a grin.

"I knew you were going to say that, I saw it coming."

"I'm kidding, I already have a couple of people in mind," said Maya.

The Global Communications project would finalize the huge upgrading of media and entertainment industry content. Because all programming would be produced for a global audience funding for production of all projects would sky rocket allowing more diverse content and innovation in all audio visual media. A demand for diverse educational content had continued to grow and now had proper funding in place to help it thrive. Chantal's involvement and love of her Culture portfolio had resulted in her obsession to unearth any and all innovative minds that had developed enlightened content for documentaries, film, music, theatre and other areas of media and entertainment. She had opened the doors for many obscure but brilliant authors and artists to get their vision seen and heard to the delight of the public audience. Real progress in media and visual arts moved forward as new content had a substantial impact on shaping citizens changing tastes for knowledge and entertainment.

"Lorne is returning on Monday also?" Julio asked

"Yes, he is joking about having gotten out of shape since he stopped chasing trains planes and cabs. Plus eating all Anna's delicious cooking does not help."

"Well tell him to fire Anna and I will come cook for him. He will be back to his usual skinny ass self in no time." Julio taunted.

Maya laughed, "God, that's enough to scare anyone back into shape!" Julio was known for living off take out and burning toast even with the latest technology that grilled bread to perfection in seconds.

"I promised I would bring back a little something for Lisa from the Sweet Shop. Want to walk over with me?" Julio asked. His nine year old daughter adored most everything from the little confectionary across the street.

"Sure," replied Maya.

Julio took Maya's arm as they crossed Forest Drive. He was such a light hearted being that it was easy to overlook his awesome abilities as an initiate, she thought to herself. That characteristic united most initiates; they appeared as humble, common citizens who could do remarkable things.

Generally none of the initiates used their adept abilities openly except for amongst themselves since most of the general population had not received such training although interest in personal evolution of that nature was increasing and encouraged.

Mary opened the door to the Sweet Shop with a plump hand and greeted Julio and Maya, "I saw the two of you heading my way, have you been getting into trouble again?" she chirped.

"Always," they replied in unison, looked at each other and smiled.

"I'm here to get a little something for Lisa," said Julio. "Sure, that's what they all say," Mary quipped. "You have to sample one of my spiced candied apples." She had brought her most decadent candy making formulas from old Scotland that had been handed down for many generations.

Julio groaned, knowing that he would walk out with the object of that maddeningly delicious scent that had found him at the tavern. He took a candied apple and some of his daughter's favorite chocolate and peanut smothered toffee brittle. Maya marveled at all of Mary's creations. She hand crafted every confection in the shop. Some of the candies resembled little toy sculptures like rocking horses, cars, dolls, truly amazing creations. She did not have a sweet tooth but loved looking at everything and was tempted to get something for Lorne.

"Here is a little something for Lorne," Mary said as she handed Maya a little bag of dark chocolate whiskey truffles."

Maya smiled and said, "You read my mind, Mary."

Maya and Julio left the store laughing as he bit into the brilliant red candy apple and a big chunk got stuck in his neatly trimmed mustache. He grabbed Maya and kissed her cheek with the sticky mess, then before she could scold him disappeared and in an instant reappeared having teleported next to his car a block away, waving good bye. She waved back with a mildly annoyed grin, wiping her face with a handkerchief.

FOUR

The holographic display came to life once more in the centre of the classroom as Chantal inserted the next segment of her presentation.

"We are now going to examine the technology of weapons systems like HAARP and understand exactly how they were used before the great cataclysms." Chantal continued, "HAARP and other scalar electromagnetic instruments used radio telescope technology in reverse. Usually a radio antenna receives frequency waves but these weapons send an electromagnetic beam out to heat the ionosphere, which is Earth's protective shielding from highly charged particles from space. This plasmic field traps the dangerous cosmic plasma and prevents it from reaching our surface. Resulting from the atomic age Earth already had too many highly charged particles that contributed to geophysical activity like earthquakes and volcanic eruptions. With the use of HAARP and other similar weapons the ionosphere began to have huge holes in it that allowed large quantities of highly charged, destructive particles from space to bombard the planet." Chantal continued, "any change in the ionosphere also affects our lower atmosphere and these tears caused erratic, out of control weather patterns that had not been anticipated. The government continued however to attempt control of weather patterns and to create geophysical effects like earthquakes for military purposes."

Dead silence and wide eyed disbelief appeared in the children's faces as explicit details of a dark, former reality that preceded their current life played out on the holographic projector and registered in their minds.

Chantal had seen this response before in other school groups around the sector. Currently youngsters enjoyed a pristine natural environment and a peaceful society; the contrast of the former reality strongly registered in their minds as they watched the presentation.

Chantal continued, "now, on a more uplifting note I can finally get to the beneficial potentials and application of our current chip technology!" Chantal exclaimed with some relief and tension in the room broke with applause from the children. "Already the brain chip and electromagnetic field technology has enabled leaps of advancement in education of which all of you have been benefactors. No more toiling to learn language arts and mathematics by rote like the homework entrenched students of the past, hey?" Chantal said and garnered some laughter form her young audience. "This group is too young to remember the days when no chip and program that gave you instant access to those skills and so many others that you have had the privilege of taking advantage of, was available."

Chantal's compilation of images continued to display as she wrapped up her presentation with highlights of future technological application research.

Back at her office at CIV Central Chantal's fingers skimmed over the touch pad of her quantum lap top with lightning speed. The image on the holographic 3D display viewer morphed with each stroke as an artistic design for her Global Communications presentation formed. Colors swirled around the CIV emblem as emerald green, shimmering leaves sprouted from the oaks branches accompanied by high, string like sound. "Beautiful," Chantal whispered to herself.

A cool breeze from her cracked window moved through the office and bathed her in the scent of exotic, white orchids with violet centers. She allowed her eyes to close and inhaled the fragrant air for a timeless moment. The energy along her spine began to stir and rise as a heat grew at the base of it. She held the roller curser in her palm and music filled her space. Chantal's breath deepened and the energy moving up her spine intensified. She felt the energy pass through her throat and inhaled sharply as it flooded her brain. She swam in remote consciousness for a moment then exhaled deeply feeling the field around her body begin to form into a sphere and move. She continued the breath from her training at Sacred Rose and increased the velocity of her field's momentum. The frequency emanating from her began to increase and her pulse quickened. Rushes of energy continued to explode up her spine into her brain as the oscillation of her field increased to an exquisite brilliance. Rapture filled Chantal's entire being as her whole body bathed in a soft glow began to rise off her chair. Eyes closed and head slightly back she steadily increased her elevation till she hovered directly above her holographic display. She continued to float, slowly opened her eyes and observed her creation from a new vantage point. With the roller curser in her hand she began to manipulate the colors of the design.

James walked into her office and his heart did a little flip at the sight of Chantal, hovering weightless over the holograph. Her dark hair hung around her shoulders and skimmed her fair cheeks now flushed from concentration. When she levitated the grace of it was breathtaking. "Sorry to disturb you," he said as he began to back out of her office.

"No it's alright," she said with a deeply relaxed, velvety voice characteristic of someone in trance. Her eyes turned on him almost knocking him over with their luminosity. "I can work better to complete this from up here and I desire your input, what do you think of this design so far?"

James did his best to compose himself and turned his attention to Chantal's design. The CIV emblem twirled to the sound of beautiful string accompaniment and the whole tree, danced with flashes of gold and emerald sprouting leaves. The words CIV Global Communications rotated around the tree and faded in and out as if appearing from hyperspace. "It's perfect!" He managed to utter. The charged air in heady scent of orchids encircled him. He could feel his face begin to flush as he quickly backed out with a quick, "I have to go, nice work!"

Chantal continued to float and work on her design, completely unfazed by James's awkward intrusion. She glanced once towards the door and smiled.

James walked back to his office and drank a tall, cool glass of water. He knew Samantha and Richard would be waiting for him to return to the meeting downstairs with John. He leaned against the wall and peered out the window. It was beginning to snow. He smiled knowing that Chantal would not close her window and flakes would be drifting into her office creating a bizarre scene of tropical orchids and swirling snowflakes. He had known her for five years and had developed strong feelings for her. Chantal remained somewhat enigmatic towards him in their friendship. At times he believed she may be open to a more serious relationship but she always avoided any discussion of it, changing the subject or ducking out of a conversation because of a convenient interruption. It was as if something else had a hold on her emotionally that she would not discuss. Chantal had never married and buried herself in the work of the CIV, hardly dating. He sighed, knowing that he was nowhere nearer to solving the mystery of her and began to head downstairs to reconvene the meeting with John Willowby.

Samantha and Richard had just escorted John back to the meeting room when James joined them. "Did you find everything to your satisfaction?" Roger asked John.

"I am somewhat overwhelmed," John admitted. "This is an extremely well planned endeavor and the financial compensation is more than I would have imagined. I am very honored and pleased that you would ask me to oversee this advisory group of great scientific minds. This will truly be a revolutionary move in government policy that will ensure the stability of the ecosystem and the application of safe technology for future generations."

All the IM's smiled and Samantha responded, "We had hoped that you would like the design of the program and are very open to the input of your group should you have ideas on improving the overall vision in any way."

"Your first meeting with the advisory group is scheduled for next Monday at 9 AM if you are available," said Richard.

"Yes, that will be fine," replied John.

"Hold on a moment, I have two tickets for you to attend Friday's CIV New Year celebration," James said handing the tickets to John.

"Oh thank you, may I bring my daughter?"

"Absolutely, said Samantha, one of our other IM's has a nine year old daughter that he will be bringing as well, perhaps they will get along."

"Great, she'll be thrilled," said John as he continued with Samantha towards her office.

James watched the two of them walk away. He glanced at Richard who seemed somewhat distracted and tense. "Everything all right?" James asked him.

"No, as a matter of fact it isn't," replied Richard. "Come back to the office with me, I have something to show you."

FiVE

Romanius sat at the edge of a multi spectral pool and dipped his silvery green hand into it. The liquid appeared phosphorescent as burnished orange droplets ran down and magnified the colors of his arm. Rays from the sun overhead warmed his skin, immersing him in its explosive consciousness. He called forth the vision of Larina and suddenly the liquid rose out of the pool and began to swirl in mid air. It created a fine, glowing mist that revealed her face in the current embodiment she wore as a human girl child. He reached out and touched the image with his fingers, creating a slight ripple. Romanius entered her consciousness knowing that she would feel his mind and unified with her. He watched the girl's face floating in the mist before him and she smiled, closing here eyes; his being filled with her presence. The mist dissipated and washed over his face as he lay in a timeless moment illuminated by the violet sun.

At some point a scarlet and yellow anatoa hopped next to him and took his hand, peering into his copper eyes, making its inquiring little sounds. Momentarily startled Romanius looked into its triangular little face, merely inches from his own and sat up smiling. He watched the creature scamper off and lunge into the treetops high above ground.

Romanius moved to rise when suddenly rapidly changing images appeared in his brain. He fell forward and gripped his temples, witnessing violent ripples in time in the world where Larina existed. Like waves of heavy energy tearing its fabric and something sinister entering that place. He could not get a fix on what it was as it moved quickly but it impacted and disturbed the frequency of the reality.

Richard led James into his office and closed the door. "Amit just sent these pictures over from the surveillance cameras in various areas of the North American Sector," Richard said as he loaded the disk into the quantum computer.

"What am I looking at?"

"Can you see the distortion in this image? Look, it appears like a mirage with a glowing mist in it and then in the next one it is back to normal and the mist is gone."

James looked closer, "ok I can see now what you are talking about but what does it mean?"

"We're not sure but in all of the areas where these images were taken people have been exhibiting the same physical symptoms of malaise such as nausea and vertigo." Richard paused in thought for a moment then continued, "you know some of the IM's teleport and have experienced observing parallel universes. Those of us that do have experienced odd dreams and some disturbing visions over the past couple of weeks. This is the first time any of us have had this occur and no one was certain of the cause but a fluctuation in our reality has been felt."

"Yes, Chantal mentioned that," replied James.

"Well when we first received our training we experienced similar side effects to what is happening to people in the vicinity of the phenomenon that is being observed till we grew accustomed to the process. When you move from one location is space time to another you are in effect creating what has been termed a time storm. If artificial time travel technology is being used the effects may be amplified."

"So what are you saying that someone is creating time storms? And if so, who?" Asked James

Richard rubbed the back of his head, "I don't know but the only group that had time travel technology before the great cataclysms was the old government, it was one of their black projects. You know that there has always been speculation about what happened to the key members, they just disappeared. Everyone thinks they left in their time machine because they knew about the impending destruction." Richard paused for a long moment in thought and then looked at James, "I think we had better get John Willowby back here with the scientific advisory group and brief them on this. Perhaps they will have some answers."

"I'll ask Samantha to get a hold of him right away," said James and headed out of Richard's office.

Romanius opened a grid portal in the atmosphere around him and rapidly activated the coordinates for the great ship Lycos. He instantly appeared as a living holograph in the matrix grid of the ship. The Shining Ones knew why he had contacted them; he had concern for Larina's safety. They had been observing the events on Earth and were aware that someone was creating the recent time warps. They had decided not to intervene in the situation but to allow Earth's leaders resolution of it while continuing to observe. Romanius understood the events and informed the Shining Ones that he planned to join Larina. They were not pleased but knew that he was beyond dissuasion and gave him coordinates for a smooth merger into her reality. He thanked them and disconnected. Immediately he entered the new coordinates into the grid portal and disappeared.

A bright, yellow sun filtered through bare branches of a birch tree as Romanius lay on his back and squinted. "Come on, Trent what are you waiting for?" A boy's voice called out.

Romanius sat up, startled by the cold snow against his hands and looked at himself. He was sitting on a red toboggan wearing waterproof pants, snow boots and the body of a ten year old boy. A mildly amused knowingness crossed his face as he realized the Shining Ones had taken the opportunity to have a bit of fun with him.

"We have to go, the voice continued; your grandmother said she wanted us back by three."

"Coming," he answered as he got up, slinging the sled onto his back.

Diana watched out the window of the Victory building as thieves smashed the glass door of the electronics store on the street below. The alarm rang as she sighed, so tired of this repetitive scene. The crime rate escalated daily and law enforcement had become stretched beyond the capacity to be effectual. She knew that similar events took place at night all over the city. It had become normal to walk the streets by day covered in glass shards from the night's rampages. Colonel Stark moved close to Diana, his presence gave her the creeps. "At it again I see," he said surveying the scene below.

"This is never going to change, these people are living in insanity," she said. Thick clouds had covered the sky for days now producing nothing but torrential rain. The Omega Group had avoided the great cataclysms by jumping ahead in time but the timeline they had arrived at in 2014 had proven to be riddled with problems. The weather still exhibited erratic patterns and the population that had survived and appeared here showed high levels of aggression and competitiveness. No cooperation existed among the people. They fought over resources like animals. Diana believed that these behavioral side effects resulted from use of their mind control weapons. Once people had recovered from mental confusion, intense paranoia and aggressive tendencies had likely formed in them as part of the survival mechanism. Worse, implementing mind restructuring on the population upon the Omega Group's arrival through time appeared to have deteriorated the public's mental stability further. Citizens were programmed to believe that the group had always governed them but social problems raged on. The group never discussed this among themselves but they were afraid to use the weapons again to control the minds of the population.

"We're making progress moving forward again, thanks to you. Soon we will be out of here," said Colonel Stark.

"We haven't solved the problem of bringing the rest of the group through. So far only I have made it and you know at what expense." Diana had located a progressive timeline in 2019 that looked promising. She had made several trips to gather data on the society so as to plan the best entry point for the whole group. She had brought back information about their government, technology and way of life, which starkly contrasted the current time they occupied. In addition several trips had been made by her to plant devices in each sector that would coordinate world wide memory eradication and replacement. Each time she returned she became ill and spent a few days in bed recovering from nausea and aches. This had not occurred to the same degree when they had arrived at their current timeline. They all felt some vertigo and queasiness but none of them had gotten ill to the degree that she did when she moved in and out of the new time. She suspected it had to do with a higher frequency of that timeline that she was unaccustomed to.

"We're confident that once you perform the memory reprogramming we will be able to come through without any problem," Colonel Stark replied.

Diana looked at his smug face knowing he disliked her but they mutually tolerated one another. These people had the technology to arrive at any destination in time, erase all the memories that people had, create new ones and thus establish themselves as the new governing order. The Omega Group was ruthless in it's pursuit of power a quality that Diana did not overly admire. Her membership in the organization did however assure that whatever timeline they traveled to she would retain her status in the government they represented. She had no guarantee of status without them; their scientists had developed the new memory interface program (MIP) that would be implemented upon their insertion point in the new timeline.

Dr. Rechter walked in and smiled at Diana, "are you ready my dear?"

"Yes," she replied.

"Then let us proceed," he said and escorted her to the basement laboratory. Dr. Rechter slid his key card into a lock and large steel doors slid open revealing an austere white room with grey flooring. Only computers and the Time Intervention Interface (TII) device occupied the space. Diana took her usual seat in the chair at the centre of the device. Dr. Rechter placed the head gear on her and turned it on. He brought her a leather overnight bag that contained all her supplies. "Your SCC card to get in at the CIV New Year Celebration is in here. Your profile as a member of the press has been encoded. The last MIP cone is programmed and ready for placement in the North American Sector. We have scheduled your return time for 1AM after the party. Make sure you reach your transport location to avoid creating suspicion."

"Yes, I'm aware of the protocol. Hopefully my body will have adjusted to the travel and changes by then so you won't have to greet me with a sick bag." Dana closed her eyes and listened to the hum of the field generated by the TII device. This day it soothed her and she could not wait to get out of her current location. She focused on the frequency of her destination in her mind as Dr. Rechter set the coordinates. The field grew around her and hummed as she relaxed and surrendered to the lifting sensation that accompanied the sound. Every molecule of her being felt the magnetic pull of the place of her focus as negative energy began to form. She pushed the time jump button and her body began the familiar dissolve propelling her through a wormhole and she momentarily lost consciousness. In the next moment she appeared outside the Harrington Inn at midnight in 2019. She reoriented her senses, smoothed her silver blond hair and walked into the building to get a room.

SiX

Chantal floated above the grass where her body lay. She knew she was having a lucid, out of body experience, had done this many times and did not fear it. She watched as a figure sat behind her body below and gently cradled her temples, speaking to her softly…it was the same scene she had revisited many times right after the great cataclysms. Suddenly the form sitting behind the body looked right up at her. For a moment Chantal felt confusion because the face that looked up at her was her own. She knew that the body stretched out on the grass was hers but so was the person sitting behind it.

Chantal studied this version of herself; she wore unfamiliar clothing, a long cloak with a simple one piece garment resembling a bodysuit beneath it made of a fabric she did not recognize. The hair was hers, dark but longer and her face had a glow about it, the eyes somehow lighter gold, emanating more light. The figure held her gaze and spoke, "it is time you remember your future and change the past that is approaching," it said as its eyes continued to pull Chantal in to their depths. "Come closer to me."

Chantal floated down and stood before this being, "Closer," it said. She could feel a magnetic pull on her light body coming from this version of herself and could not look away. "It's alright, it is time," the being said. Chantal allowed herself to be drawn closer to the being till finally, her light body merged with the other. Instantly she experienced an energetic surge as she and the other aspect of herself became one. Chantal looked at herself and realized she was dressed in the others clothes, that she had become integrated. The body on the grass was gone. She stood and experienced visions of the future and watched as an image of a white building formed in her mind. At the instant that she viewed it, she appeared there.

Chantal stood in the middle of a huge, circular room. It had curved glass windows that looked out onto an ocean, so close that she could hear the waves drenching the shore of ivory sand. A burnished, setting sun fell into the glistening waters coloring the sky orange—peach with gold and lavender hues. Gorgeous gardens surrounded the building; she could see lush flowers and plants all around the windows. The room itself had furnishings that looked oddly alive as if at any moment they could morph and change. She fixed her gaze on suede like, turquoise covered armchair with curved metallic legs. Its form began to undulate and animate displaying various styles of design; she smiled and selected her preferred one with her mind. Instantly the chair froze in the design of her choice. She sat in it and her eyes followed the circular walls up to a domed ceiling that displayed emanations of moving light, creating a beautiful illusion similar to renaissance artists' renditions of the heavens. All this was new but at the same time very familiar like she had always known this place.

Chantal laid her head back in the chair and watched the mesmerizing movement of hues across the ceiling while the surf washed over the sand outside. The sun had set now and she wondered what the sky here must look like at night. Instantly the ceiling began to dissolve revealing an azure sky of twilight decorated with a sliver of moon. She could see the rest of the silver crescent's shadowed, circular form coyly hiding behind it. To her delight as the sky grew deeper blue a smattering of stars shone through brightly.

"When the sky is the color of midnight they shine like diamonds," a quiet but deeply resonant male voice spoke from across the room. A shockwave went off in Chantal as she bolted up...every fiber of her being recognized that voice. She slammed back into her body and opened her eyes, her pulse racing and looked around her bedroom. Tendrils of hair clung to her damp brow. Her Burmese cat, Morocco, came over to her with inquisitive eyes and a questioning 'meow.' She stroked his plush, sable colored coat and lay back down allowing hear heart rate to return to normal. The vividness of the out of body experience still flashed in Technicolor through her mind. Chantal lay in her bed and contemplated what had just occurred. She was able to recall new memories from what appeared to be a future time.

Whenever she closed her eyes and focused on where she had visited more images like bits and pieces filled her mind. They seemed new but at the same time strongly familiar. She could not get the male presence who spoke to her out of her mind. Something about him and his voice tugged at her heart; but she did not know why. Chantal curled up into a ball on her side and buried her face in the covers, suddenly feeling very exposed and vulnerable. She finally drifted of into a deep, dreamless sleep.

All twelve IM's and the scientific advisory group, headed by John Willowby, gathered at CIV Central for an emergency security meeting. Amit proceeded with the briefing, "these images have been collected by security cameras form all over the North American sector," he said as the holographic projector displayed the collected data. Amit continued, "As you can see, in each area of the sector that physical symptoms have been appearing in the general population, a distortion of some sort has been recorded by the cameras. Then in the next frame, everything appears as normal again.

The members studied the images closely, "what is happening exactly?" asked Samantha.

"I am going to allow John Willowby, our newly appointed head of the Scientific Advisory Group, to answer your questions," replied Amit.

John rose and moved to the podium. This was the first time he actually was meeting the rest of the IM's since he accepted his new position with the CIV and consequently felt a little nervous. He was not accustomed to public speaking but composed himself as best he could and proceeded, "the group and I have studied these images and agree with IM James's suggestion that we may be witnessing the evidence of manufactured time storms. This basically means that someone is attempting to enter our current timeline likely by technological means." Having the total attention of all IM's John continued, "this mirage like effect in the atmosphere and the presence of yellowish mist is characteristic of movement through the time domain and appearing into current space time. These are the last set of images that were taken two days ago in downtown Olympia. As you can see it is the same phenomenon that is occurring in the other pictures. Soil samples of the area show elevated radiation levels that are theoretically concurrent with the use of this type of technology."

"Do we have any idea as to who is attempting to enter our time?" asked Maya.

"Or why?" added Julio.

"We don't know but suspect that it may be members from a secret organization and or certain previous government officials from before the great cataclysms that used electromagnetic technology. Key members from these groups disappeared after the cataclysms and it is unlikely that they were all killed. Many of us believe that they used a time travel device to leave before the tragedies they helped create began to occur. From my time as a physicist involved in military weapons development I know that such technology was being developed by a select group in a government black project. It is likely that they succeeded and may be attempting to enter our time with it."

"If they had already left prior to the cataclysms then why would they want to enter our time now?" Asked Amanda Bridges, IM of Agriculture.

"We're not sure. Perhaps the time they traveled to initially is not suitable for some reason. The other option is that the travelers may be of extra terrestrial origin. I and the Scientific Advisory Group have doubts about this second option."

"Can you explain that a little more, John?" asked Richard.

"Yes, we all strongly believe that Extra Terrestrial intervention played a role in our move into this current timeline after the great cataclysms." John continued, "we all lost a gap of six years. The memories we were seeded with contain more advanced technologies and a highly organized and efficient social structure which we are enjoying today in total freedom. In addition, no one suffered adverse health effects of the nature that are being reported in the sites of disturbances. Our transition was seamless. What is occurring with the creation of these time storms appears more amateurish and frankly like the work of hackers."

Most of the IM's nodded in agreement with John's logic. It was true, Chantal thought to herself and spoke, "if off world beings helped relocate our population to the present time they created as little disturbance as possible as if the goal was to have a totally seamless transition for all people. I don't believe that what is happening with these disturbances is consistent with a beneficial objective. It looks like someone is moving in and out of our time without regard for the consequences of his actions."

"What potential risks have been identified that these maneuvers could cause us?" inquired Lorne, IM of Justice.

John paused for a moment and surveyed the room. He could see genuine concern in the faces of the IM's. "There is no way to deliver this that will be of any less impact so I'm just going to say it, the same technologies that contributed to the earth's instability and mental disorientation in pockets of the general public could be used to manipulate our state of mind. Ultimately the possible scenarios all depend on the objectives of whoever is doing this."

The council became silent and pensive. "Amit, do we have any technology that could act as a defense against the more extreme potential that John has just presented?" asked James.

"At this time no defense system of such nature exists. This is because it was universally agreed by the World CIV to only use the electromagnetic and other advanced technologies for beneficial purposes and to ban their military application. We did not anticipate the possibility of having to defend ourselves against warped time travelers with malevolent intentions."

Someone from the council chuckled at Amit's comment. What he had said was true but strangely surreal. "Perhaps they don't have good take out in their time...that might lead me to take drastic measures also, said Julio," garnering more giggles from the rest of the council.

"We're beginning to loose it folks, but at least this proves we have a sense of humor in any situation," said Richard.

"I am going to work closely with our remote view team and John's group to investigate this matter further and explore all our defense options," said Amit. "We will keep the council abreast of the situation and as per our protocol we will inform CIV factions form all sectors of our security problem and potential risks. In spite of these events I would like to wish everyone an unprecedented happy New Year and encourage you all to enjoy this evening's celebration. Rest assured we have arranged extra security for your safety."

The council meeting ended and the IM's began to depart. Samantha touched John's arm, "John, you did a fabulous job with the briefing, thank you," she said.

He smiled at her, "I wish the circumstances of my first address to the council were different, but I'm pleased that you are satisfied with my contribution."

"See you tonight John," she said and smiled warmly.

SEVEN

Diana lay on the bed inside her hotel room and slowly sipped a glass of water. Having arrived three days prior finally her nausea was subsiding. She had sustained herself with water, crackers and a green powder supplement during that time so as not to loose her strength totally. She looked at the clock, the CIV New Year celebration would be starting in half an hour. Diana sat up and got off the bed. The vertigo had not completely gone away and she leaned against the wall momentarily, regaining her balance. She took a deep breath and headed for the closet where her black evening gown hung. Diana put it on and glanced at herself in the mirror, applying lipstick. She stopped for a moment and took a long look. She appeared different somehow. In spite of the bout of nausea she had suffered, her face seemed brighter. It was as if her body had responded to the clean energy of this place, softening her features and generally making her feel lighter. In the previous visits she had never stayed long enough to notice that this reality had an incredible lightness of being to it. She could breathe more deeply for the first time in months and the tension she usually carried in her solar plexus was gone.

Diana put her hotel keycard into her evening bag, called the front desk for a taxi and headed downstairs to wait.

James adjusted his jacket and put on some cologne. Satisfied with his general appearance, he grabbed his car keys and headed out to pick up

Chantal to escort her to the 2020 New Year celebration at CIV central. The day had worn him out so he entered Chantal's address into his car's auto navigation system, reclined his chair and closed his eyes. The near silent engine purred softly as the vehicle transported him onto the highway. Chantal's house was only twenty minutes away, just enough for a quick nap before the party James thought as he drifted off.

"Hello...hello!" A voice and loud knocking on his car window startled James awake.

"Oh shit," James mumbled to himself, getting out of the car, "Chantal I'm sorry...I was really wiped on the way here and dozed off."

"Yeah, I could practically hear you sawing logs from my house," Chantal teased and got into the car."

James looked at her; she had put her hair up in a chignon clipped with an antique dragonfly gem studded clip. A few pieces of hair framed her beautiful face and she wore a simple white silk dress with fabric draping low down her back to the waist. "You look lovely, he said, its cold, here, let me help you with your coat," he said and put it on her.

"I didn't sleep well either last night, why don't we get some coffee on the way to the party," she suggested getting into the car.

"Good idea, I could use some to perk me up," James answered, pulling out of her driveway. "You're having trouble sleeping?"

"No, I sleep fine, just last night...I don't know. I had some intense dreams," said Chantal.

"Anything you want to share?"

Chantal paused for a moment. James was the only one she had ever told about her experience immediately after the great cataclysms when she was transported forward in time. "Well remember what I told you happened to me, when I found myself laying on the grass after the earthquake in Seattle?"

"Yeah, you said there was someone else present with you but you didn't know who it was and this person told you that you had been brought forward in time," he replied.

"Good memory. Well I often dream of that day and it is always the same as what happened only this time it was different."

"Different how?"

Chantal paused again, not sure if she should proceed.

"You ok?" James asked looking at her with concern.

"Yes, I'm fine, it's just that my dream...actually it was a lucid out of body experience, not just a dream. Anyway, this time the person sitting behind me looked right up at me where I was floating in my astral body and I saw her. This person's face was my own."

James thought about what she said for a moment. "Do you mean that you were on the grass, plus with yourself on the grass, plus watching all this from above?"

"Yes."

"That's trippy, now I really need a coffee to clear my head," he joked. "So what do you make of the dream or experience?"

"I'm not sure but some memories have begun to surface for me that I didn't know I had and I think they were this other 'me's' memories...I know it sounds odd but it's like her and I merged into one."

"But do you think you were really in two places at once and possibly had something to do with transporting yourself to the future, our time now or did you appeared there symbolically in your dream?" James asked.

Chantal thought for a moment. "I don't know but you know, I never thought about that."

"About what?"

"That I may have had something to do with transporting my self here...now that is interesting."

"Well most of you from Sacred Rose have bilocated, even teleported so why not through time...anything is possible," said James.

"I know it's just weird that I had this experience last night right after the security briefing we got."

"You said that you also had some new memories, what did you mean?"

James was a good listener, Chantal though to her self. "Yes, they are memories from the future, and that unpleasant feeling about something not being right in our time but I can't tell you anything more than that."

He looked at her for a long moment and decided not to pry. "Sure, he said, whatever you want."

"Thanks for listening an understanding," she said and gave him a dazzling smile.

His heart did a little flip as he pulled into the drive through coffee bar and ordered two espressos.

EiGHT

Julio walked into CIV central holding his nine year old daughter Lisa's hand. "Wow, look at all the decorations!" Lisa exclaimed. In the centre of the room a holographic Happy New Year 2020 visual rotated. The letters appeared to be blooming out of the CIV Oak tree emblem and sprinkling the air with virtual sparkles as they formed and dissolved in a continuous, repetitive loop. The room was subtly decorated with holly branches, whose tips were dipped in gold, fabric bows with lacy accents and virtual candles embedded in the leaves of the holly, creating a warm glow.

"Chantal designed all this pretty neat, hey?" Julio told her.

"Yeah," Lisa spotted Maya across the room and ran to greet her, diving into her arms, "Maya!" she exclaimed.

"Look at you, you're getting so tall!" Maya gave the child a big squeeze as she giggled. She and Lorne did not have children of their own but she adored them and took pleasure in spoiling all her closest friends' youngsters. "There is someone here I want you to meet," Maya said and led Lisa by the hand over to where John and Jena loaded up their appetizer plates. "Hello John, this is Julio Mandera's daughter Lisa, she's nine, just about Jenna's age I think."

Jena smiled at Lisa, "hi" she said.

"Hi, Lisa answered eyeing Jena's plate, that stuff looks good, I'm hungry."

"Come on I'll share with you and then we can get more." The two girls went off and sat together at a nearby table.

Julio watched them go and smiled, "Your daughter is sweet, he said to John. She doesn't look a thing like you though; does she take after her mother?"

Julio's candor did not offend John, as the man obviously liked to speak his mind. "Actually Jena is my adopted daughter. She's been with me now for about a year."

"It must be a real blessing to have her in your life," said Julio.

"She looks like she has made an excellent adjustment," Maya added.

"Yes, I'm very fortunate to have her and thankful that she puts up with me," John replied.

Amit approached the small group, "good evening everyone, John may I take you away just for a moment?" he asked.

"Sure, Julio, would you mind watching over Jena?" John asked.

"Of course, go on, she'll be fine," said Julio.

"Excuse me," John said and followed Amit.

Julio turned to Maya, "you think everything is ok?" He asked.

"I wouldn't worry, if it wasn't we would know by now," she replied.

"So how is the Global Communications project coming along, have you formed your liaison group yet?" Julio inquired.

"Just about, I'm interviewing the last two candidates the day after tomorrow. With the liaison group in place we'll be ready to deal with the media stations. Chantal has finished her presentation document so providing everything goes smoothly, after our meeting at the World CIV in a couple of weeks we'll be ready to begin structuring the global network."

Lorne walked over to the two of them with a tray of wine filled glasses. "Lorne, what are you doing? Said Maya, where is the server?"

"I don't know and I was getting tired of waiting around till someone noticed me so I just went over to the bar and decided to take matters into my own hands."

"Well they are pretty busy I guess," she said taking a glass.

"You do that so well, can I hire you for my daughter's birthday party?" joked Julio.

"You mean you intend on serving alcohol to minors?" said Lorne with mock seriousness.

"What kind of father do you think I am? The booze is strictly for me. I figure that after entertaining a bunch of ten year olds all day I will need a drink or three."

Lorne paused and watched as a tall, slender woman with shoulder length, light blond hair walked into CIV Central, "hey, who is that? I don't recognize her, do either of you?"

Maya and Julio both looked in the direction of Lorne's gaze at the female. "I don't know who that is," said Maya.

"Neither do I, she does not look familiar, very attractive though," added Julio.

"She doesn't appear to have a date, Julio why don't you go over there and introduce yourself, my man," suggested Lorne.

"We'll watch the girls for you," added Maya.

"Thanks, don't mind if I do," he replied, taking the drink tray out of Lorne's hands.

Diana had just checked her coat and studied her surroundings. She had never been inside CIV Central and it was truly stunning. The marble floor, vaulted ceiling and ornate moldings gave her the sense of being transported to the Italian Renaissance. Some of the light fixtures were exquisite antiques chandeliers, likely worth a fortune. Subtle but beautiful decorations gave warmth and festive appeal to the rooms. Diana sighed deeply and welcomed the light hearted, celebratory atmosphere that contrasted sharply to the intense, troubled world she had recently left behind.

Julio approached her bearing a tray with two filled glasses. "Would you like a glass of wine?"

"No, but if you have soda I would love it."

"Sure, I'll be right back," he replied as he headed back to the bar.

Lorne watched Julio walk by him with the wine. "Strike out so soon?"

"She wants soda," Julio replied, causing Lorne and Maya to snicker at the sight of him playing waiter. He approached the bar and surveyed a lengthy line of guests waiting. Clearly they had not hired enough servers. Julio discreetly placed one of his hands over the wine glass on the tray. He closed his eyes, focused for a moment and then removed his hand. Where the wine had been now sat a tall glass of soda garnished with a wedge of lemon. Julio smiled and headed back to find the blond lady awaiting her soda.

Diana wandered through the CIV rooms admiring the art and observing the guests. This would be her only chance to meet some of the IM's and gather more information on the workings of the CIV. Identifying the best entry point in this time for the Omega Group depended on that information. Inside her handbag she carried some surveillance chips that Colonel Stark had given her to plant while inside. Diana turned to enter the next room and was startled by the presence of a young red haired girl. "You don't belong here," the child said to her with a penetrating gaze.

Surprised, Diana's eyes darted around the room to see if any one else had noticed them, then looked at the child, "excuse me?"

"You don't belong here; this is not your time. I know why you came, go back, go back now before you do something you will regret. These people are happy," Jena said with intensity totally uncharacteristic of a ten year old.

Diana was stunned. Her mind reeled from this assault coming from a child.

"Ah there you are, one soda for the beautiful lady," said Julio, handing Diana the glass.

"Thank you," Diana stammered quickly grabbing the glass and gulping it all down. She looked around for the strange girl but she had disappeared.

"My you are one thirsty lady!" Julio held out his hand. "Julio Manderas, IM of Sector Building and Planning at your service."

Diana composed herself, "oh my, I'm so sorry, I had no idea…I saw you with the drink tray and assumed…"

"It's alright, that is my fault, my colleague was being humorous and started a trend this evening; we seem to have found ourselves moonlighting as servers."

"Mr. Manderas."

"No, please call me Julio."

"Very well, Julio it is an honor to meet you. My name is Diana Manning; I'm a writer for the Seattle Journal. I'm here to cover the festivities and ask probing questions of the Illuminated Members," Diana said with a convincing smile.

Julio groaned inside…press. He knew that they let select media and press members to their functions. Usually these people blended in without creating any disturbance and collected their information respectfully. The woman before him fit right in with that profile and obviously had presented her credentials to security. "Well, as you've probably surmised by now I'm an easy target for probing questions so ask away."

Diana smiled, beginning to relax.

Chantal and James finally walked in, tossed out their coffee cups and waved to Julio. "Who is that woman with him?" Chantal asked.

"Haven't got a clue," said James. He looked around and noticed the increased plain clothes security staff convincingly mingling with the guests and a few uniform guards near the doors. "Hey, look at this place, all decked out, you did a fabulous job on coordinating the décor, Chantal."

"I know, it does look amazing, but thanks!" She smiled.

"Let's check out the food I'm starving," said James.

Chantal knew James had a hearty appetite. He stood almost six foot four and had a fast metabolism. "You go ahead, I am going to say hello to Julio."

"Ok, I'll catch up with you shortly."

"Julio!" Chantal exclaimed and gave him an embrace. "Who is this lovely lady?"

"Oh Chantal, this is Diana Manning; she is here from the Seattle Journal covering our event."

"Really? Pleased to meet you," she said shaking the woman's hand. Chantal examined her face, "you know, I was just at the journal last month and I would have remembered you…"

"Oh, I was away in the tropics on vacation," Diana interjected.

"That must have been why I didn't meet you." Chantal could not put her finger on it but there was something insincere about this woman.

"I've been filling Diana in on our progress with Evergreen Village," said Julio.

"So as a journalist how do you feel about the consolidation of all the media stations that's in the works, Diana?" Chantal asked casually.

Diana was silent for a moment. She had no idea what Chantal was talking about. She had studied the Global Communications effort that was being developed by the world CIV but was not aware of many of the details as they had not yet been finalized and released publicly. "Ah, well…I'm sure it will all go smoothly." She replied with a forced smile.

"Yes…excuse me for a moment." Alarms were going off in Chantal; this woman was lying. She walked over to Maya, "You know the blond that Julio has been talking to over there?"

"Yes, do you know who she is? Lorne and I have never seen her before."

"I had a feeling you were going to say that."

"Really, why?"

Chantal turned and looked Maya squarely in the face, "because she told me and Julio that she works for the Seattle Journal."

From across the room Diana had been following the exchange between Chantal and Maya and she could tell that Chantal had not believed her story. Beads of perspiration started to break out across her chest. As Julio continued to tell her about some CIV projects Diana interrupted him, "excuse me Julio, I need to find the powder room," she said and walked away abruptly.

"It's right over...." Julio's sentence trailed off as he watched Diana's speedy departure. Strange woman, he thought to himself.

"That blond does not work for the Seattle Journal. I personally know all the staff there and she isn't one of them," said Maya firmly.

"Thought so, we had better alert security," said Chantal.

"I'll find Lorne," replied Maya and headed off to look for him.

Diana managed to plant a few surveillance chips in discreet places on her way out of CIV Central, knowing that if they suspected her they would likely comb the place and find them, making her attempt to bug the place futile. She was a physicist, not a spy and this whole situation was turning into one giant disaster, she thought as she hailed a taxi and headed for the hotel.

Amit, Lorne and several of the other IM's gathered in the security room. "She's left the building," said Amit. Our people have searched everywhere and she is definitely no longer anywhere on the premises."

"I think she sensed that I was not buying into her story and I may have accidentally alerted her. Sorry," said Chantal.

"It's not your fault, she checked out at the door and had a valid SCC card," said Lorne.

"Looks like I missed all the fun," remarked James.

"We are issuing a sector wide alert as we speak. We got some good images of her from the surveillance equipment. If anyone sees her they are instructed to contact the CIV intelligence unit immediately. I am also putting the Remote View team on this right away to see if hey can pinpoint her location," said Amit.

"She seemed out of place from the start and behaved a bit nervously, like she was not accustomed to doing whatever she was here to do," Julio interjected.

"I agree, and she was definitely a lousy liar," Chantal added.

"Ok, well it looks like we have everything under control here without disturbing the flow of the party so why don't you folks return to the festivities so we don't alarm the guests," suggested Amit.

The IM's returned and joined the rest of the party. James was chatting with Maya so Chantal went to the bar and got a glass of wine. She stood in the far end of the main room by the French doors and sipped it. Seemingly out of nowhere Jena appeared beside her. "Oh hello, I didn't see you there, you are John's daughter, right?" She asked.

Jena ignored her question and looked long into Chantal's eyes, "You are remembering," she said.

Her comment caught Chantal off guard. Surely this child could not possibly know about her recent experiences.

Jena continued, "you will be needed again to help protect the present and your future. Don't be afraid of what is to come," the young girl said, smiled and walked away.

"Wait!" Chantal called after her, but Jena had disappeared into the crowd.

Chantal's cheeks flushed. The potential security problems the CIV faced her strange experience in the future and now this evening's events had left her feeling somewhat overwhelmed; her head began to ache. She opened the French doors and stepped out onto the balcony. The night air chilled her, raising goose bumps on her arms but it felt good to get away from the party for a moment and her head cleared. Chantal loved the beautiful gardens below but this time of year the trees stood bare to the winds and snow while no flowers bloomed. In the quiet she allowed the frigid night to envelop her like a dark cloak as she stood in the shadows of the trees, huddling her arms around herself for warmth.

Chantal felt someone's eyes on her and turned squinting into the dark corners of the balcony. 'I must be getting paranoid, no one else would be out here freezing his ass off,' she thought to herself and began to turn back towards the garden. "You look cold," a familiar voice spoke out of the darkness.

"Brilliant observation...who's there?" She asked as the answer already swam to the surface of her consciousness. Hear heart began to beat faster and she clutched at her shoulders more tightly.

"I think you know me," he said in his quiet, resonant voice and proceeded to light a cigar. In the glow of the flame Chantal could momentarily see the strong contours of his jaw and vivid green eyes that stared back at her. Dark, wavy hair framed his face.

Chantal's mind began to swim in the sur reality of his presence. "You're the voice from my dream," she said faintly as he walked towards her.

"Was I a dream?"

Chantal pressed her spine into the balcony railing, unable to back away from his tall, broad, approaching form. "Who are you?" she repeated, her throat dry, emitting only a whisper.

"Here, let me give you my coat before you freeze," he said removing a long, beautifully cut, dark coat and draping it over her shuddering shoulders. "Better?"

"Yesss," she said through quivering lips. His warmth still radiated off the fabric scented with tobacco and musky spice. She made herself look up into those deep green eyes, her heart thudded in her breast and her mind began to open like a river in remembrance. His gaze drew Chantal deeply into his eyes and she began to feel gradually more lightheaded.

"I want to show you something," he said and took hold of her hand.

"Where?" She asked.

"Elsewhere," he said simply.

Perplexed but intrigued Chantal responded, "why not I had my fill of the party," she said. He looked to the heavens; his ship had arrived. With a flash of light, Chantal and her mysterious visitor disappeared from the balcony of CIV Central.

NiNE

Inside CIV Central streamers and sparkling confetti came down from the ceiling as the clock struck midnight. The guests began to resemble fairies gilded with sparkling hair and clothing as they cheered and clapped in celebration of the New Year. Lorne and Maya embraced and had a dance. "I have a fix on that blond woman," she whispered in his ear.

"Great! I'll get Amit"

"No! You know how it sometimes works, I don't know exactly where she is but I see her in a hotel room and if I focus I can get us there. You up for a little adventure?"

"Maya, we should really tell Amit so that he can locate her with his team."

"I know Lorne, his RV team is already working on it but that could take too much time and we could loose her. I could try to take him through but you know Amit is not trained the way we are, he can't teleport. It might not work or the effects may put him out of commission for a while. I think it is best if we go. Just leave him a note that I've viewed her being alone in a hotel room with lime green and gold 1940's style décor, it is very distinct. That should serve as a good lead for the RV team. By the time we've gone he'll figure out we're there."

Lorne hesitated for a moment, "fine, jot it down and I'll make sure he gets it."

DRUMS OF THE WINGED CARRIER 2020

Maya quickly got her hand held Q out of her bag and inserted a diskette. She rapidly relayed the information through the touch pad and took out a diskette, giving it to Lorne who discreetly handed it to a security person with instructions that Amit receive it.

"Let's go," said Lorne taking Maya by the hand and moving to a discreet room away from the party.

"As far as I can see she is not armed and is alone." Maya held Lorne's hand and began to move her energy up with the breath and watched him do the same. She held his loving gaze for a moment as the energy began to build and leaned forward kissing him on the mouth. He embraced her and felt their heat rising up their bodies to their heads till their temples throbbed. Maya stared deeply into his pupils seeing Diana in her hotel room, as a powerful vortex of energy encircled her and Lorne. He began to see the same scene expand and become more real. The energy grew in intensity till their bodies began to dissolve and they momentarily lost consciousness. In the next moment Lorne and Maya appeared in the hotel room directly behind a greenish, velveteen armchair where Diana had dozed off.

Maya looked around the room glancing at Lorne. "Nice to see you made it but you better wipe that off," she whispered, reaching for Lorne's face. "Lipstick."

Lorne reached in his pocket and found a crumpled tissue and used it to clean his face. As Diana slept he moved silently to lock the door and disconnected the phonecom.

Maya moved towards Diana who slept soundly and put her hand gently on her shoulder, whispering in her ear, "we're here to have a little chat."

Diana's eyes flew open and she bolted up in her chair. She looked at Maya and Lorne with shock, her heart pounding in her chest, "how did you get in here?"

"The question is, who are you and what were you doing at CIV Central? You sure as hell don't work for the Journal, I personally know all the staff there," said Maya, her demanding eyes boring into Diana.

Diana's mind raced for an answer but she knew that there was nothing to say that would be believed at this point other than the truth.

"You have been asking questions about the workings of the CIV and our activities, why? asked Lorne.

"Look, I can't tell you anything."

"Fine, then we will escort you downtown to the justice centre where you can meet with our intelligence personnel. The room that they'll have for you will be much less comfortable than your set up here," he replied.

"It doesn't matter where you take me they are going to retrieve me shortly."

Lorne looked at Maya. "Who is going to retrieve you? What do you mean?" Diana was silent.

"We're a progressive society and we openly share technology and knowledge. I don't know what exactly you're up to but is all this really necessary? What do you want? Have you ever thought about taking the civilized approach and just asking?" asked Maya.

Diana sighed deeply and momentarily put her face in her hands. She looked up at Maya, "this time is beautiful, more than I had ever hoped to find. The group I'm with is very interested in this timeline. Where we are from things are very bleak. We cannot stay there." Diana knew she had revealed too much but after all she had been through this night she didn't care anymore. There would be serious repercussions for her upon her return because of being discovered, that fact she was certain of. The peace and sanity of this place starkly contrasted with 2015 in New York and the insatiable appetite of the Omega Group for power. In a way she couldn't quite understand the frequency of this time had changed her. Diana knew that she was not the same person that had arrived here four days prior.

Maya and Lorne looked at each other. "So you're the one who's been creating the time storms," Lorne said.

"Yes, you know about that?"

"Symptoms have broken out in the general population around the vicinity of the time rifts. We suspected that someone was using technology to enter our time," Lorne admitted.

Diana glanced at the clock on the wall, 12:46 she noted. "I can't tell you anything more; you don't want to mess with these people."

"Well by virtue of your presence here they are already messing with us. Are they ex government?" Lorne asked her. "We suspected that key figures of the old government and possibly members of the Illuminati had left just prior to the great cataclysms. We also know that one of the governments black projects funded by the organization was time travel."

"Then you already know more than I can tell you."

Maya looked at Diana, "Do they want to take over this timeline?"

"Look, I'm a physicist. I helped develop some of the technology we are using. The only reason that they sent me is because I was the only one who discovered and could access this timeline. The others have tried and cannot get through. I am obviously not gifted at espionage; I bungled up this operation quite thoroughly."

"Please answer the question Diana," said Lorne.

"Yes."

Silence filled the small hotel room. Diana's stomach became queasy again; the lime green walls of the small room closed in on her. "The group consists of very power hungry, obsessively driven people. The will do whatever is necessary to ensure their success."

"Then don't go back. Stay here, we will protect you and give you amnesty for your cooperation. If they can't enter this timeline without you then there is no danger to anyone," said Lorne.

Diana's lip began to quiver and her eyes welled up. She looked at both of them with futility. "Too much has happened, they're coming to get me," she said and looked at the clock once more…12:59. "I don't want to go back!" She took hold of Maya's arm, her eyes wide with fear. In slow motion Diana watched the dial on the wall clock turn to 1:00 am. Suddenly Maya could feel an electrical surge traveling from Diana's hand through her arm. Her consciousness began to swim as a force drew her sharply to its centre. The whole room became illuminated with an unnatural light. The last thing Maya remembered was Lorne grabbing her and pulling her towards him.

On board his ship Zain watched Novara, the equivalent of a medical science specialist, regulate the neuronal conductor around Chantal's head. "Her memories will flow more smoothly now. The ones that were blocked will reactivate upon her return when she reads her notes." She removed the unit from Chantal when the procedure completed.

"Thank you Novara."

"I will leave you now." She left the cabin and the opening that she had walked through reformed into a wall with no sign of an entrance point.

Zain watched Chantal sleep, her cheeks bloomed roses and soft breath escaped slightly parted, cupid bow lips. A wisp of dark hair fell across her face down to her clavicle. He studied how her skin draped over that smooth, rounded bone and caught the cabin's soft light in pearlescence. She began to stir and he rose to get refreshment for her. Zain placed his hand within an illuminated, rotating matrix of glowing lines and withdrew a glass containing a bluish liquid.

"Where am I?" her voice sounded behind him.

He approached her with a smile and handed her the glass, "here, drink this, it will replenish you."

Chantal studied his face for a long moment. It appeared exotic and foreign though she could not place his genetic origins. His deep complexion dramatically contrasted those emerald green eyes. Waves of dark hair contradicted the strong line of his jaw. He was quite beautiful. Chantal knew his face and realized she was not afraid of him and accepted the glass. "What is this?" she sipped the liquid slowly; it tasted fruity but not too sweet.

"It's a manufactured essence that contains every nutrient your body needs for an entire day. The molecular structure allows for rapid, full absorption with almost no waste byproducts."

Chantal wryly wondered if this meticulous efficiency meant they didn't need toilets on board.

"If you need to use a latrine we can accommodate that."

"You can read my thoughts?"

"Yes."

Chantal slightly blushed.

"It's alright," he said and broke out with rich laughter.

"I don't see what is so amusing," she retorted furrowing her brow. She also could read thoughts though it required her to trance and focus on her subject. She was not quite as smooth with it as he appeared to be.

"I've been here before, this is a space craft. I don't know how I know that. Why did you bring me here? Oh God, the party…"

"It's all right. We've arranged your safe return. No one will know where you've been." We brought you here to help you regain your memories. Certain technologies are on board that can assist with that."

"I'm not accustomed to being poked and prodded, what do you plan to do?"

Zain smiled at her bluntness, "what needed to be done has been completed. I can return you now if you like but first perhaps you would enjoy the view a bit, it's quite stunning," he said and before Chantal's eyes the walls of the cabin dissolved revealing a deepest blue sky alight with a halo of swirling stars.

She inhaled deeply in total wonder. "This is just like the technology I experienced in that circular house by the ocean when the ceiling dissolved! Where are we, is this the Milky Way?"

"Yes, isn't it marvelous?"

"My god, I've never seen it this close."

"I can take us in a bit further if you like."

"Really? Well of course, what am I saying, we're on a space ship!"

A holographic grid made of light appeared in front of Zain. Chantal watched it as a rapid succession of lights lit along the grid filaments. Suddenly she experienced a mild sinking sensation in her solar plexus. Out the windows momentarily a flash appeared then she surveyed a new landscape of dazzling starlight and luminous gasses with particulates. "Wow! How gorgeous!"

"We just folded space time. I guess you'll be wanting go back now," Zain said with a sly grin as he watched Chantal enraptured with the view.

"I could stay here forever."

Ethereal music began to fill the cabin. Chantal had never heard it before but it transported her consciousness higher into heaven. Zain enfolded her hand in his and whispered in her ear, "this is your future."

Chantal's eyes began to mist and she couldn't speak. In silence they watched the movement of vast heavens as the ship cruised through the Milky Way galaxy.

TEN

Sparks flew in the electromagnetic field that transported Diana back to the lab inside the Victory building. Dr. Rechter and Colonel Stark moved quickly towards her. "Who was that?" demanded Colonel Stark. "You were holding someone's arm and they were beginning to appear back here with you!"

Diana gathered her thoughts, not certain how to proceed in explaining all that had happened. "I ran into some problems."

"Clearly, what happened?"

"They already suspected that someone was time traveling to their reality. People in the vicinity of my arrival began to exhibit physical symptoms. Then I was discovered."

"Jesus Christ!" Colonel Stark began to pace. "The group is going to be furious. How did this happen?"

"I'm not sure," Diana responded.

"What the hell do you mean you're not sure!" he screamed.

Diana had never seen him like this before and her blood ran cold. He had always made her feel uncomfortable in his presence and now she realized why. She took a deep breath but already felt her stomach clenching. "Lorne and Maya Savanna made a surprise appearance in my hotel room. I have no idea how they knew where to find me or how they got in for that matter. No one saw me leave the party, I'm sure of that."

"Well someone must have suspected something and followed you. How else would they know where you were staying?"

Dr. Rechter became agitated watching the heated exchange and turned to leave the room.

"Stay right there!" Colonel Stark ordered.

A little shocked at his manner Dr. Rechter sat down.

"I'll tell you one thing, that press cover you came up with did not work. Maya Savanna personally knows everyone who works at the Seattle Journal. That's what caused this whole mess."

"Shut up, you stupid bitch!" "This whole mess happened because a woman without proper training was sent to do a covert operative's job. I warned the group not to trust you with a responsibility of this magnitude."

"You're crazy!" Diana yelled back.

Colonel Stark struck Diana on the side of the head with his fist. Diana fell to her knees, her head oozing blood from where he had broken her skin. This man was a raving lunatic, she thought incredulously. "Get her out of here, lock her in one of the upper offices," he told Dr. Rechter.

The doctor just stared at Colonel stark for a moment then he took Diana's arm and led her out of the laboratory. He took her to the eight floor to one of the offices. "I'm sorry my dear I will come by a little later and tend to your cut," he said as he locked her in the small room.

Diana sat on a chair in the drab office and finally lost her composure. Tears streamed down her face, mixing with blood from the gash in her head and dripped onto her blouse. The oppressive frequency of this reality crushed her heart. She felt totally disjointed and out of place. Worse, Diana was known as a successful scientist and respected by her peers. Outrage and humiliation from being treated like an animal by a sexist madman filled her being. She faced the truth however that her own choices had led to this. Diana had been involved in the mind control administration of the masses and knew the results. What she had done was no less barbaric than Colonel Stark's actions. In their quest for power and control the Omega Group had all lost their objectivity and worse their humanity. The full impact of Diana's choices overwhelmed her and she remorsefully wept hard from the depths of her soul.

In another part of the Victory building behind closed doors Colonel Stark met with the group and debriefed them on the status of the time shift operation. The Omega Group comprised of top former US government representatives, three key CIA operatives, three scientists and eight members of the Illuminati who funded some of the ex governments black projects. In total they had twenty one members.

Nicholas Sealy who lead the organization stood over six foot five in a bulky frame. Known to most as a former CIA operative, he joined the organization after the great cataclysms. Only five group members knew the deeper truth of his identity. Both the former President and Vice President of what had been the United States had been killed in the destruction of the White House and in the ensuing chaos the group formed and jointly appointed Nicholas as their head.

"Where is Diana now?" Nicholas asked.

"I had Dr. Rechter lock her in one of the small offices upstairs Sir," Colonel Stark replied.

"You should not have lost your temper with her. What were you thinking? She is the only person who has made a viable inroad in time that is a future potential for our relocation. Regardless of her failure to remain undetected she is still the key to the success of this whole project."

Colonel Stark could not believe that after Diana had proven to be so incompetent and untrustworthy Nicholas still had any use for her. He bit his tongue and said nothing.

"I want you to bring her here immediately; she should be a part of this meeting."

"Dr. Rechter, would you please help Diana to ah…clean up a bit and escort her here to join us," asked Colonel Stark.

"Right away Sir," replied Dr. Rechter as he scurried out of the room. He took the lift up to the eighth floor and arrived at the room where he had left Diana. He unlocked the door and entered, startling her. "It's alright, my dear, I've come to take you down to join the group meeting. Nicholas has requested your presence." She would need a major clean up he remarked to himself upon observing her bloody soiled blouse and encrusted, oozing head. Mascara had run down her cheeks adding a more grotesque overall effect. She looked up at him through swollen eyes and clearly had no interest in attending. "Come," he gently took her arm and coaxed her out of the chair. "Let's get you all cleaned up, we don't want to keep the group waiting."

Diana reluctantly followed him down to the medical supply room. He sat her down and swabbed her face and head with antiseptic solution. "That cut is wide; I am going to quickly suture it for you so it heals nicely without a scar."

Diana complied in silence as Dr. Rechter stitched the wound shut. He got a clean blouse and cosmetic bag out of her closet. "Here, everything you need to make yourself beautiful!"

Diana glared at him; he must be kidding she thought.

"I will give you some privacy and meet you outside when you're ready," he said quickly and left the room.

She opened her compact and looked at her face. The side of her head had an ugly, purplish bruise with black sutures sticking out of a cut at least an inch and a half long. Her eyes were red and puffy and she looked pale. There was nothing in her cosmetic bag that would fix this. "Fuck it," she said and put the mirror away and wiped her face with a tissue. She took off the blood stained blouse and put on a clean one.

Diana stepped into the hallway where Dr. Rechter waited. He looked at her made his best effort to smile. "You look much better my dear."

"Yeah, I could pass as a double of Frankenstein's bride courtesy of that lunatic Stark."

Dr. Rechter had wisdom enough not to respond and lead her to the meeting room.

James searched the party for Chantal. He was annoyed with himself for not finding her to toast the New Year and give her the little gift he had bought. He could not get a mental fix on her at all. Finally, after thoroughly looking in every room and even waiting outside the ladies latrine to see if she was there he approached Amit. "I can't find Chantal anywhere, have you seen her?"

"No, Lorne and Maya have vanished as well," Amit replied.

"Where the heck is everyone?"

"Maya got a glimpse of the suspect's location. Lorne left us the details and one of our RV operatives identified the location as the Harrington Inn downtown. I think that's where they are now; we're on our way there," said Amit putting on his jacket.

"I should go with you in case Chantal is there."

"No, why don't you try calling her at home I have a feeling she is not with Lorne and Maya."

James had not thought to call her at home. It wasn't like her to just leave without saying anything. "You're right Amit I haven't tried her at home yet." As Amit left accompanied by two intelligence officers James stepped out of the party and called Chantal on his micro phonecom. The line rang and finally a mini holograph projected from the device with the words, 'picture disabled' rotating within it. "Hello?" said a groggy voice.

"Chantal?"

"Yes, is that you James?"

"Yeah, what happened? You just left the party without saying anything."

Chantal paused for a moment. She became more alert but her head still felt very foggy. She realized that she had been aboard a space ship and somehow got transported back home. Suddenly it all began to come back. She had been watching the stars with her familiar friend when he said, "it's time for you to return or you'll be missed."

She had looked at him and said, "I don't know your name."

"Zain," he had replied with a big smile and that was all she could remember.

"Chantal, are you there? Please activate the picture on the phonecom so I know you're ok."

"James I'm here but I'm in bed."

"Please just do it."

"Alright," she said and her image appeared.

James looked at her sleepy face, relieved that she was alright. "Mind telling me why you ditched me at the party and went home?"

A small laugh escaped from Chantal, "god James I didn't ditch you. I just got a migraine and took a cab home. You looked like you were enjoying yourself so I didn't want to make you drive me all the way back. I'm sorry I probably should have said something." Chantal hoped she sounded convincing.

"Well I'm just glad you're safe, I was worried."

"I'm fine."

"By the way, they may have found that blond at the Harrington Inn. Amit is on his way there with his intelligence people as we speak."

"That's good news. I'll see you in the morning and hopefully he'll have an update for us."

"Ok and Chantal…"

"Yes?"

"Happy New Year."

Chantal smiled, "Happy New Year James."

James ended the conversation. This was not how he had envisioned the evening ending. He opened the little box that contained an antique bracelet with gemstone dragon flies circling around it. He had so wanted to give this to Chantal and tell her how he felt about her. Tonight the distance between them felt vaster than ever. He closed the box and put it back into his coat. The party wound down as guests took their leave and James decided to do the same.

Back in her home and now wide awake Chantal got up and poured herself a glass of water. Morocco jumped on her lap and arranged himself in a circular cuddle, clearly not ready to relinquish his sleep. She stroked his soft back and sipped cool water. She knew that she had done the right thing in not telling James how she really left the party. Besides, it was obvious that he had feelings for her and a description of Chantal cruising the Milky Way galaxy on board a space ship with a handsome, mysterious host would be like rubbing salt in the wound even if he did believe her.

Zain, she thought. He had said his name was Zain and he clearly was as smooth as his name. Chantal realized that the whole time she had been on board his ship hardly any of her questions had been answered. In fact she had been so enraptured with the view of the cosmos the music and his magnetic presence that she had not even asked the more pertinent ones! She suspected that he knew exactly the effect all those elements were having on her. Chantal furrowed her brow. She decided not to be so easily swooned should they meet again; she didn't know a thing about him or where he came from. Admittedly Chantal could not get the sensation of Zain's hand enveloping hers out of her mind. She could easily loose her self in those intense, green eyes of his and never tire of looking into them; like peering into forever laced with a hint of mischief.

James flashed back into Chantal's mind; he had to be one of sweetest and most intelligent men she had ever met. He exuded a natural vitality that was very attractive and treated her with total respect. Chantal had often searched the corners of her mind as to why she would not allow him to get closer to her. Something inside always held her back. When she reveled in rivers of higher consciousness a 'wildness' would take possession of her bringing an intensity to her life that no one could contain. Perhaps that was it, she realized. Chantal did not want to ever be contained by anyone and the nature of personal relationships was such that it sometimes fostered such containment. She knew James was the type of man who would want to settle down to a safe, comfortable life and over time her independence and desire for solitude would annoy him.

Chantal got up with Morocco in her arms and returned to her bedroom. About to turn off her light she noticed the night table drawer slightly open.

Slowly her hand moved towards it and she pulled it open revealing a tattered, floral covered notebook. Chantal stared at it for a moment realizing the notebook was from her days at Sacred Rose. Where did this old thing come from? She wondered having no recollection of putting it in the drawer. Chantal removed it and scanned the pages. With each word lost memories of select experiences at Sacred Rose unfolded in her mind. She could not stop reading and ploughed through the entire journal to the last page.

Chantal remembered how in the last two years of her attendance at Sacred Rose she had begun to have visions of the future. A specific part of her training facilitated the creation of neuronal connections in her brain that allowed movement forward and backward in time. This resulted in vivid descriptions of life in 2020 that filled the journal's pages. Her role in a government position, some of the technologies they used and the systems of learning were all described in her notes.

Further in the book she found a rendering of the house she had visited in her out of body experience where Zain had first appeared. In addition she found depictions of advanced technologies very similar to the ones on board his ship and much more. The date of 2508 was written in the upper corner of that particular page. Many scenes that she had remote viewed created a montage that spanned two main timelines; 2020 and 2508. She found reference to a dark haired man who appeared in many of these visions and had shown her things. Chantal realized that he had also appeared in her dreams; it was Zain. Nothing more about his identity spanned the pages of the notebook or existed in her memory. Chantal only knew that he existed in the future and had interacted with her future self.

Of the entire journal one vision stood out the most to Chantal: She had been with Zain and two others in 2508 on board a space craft using an advanced holographic viewer generated from a grid like structure that they interfaced with their minds as it displayed several future timeline potentials. From these she worked in constructing a select timeline that represented her future beyond the great cataclysms. Chantal remembered the indescribable connectedness she felt with Zain and all life when they engaged viewing space time through their mind grid interface. Her consciousness reached through the vastness of space and simultaneously she existed in many places that she had visited with him. Somehow in her current environment her non local awareness was not as pronounced and stunning as when she had engaged the technology with Zain. She knew it was because Earth's collective reality matrix was not yet connected to future grid technologies that would enhance this awareness.

Momentarily she came back to the present and looked around her room observing the gentle rise and fall of Morocco's back as he slept curled up on his little red cushion at the foot of her bed. Open blinds invited a wash of waning, silvery moonlight upon blooming orchids potted by the window. She looked out at the moon's serene face and pondered the revelation that her future self from 2508 had designed her current reality in 2020. In the clarity of her remembrance no surprise existed within Chantal only the knowingness of this truth.

Exhausted from intense mental activity and the emotional surge of regaining lost memories Chantal closed her eyes and slept holding the notebook against her chest.

ELEVEN

Lorne held Maya close to him as she regained full consciousness. "What happened?" she asked looking around the room.

"Diana almost pulled you through with her. Your body was beginning to dissolve, in fact your arm did and then I grabbed you."

Maya looked at her arm and rubbed it. "Well I feel fine. She's gone?"

"Yes."

"I feel sorry for her; she's tangled up in quite a mess. She looked really scared to go back."

Someone knocked on the door, "Lorne, Maya are you in there?"

"It's Amit," said Lorne and quickly opened the door.

"Are you two alright?"

"We're fine," Maya replied.

"Please, no matter what the circumstances are never do that again, leave to apprehend a suspect without the intelligence team. Where is she?"

Lorne explained everything that took place with Diana to Amit and the intelligence officers.

"Well we now know more about who's been causing the time storms so we can update World CIV intelligence units," said Amit.

"We didn't get a chance to find out from Diana details about their weapons but if they plan on taking over this timeline it is likely they still have operational mind reprogramming capability," said Lorne.

"That means we have to come up with defensive measures immediately," said Amit as he led them out of the hotel room. "We thoroughly searched CIV Central after the guests left and found surveillance chips planted in several areas. They've all been disabled so the building is clean."

Amit dismissed the intelligence officers and headed to his car, "it's been a long night, go home and get some sleep you two and stay out of trouble."

Lorne and Maya grinned at each other and then realized their car was still back at CIV Central. "Amit wait for us we need a ride," Maya called out.

"Sure, get in. At this rate I may as well stay up to watch the sunrise." Amit knew he would not sleep but say up to formulate the agenda for a meeting with the defense group first thing in the morning. He had already spoken to John about this earlier at the party in hopes that an effective defense strategy could be implemented quickly with help from the science team. They all got in Amit's vehicle and headed back to CIV Central.

Diana walked into the meeting room with Dr. Rechter and silently faced the Omega group. Nicholas examined her forehead, "Diana on behalf of the group I would like to extend our sincerest apologies for what you have suffered. We are all under tremendous stress to solve our dilemma and obviously Colonel Stark has allowed that to impair his judgment," he said and glared at Colonel Stark.

"I would say his actions have gone far beyond sanity. Do you intend to keep a volatile person with impaired judgment involved in this operation?" She glanced over at Colonel Stark and his face flushed crimson with anger.

Members from the group began to grow restless, "quiet please." Nicholas studied her and paused. "Diana although you're an esteemed scientist and highly important to our objectives I think it's fair to say that you also suffered from impaired judgment."

"How's that?"

"Your failure to remain undetected at CIV Central which has jeopardized our plans."

Diana did not respond knowing it was futile to say anymore against Nicholas's favorite puppet. Colonel Stark's ability to effectively perform the group's dirty work made him an immovable asset. She questioned the sincerity of the trite apology Nicholas had offered her.

Colonel Stark leapt at his chance to discredit her further, "I made my opinion known to the group that this woman was not the right person to send forward and I was right; she's totally incompetent. We don't need her we can find another suitable timeline."

"Both of you have shown your weaknesses thus far which compromise this operation. However the group and I still agree that the timeline Diana discovered is our best chance to reestablish ourselves as the governing body of a progressive future. We have agreed to make certain modifications to this mission that will ensure our success."

"What kind of modifications?" asked Colonel Stark.

Diana's pulse quickened as she sensed what was coming.

"You and I will accompany her on the next trip. Diana you and Dr. Rechter are to make the necessary adjustments to the TII so that we can be transported together."

Diana looked over at Dr. Rechter who avoided her eyes, "that has never been attempted before, it's too risky."

Nicholas smiled, "I've already discussed this with Dr. Rechter. He is confident that it can be done. You practically pulled someone through with you upon your return and routinely take supplies along. As long as the modifications are performed there is no reason why we won't succeed."

Colonel Stark's mind raced as he contemplated the implications. He didn't like the idea that Diana would still be allowed to time travel but at least now he would be there to keep her in line. "Excellent idea Sir," he said.

Growing horror filled Diana as she thought of taking the two of them along knowing they intended on total memory eradication and restructuring of the population. She wanted to yell out that they were making a mistake and that the CIV had made such astounding progress in fostering a remarkably elevated way of life for all people. She knew however that doing so would be suicide and a waste of time since the group was not interested in preserving a way of life without their rule over it.

"Diana what exactly did you tell the two IM's who discovered you?"

"Nothing, they appeared in my room just before you retrieved me. Maya Savanna grabbed my arm and you know the rest," she lied.

Nicholas looked intently into her eyes, "are you sure there is nothing else?" he asked with a menacing undertone. He didn't completely trust anyone.

Diana looked back at him defiantly. She was not going to let him intimidate her. "I've told you everything."

"And you planted the last MIP cone as instructed?"

"Yes it is located in the vicinity of the hotel."

"Very well, then I would like you and Dr. Rechter to start working on the

TII modifications immediately, I'm giving you three days."

"That's not enough time…." Dr. Rechter began to protest.

"It has to be. I'm not willing to wait on this any longer since the CIV is aware that time interference has already taken place. We are adding risk each hour we postpone.

"Yes Sir."

"Good." Nicholas turned and addressed the scientist from the Omega group that had created the memory restructuring program for the new timeline. "Dr. Ospov have all the bugs been worked out of the mind interface program? We need it ready for us to implement upon our arrival."

"Almost. Since the population we will use it on does not exhibit the added complication of mental instability I am confident that this time we will achieve success."

"Excellent."

Diana had assisted Dr. Ospov in implementing the last MIP on the population in their current time. While the people did accept the Omega group's ruling presence the process had aggravated their mental state resulting in further problems and anti—social behavior. She knew that citizens of 2020 exhibited excellent mental faculties but in her opinion MIP had not been sufficiently developed to avoid risk to mental coherence. The idea of radically altering that beautiful world made her sick inside. Diana realized she had to find a way to stop Nicholas and the group from destroying everything these innocent people had created.

"John, wake up."

John opened his eyes and saw Jena sitting next to him on his bed. "Child, what are you doing here? It's very late."

"I have to show you something," she said and placed her hand over his forehead. Instantly a mild electrical sensation filled his brain and John's consciousness disassociated from his body. He felt as if miles away, floating in a void. "It's all right John, I'm here. You're going to remember something important." He could still remotely hear Jena's voice. A scene appeared of him in a mountain forest of western Canada. He watched himself dwelling in a shabby cabin, foraging for food and tending to basic survival. Inside he observed himself working on something. He looked closer…yes now he remembered. John was preparing the photonic shielding device to counteract the effects of electromagnetic weapons. Once completed John had kept the shield on everyday protecting the parameters of his immediate vicinity until Jena had appeared to him in the forest.

"Open your eyes, John."

John's consciousness engaged his body once more; he opened his eyes, sat up and looked at Jena," how did you do that?"

"I just knew you needed to remember something."

He examined her face for a moment and thought to himself how different this child was and so intuitive at times. He contemplated his retrieved memories and became very animated, "I remember before now.before this time. I was in the forest and I survived the great cataclysms…I remember!" I left the city just before they happened and created the photonic shielding device. They never got a chance to scramble my brain."

"John, everyone that is now in your time was relocated forward to 2015 five years ago. You missed this time placement because the device you created also blocked the technology advanced beings used to move everyone forward with new memories. You had to be retrieved and placed in your proper timeline. All recollection of your months in the woods was erased to facilitate your smooth transition into this reality. John, your memory of the photonic shielding technology you created had to be recovered and you know why."

"Of course, it will serve as a defensive measure against any future mind tampering effects."

"Yes."

"But who moved us forward, how did we get here?"

"That's not important but protecting this time and your way of life is."

John looked deeply into Jena's eyes for a long moment and for the first time she revealed ancient consciousness that dwelt there. His eyes misted over. "You're not really a child are you?"

Jena's youthful face smiled, "I wear this garment for my mission and I will remain here until your world is safe again."

In his heightened state of consciousness John knew that he could not ask her questions about her origins. As a scientist he had always been intrigued by the unsolved mysteries of life and finally here one sat before him.

John took Jena's hand and held it, his eyes welled up knowing that she would leaving him one day and a tear ran down his cheek.

Jena hugged John with her small frame and pressed her curly red hair against his face. She pulled away and looked at him, "get some sleep now," she said and left his room.

Fatigue began to overtake John but the photon shield design filled his mind. He could see himself designing and constructing it again. This time it has to be much more powerful, he thought as he drifted off. The clock showed 4:15 am and John tossed restlessly in his sleep.

"Jena, Jena!" John called out and his voice echoed back to him explosively reverberating in his ears. He stood at the edge of a steep incline and a few yards away Jena floated in a transparent cube that turned and twisted in the air. Her hands pressed against the glass and he could see her lips forming his name in silence. John looked down from the incline onto menacingly jagged rocks. He could not find a way to get to her. Inside the cube he watched as a door opened and someone stepped inside with her. The person leaned forward, his face distorted by the cube but John could see a hand grabbing Jena's shoulder with a gold signet ring on the middle finger. Her eyes showed alarm as she opened her mouth to scream. John's frustration at being stranded on the edge of the cliff intensified as the cube began to twist more rapidly and float away from him. "Create the path to her," a voice in his mind sounded. He paused and collected his thoughts envisioning a walkway between himself and the receding cube. As he watched a narrow strip of light began to form before him and solidify reaching all the way to Jena. John backed up and took a running start across the path. As he launched towards her he looked down momentarily not feeling the ground beneath his feet and the path started to dissolve hurling John backwards towards the rocks below. As he hit the ground he woke up from the force of the impact.

Perspiration soaked John's night shirt and his heart thudded wildly against his ribs. He realized he had been dreaming but in wakefulness the fear for Jena's life remained. John got out of bed and walked down the hall to her room. He cracked her door and looked in and saw an empty bed. He turned the light on; she was definitely not in the room. "Jena?" he called out and headed down the hall to the living room, "Jena!"

"I'm in here," her voice sounded from the kitchen.

"I couldn't sleep so I'm having an orange, want one?"

"No thanks," he said hugely relieved to hear her voice. "I just had a strange dream and wanted to make sure you were ok."

"I'm fine John."

"Alright, good night, don't stay up too late," he said with his habitual protectiveness. She merely smiled and he wondered if she even needed sleep as he walked back to his room. He knew she was safe here with him but uneasiness about the disturbing dream remained in his psyche.

TWELVE

James ran up the stairs of the entrance to CIV Central catching up with Chantal. "Hey there, how'd you sleep?"

"Not enough."

"I'll bet that will be the universal statement of the day."

"Maya said this meeting shouldn't be long, apparently Amit has already run through everything with his intelligence unit and been advised by John regarding some progress in defensive measures. The rest of the IM's have agreed to take what's left of the day off afterwards."

"I missed the call this morning and wondered what the plans were."

James and Chantal entered the building and headed to the meeting. Most of the members were already assembled waiting for Amit to commence. "I have something for you that I didn't get a chance to give you at the party," James whispered in Chantal's ear catching the tropical warmth of a rare floral scent she wore.

"Ok," she smiled.

Amit walked into the room, "good morning everyone and happy 2020."

The IM's gave a round of applause and cheered in acknowledgement of what they would ensure would be another joyous and productive year for all citizens in spite of the complications they now faced.

"We are grateful that you all assembled here so quickly again a few short hours after just having left."

"Well next time we have a party here I am packing my sleeping bag just in case," Julio remarked.

The IM's chuckled, "I was waiting for someone to throw something like that at me this morning," replied Amit with a grin. "We're well prepared with defensive measures to fend off any more hecklers," he joked as a catering service wheeled in fresh coffee and pastries. "Please everyone help your selves before we start."

"Heaven," Maya said as she poured herself a cup of coffee.

Once everyone had settled again Amit commenced the meeting.

"I am pleased to report that we have made significant progress in our investigation. This is partly due to efforts of Lorne and Maya in identifying the persons responsible for the time storms we have been experiencing." Amit continued to brief the IM's on the events that had occurred the previous evening and revealed the identity of Diana as the central person who had intercepted their reality through time. He concluded with confirmation that the group she represented was in fact comprised of ex— government and likely secret organization members from their pre cataclysmic time.

"Did this woman give any details about this group's weapons capability or how they intend to take over our reality?" asked Richard.

"No but we are confident that they will attempt memory erasure and reprogramming because unless they plan on transporting a huge army here that's the only feasible method for achieving what they want efficiently." Amit continued, "as we meet here John's team is working on defense measures. I've asked him to briefly update you on what that entails from his scientific expertise."

As if on cue John walked into the meeting room. "Am I late?"

"No, perfect timing I was just beginning to talk about your defense project why don't you continue, John."

"Thank you Amit." John stepped up to the front of the room and continued, "Well as you all know last night proved to be full of surprises and I was also on the receiving end of one of them. I am thankful that in our current reality people are more enlightened so I hope the experience I am about to relay will be received by open minds." He proceeded to share the previous night's events and described to the IM's how he had retrieved his memories of his months just before and after the great cataclysms but leaving details of Jena's involvement out.

"Are you saying that you did not loose time the way everyone else did here after the great cataclysms and remember everything up to now?" asked Chantal.

"Yes, for me it was different. The device I used to protect myself from the mind scrambling technology prevented me from being placed in our new time probably because whoever moved us forward uses similar technology to do so. However I was eventually intercepted and placed in this time flow later than all of you and my memories of the months in Canada were gone till last night."

"What made them come back?" asked James.

John resolved to stay composed and new that he could not divulge anything about Jena or what he had learned from her to anyone. "I'm not sure, it just happened and I'm glad it did because that is where my memory of building the photon shielding device had gone. It is this technology that is being built as we speak by select members of the Scientific Advisory Group."

"How long will it take to complete, I mean the perimeter of your property would be much smaller than our requirements. Also will the device still be as effective covering larger areas?" asked Richard.

"We've embarked upon a two stage process. Because of the urgency of this matter a device will be completed within 48 hours that will protect all of the immediate area around Olympia and some of the neighboring cities. The next phase is more complicated because it involves constructing a device that covers the entire North American sector from it's installation in space. In answer to your last question, the photon shield has never been tested over larger areas but I am confident that it will be effective."

"We're also going to share the schematics of this defense device with the other world sectors so they will have the option of implementing the technology for their security," added Amit. After finalizing some additional personal security measures for the IM's he closed the meeting and everyone prepared to leave.

Chantal gathered her belongings as James approached her, "care for some lunch?"

"No, I'm not hungry yet but I'm heading over to Helios Books at the village if you want to join me."

"Sure, let's go," said James as he helped Chantal with her coat. They left CIV Central together and got into James's car. He cleared his throat and took the little gift. "I've been carrying this around since New Year's Eve it's starting to wear a hole in my pocket. I think it has your name on it," he said with a sly smile.

"How sweet, thank you," Chantal replied pulling the silver satin ribbon off the little violet colored box. She opened it and took out the gemstone bracelet, her eyes suffused in wonder. "James, this is gorgeous!"

"I know how much you love dragon flies and antique jewelry. This is an authentic piece from circa 1925. All the stones are hand cut and set in platinum."

"This must have cost you a fortune!" Chantal studied the little dragonflies circling the bracelet. Each one had topaz eyes and the wings were studded with aquamarines and a sprinkle of white diamonds.

James reached over to help Chantal fasten the bracelet around her wrist. "Chantal you know I've had feelings for you for a long time now…"

"James, I know what you're going to say and that's why I can't keep this. I care a great deal for you and trust you more than anyone I know but I can't get involved with you," she said trying to undo the bracelet.

James didn't move to assist her. "I don't understand, what is it? We have a great time together no matter where we are or what we're doing; I always make you laugh. Why won't you let me get closer to you?"

"James, you think you know me but there is more there that you don't know."

"But I want to if you would just let me in. I want to know all of you," he said and put his hands on her shoulders drawing her closer to him.

Chantal skillfully maneuvered her arms out of his embrace and put her hands on his face. She looked into his eyes with an intensity he had never seen before. "I can't be contained James, not by anyone not ever." She released her hands, "I am not the woman who will settle down with you or have your children. You deserve to be happy James, you are a wonderful man, a real gentleman and a very precious friend to me but I don't want anything more from you." Finally saying those words to him pained Chantal greatly. She cared so much about him and had always avoided this moment. She so hated to see the sad look in his eyes.

James didn't know what more to say.

"Please, you must return this," Chantal said struggling to undo the clasp. "Help me."

"No, I want you to keep it."

"I can't!"

"Please, I want you to it would mean a lot to me if you did. I won't ever mention anything else to you. You're the best friend I have Chantal and when you look at your wrist I want you to remember how much I care about you and that if you ever need anything I will be there…as a friend to you."

Chantal felt his sincerity in her heart and was deeply moved by it. "Alright, I will treasure it always," she said with a warm smile and hugged James.

He held on to her for a long time, aching inside but glad to know their friendship really meant something to her. James finally released Chantal and started the car. "Well let's get you to that bookstore."

"Are you ok? Sure you want to come?"

Absolutely, there are some new books on the latest innovations in the auto industry that I want to check out."

"Ok, I'll buy you a double cappuccino."

"For once, I'm going to take you up on that."

Chantal grinned at James and squeezed his hand glad that despite the disappointment she had caused him he chose to maintain his usual light heartedness.

James started the car and headed for the highway to Evergreen Village. The sun shone high overhead in a clear blue sky enhanced vibrantly by the absence of air pollution. Chantal reclined her seat and enjoyed the sensation of dissolving in the momentum of the car. Its subtle vibration and the heated seat cradled her back and she closed her eyes floating into lucid sleep. Disjointed images of the past two days events faded in and out of her mind. From a detached state she observed the New Year's party at CIV Central, orchids blooming in her office, her tattered notebook from Sacred Rose as she fell deeper into sleep. "Chantal," a far away voice called her. Zain's face appeared hovering above her. "Chantal, we're here." Startled she opened her eyes momentarily confused to see James there and then realized she had been dreaming.

Chantal adjusted her seat and sat up, "that was quick."

They got out of the car and walked towards Helios Books, their heels audibly clicking against the cobble stone road. "Watch the holly; I lost a chunk of my pants on that the last time I was here," said James pulling her towards him and away from the prickly bush. Chantal giggled as he opened the door for her and they entered he store. Inside rich, deep colored wood molded around tall shelves that displayed seemingly endless quantities of books. A circular staircase lead up to the second floor of the store where more shelves wound around the walls. Each one had a brass ladder attached to the side that swung out allowing access to the out of reach volumes. At the front on the main floor a coffee bar offered hot beverages and baked goods. Antique leather armchairs surrounded a genuine fire place that crackled and emitted welcoming warmth during cold winter months. Sunlight refracted through stain glass windows onto the store's hardwood floor creating dancing prisms of color. Chantal went over to the coffee bar and ordered two cappuccinos with chocolate dipped biscotti. The espresso machine whirred as it heated the milk to foam. Chantal paid and took the coffees over to James who was glancing through a photography book. "Fresh baked biscotti," she said handing him his goodies.

"Beautiful, thank you!"

"So where's the automotive stuff you want to look at?"

"Not sure, I can't seem to find it down here. I'm going to head upstairs to take a look."

"Ok," replied Chantal as James went to the second floor. She browsed through the shelves searching for the section on quantum software.

"May I help you find something?" A store clerk inquired with a friendly smile.

"Yes, I'm looking for a book called Holographic Art Rendering and Design by William Morris.

"That's a new title we just got it in yesterday. It's in the Quantum Software and Design Applications section," replied the clerk and lead Chantal to the other side of the store. She handed Chantal a copy. "Is there anything else I can help you find?"

"No that's it, thank you."

"My pleasure," she replied and left Chantal to shop.

Chantal tucked the book under her arm and browsed through other titles along the bookcase. She could feel the heat from the fire behind her as she leafed through pages. Chantal sensed a strong presence and turned around somewhat perplexed to see no one there. One of the armchairs facing the fireplace was occupied. She could see a dark coat casually draped over it that she recognized immediately. Chantal approached the chair and stood at its back momentarily, "Zain?" A curl of smoke floated above the chair and filled the air with the smell of imported cigars. "I don't think you're supposed to smoke in here," she said moving in front of him.

"Probably not," he replied watching her as he took another puff. "Want to go for a walk?"

"I'm here with someone I shouldn't just leave." She glanced up towards the top floor of the store and could not see James. Oh what the heck, she thought to herself. "Just wait a minute, I'll be right back," Chantal replied and went over to the cash desk. "My name is Chantal Colombe. Can you please hold on to this for me for about half an hour?" she asked handing the book over to the sales clerk. "I came here with the tall blond gentleman upstairs. If he asks about me tell him I had to step out but I'll be right back."

"I know who you are Miss Colombe and I'll be happy to put this aside for you," replied the clerk taking the book and putting it under the counter.

"Thank you." Chantal could see Zain standing outside the store smoking his cigar and waiting for her. She stepped out into the crisp winter air and began to walk with him through the village. "I've remembered some things," she said and looked at him. "I remember certain events from my days at Initiates of the Sacred Rose mystery school. You appeared to me when I created future timelines for myself and specifically this one that I'm living now."

"I know that's why I brought you on board my ship so that we could help you retrieve the memories that you chose to put aside."

"Yes, I also remember you telling me that. It happened right after the visit when I found my old notebook from school." Chantal stopped walking and faced Zain. "None of those memories explain who you are though and where you come from. All I know is that I met you initially in what I believe to be the twenty sixth century and that is when I designed my timeline."

"You've remembered the most important elements," he replied and began to walk again. A small group of you at Sacred Rose made real contact five hundred years forward and created a presence there. Over time the richness of that reality grew as you continued to explore it with your minds. Several of you began to interact with their future selves and some touch the consciousness of others; I happened to be one of the characters you encountered there," Zain said with a grin.

Chantal looked into his eyes and was glad to finally understand how she had come to know him.

"In the future Earth's reality matrix which is the fabric of Divine Intelligence is interfaced with synthetic grid technology. That is how advanced cultures throughout multiple universes or what we call the multiverse have been living for thousands of years. Once a world is connected in this way through the universal, intelligent matrix not only is technology and its application greatly enhanced but connection to all life everywhere is made possible. In five hundred years Earth is part of a vast cosmic community without boundaries. In this future you already have a presence. That presence is the mind which created your current 2020 timeline with others who wanted change."

Chantal contemplated everything that Zain shared with her as they walked. Bells chimed as someone entered Pixie's Magical Gifts. The store's display window featured figurines of unicorns, fairies, and elaborately constructed miniature castles surrounded by live plants and flowers. A family of five walked by eating giant freshly baked pretzels which emitted the aroma of vanilla sauce and cinnamon. A boy cruising on a hover board passed within inches of Chantal and popped pink bubble gum. She looked back and glanced at his face half covered in a film of gum as he smiled mischievously. Incredible peace and happiness permeated the day and Chantal's heart filled with gratitude for the beauty of life unfolding before her eyes.

"So many people died though, why didn't everyone move to this reality?" Chantal paused, "I know the answer. It has to do with frequency compatibility of the mind, doesn't it?"

"All the people who made it to your current time on some level were dissatisfied with life before the great cataclysms. They dreamed of freedom, peace and a better way of life. Their minds telegraphed enough of the correct frequency signature that was compatible with placement in this reality. The ones that died resonated with attitudes of control, tyranny, greed, apathy and very deep destructive addictions. There are other timelines however where some of them survived and live in chaotic conditions."

"Wait a minute, what about that woman Diana who has been traveling here from another time. From what she told Maya and Lorne I think that she comes from a chaotic world like what you are describing."

Zane looked at Chantal for a long moment. "Yes, and that's where your problems here have begun. Usually timelines of frequencies that are incompatible with the mind that is viewing through time are not seen at all. No one else from her world could see this reality. Diana's consciousness though corrupted was elevated enough in moments that she found it. She is the only one that can bring others from her world through to this one unless they change."

Chantal became psychically aware that James would be looking for her shortly. "Zain, we should turn around. The friend who brought me to the book store will be wondering where I am." They began to head back towards Helios books and she continued, "if Diana did bring the others from her time through would they adapt to our frequency?"

"If they stayed without changing anything immediately physical symptoms of malaise would begin in their bodies and within a short time all of their mental demons would be upon them. Literally they could go mad from suppressed emotions and destructive attitudes that would be unleashed in their conscious state by being exposed to the higher vibration of this current reality. They do not however plan to do that. Their agenda is to take over this timeline and plant new memories in the population. As you know mind is what creates reality and when you change a person's mind the entire reality will shift. The face of this world would once again become different according to the program that they implanted into the minds of all citizens. Tragically if they succeed the general population would not know it's happened."

Chantal felt chilled all of a sudden and a wave of dread washed through her. "Maya said that Diana was afraid and did not want to go back when her people intercepted her with their time travel technology. It doesn't sound like she wants to bring them here anymore."

"She may not have a choice in the matter," replied Zain.

Chantal turned to Zain, "is that why you're her now because of what's happening? I know so little about you."

He stopped and looked at her for a long moment. "That's part of it but whatever else I share with you will depend on decisions that you are going to make," he said and resumed walking.

Perplexed Chantal was not sure what he meant and didn't mentally probe his mind as he was too aware. "What decisions?"

"It is vital that you and your people preserve of all that has been meticulously crafted here."

Knowingness filled Chantal that Zain would not intervene in the security challenges that faced the CIV. His involvement was creating more awareness in her about the situation the council faced but she understood that ultimately they alone had to protect their world. She had no time to examine further the rest of what he had said as Helios Books now stood a few yards away. A thick scent of roses pierced the crisp winter air from a nearby flower stand momentarily distracting Chantal. "Oh look!" She went over and could not resist sampling the selection. They had her favorite color, fuchsia mixed with orange hues, most unusual with a heady fragrance. She took a quick inhale and ran back to Zain.

"He was smiling as she returned, "contemplate all I've said."

"I will thank you," she said as she impulsively reached for his hand, not knowing when she would see him again. He squeezed it giving her a penetrating look then turned and walked away from her.

"There you are," James said from behind her as she watched Zain go. You're developing this obnoxious habit of disappearing lately, where did you go?"

"Sorry I remembered that there was something I wanted to see in Pixie's Magical Gifts, Chantal said a bit awkwardly, not accustomed to bending the truth quite so far.

James examined her face, "There is something you're not telling me."

"There's a book inside I have to pay for before we leave, I'll be right back," she said avoiding his accusation and going inside the store.

James sighed and resigned himself to waiting for her. She came out with the book, "I'm ready, let's go I'm really tired now," she said with a yawn. "This is my last day of rest before a busy week begins and soon after Maya and I have to fly to Vienna for the Global Communications launch."

"Fine, I'll drive you home," he replied deciding not to ask her any more questions.

Back at her house Chantal put away her purchase and stretched out on her suede sofa. Sunlight filtered by a naked tree outside her living room window gently warmed her body as she sank into the cushions, fatigue overtaking her. She had begun to peacefully drift off when her cat jumped up and landed with great precision on her stomach eliciting a squeal from Chantal. "Ouch! Jesus Morocco, I'm going to have to put you on a diet, you're not exactly a light weight," she said to the cat as it settled on her chest looking lovingly into her eyes not in the least offended by her commentary. She smiled and stroked his face closing her eyes again. 'I must be dreaming,' she thought to herself because the scent of the roses she had smelled at the village filled her nose. She became more alert and the aroma grew stronger. "What the…." Chantal sat up and looked around. Her eyes fixed on her work desk across the room and there in a slender, glass vase stood the most gorgeous fuchsia and orange rose on an elegant, long stalk. She got up and walked over to it completely mesmerized. The flower had just begun to open its large, vibrant petals. She bent down and smelled it inhaling deeply and felt the energetic essence of the flower permeating her aura. Chantal was certain that this was the same rose she had seen in the village. "Zain," she whispered.

THiRTEEN

Maya met Chantal at the airport ticket counter where they checked in their bags and headed to the boarding gate. "I just got off the phonecom with IM Romy Lindt in Vienna and they've done it. The whole global communications technology is in place and before the programming approval is finalized at tomorrow's meeting they will be able to give us a real—time demonstration," Maya reported excitedly.

"That's incredible. I can't believe the tech people got the new system in place so fast!" said Chantal.

"I now, I can barely contain myself. This is a total surprise since Romy had told me that it would take at least till spring to get the system up."

Chantal and Maya scanned their SCC cards and prepared to board the Starlight 4000 supersonic aircraft. These were incredible planes powered by satellite laser beams and used liquid hydrogen as a propellant. They flew at very high altitudes several times the speed of sound resulting in smooth flights with no turbulence. Since laser pulses virtually powered and maneuvered the planes through advanced flex wing technology the weight of the planes was greatly reduced. Travel time to Vienna from Seattle was effectively reduced to four and a half hours.

A flight attendant greeted Maya and Chantal and directed them to their private seats aboard the aircraft. Once settled in Chantal prepared her quantum data files to review after takeoff. Eventually the plane began its quiet ascent climbing till it reached the designated altitude. They flew high above any visible cloud cover in the thinnest part of the atmosphere. Maya looked out her window and observed the weather patterns below them. A flight attendant came by with a tray of Mimosas. "Would you care for a champagne and orange juice?"

"No thanks, just coffee for me, one cream and sugar," said Chantal.

Maya took one and sipped it. "Mmmm Chantal, these are yummy."

"They look delicious," she said smiling.

The attendant returned with Chantal's coffee. Chantal loaded her files on her quantum laptop and watched the holographic display as she reviewed her presentation with Maya and they finalized some changes in additional documents together during the flight. Briefly they paused from working to enjoy the in flight lunch feature: roasted duck in a strawberry ginger sauce over wild rice with a butter lettuce salad followed by new york style cheesecake for desert. Shortly after the meal the plane began it's descent as Maya and Chantal packed up their work.

One hour later Chantal entered her suite at the Grand Hotel in the heart of Vienna. This was one her favorite places to stay in the world. The hotel blended a rich opulence in grand Austrian tradition with an old world elegant but comfortable ambiance. The main entrance featured sprawling intricate marble floors, pillars that reached to high ceilings adorned with breathtaking moldings. Warmly lit colors decorated the interior and tall potted palms grazed panels of amber colored wood. Antique furniture and hand woven rugs of the most exquisite quality filled every room. Artwork from various periods set in gold; hand carved frames adorned the walls.

Chantal's deluxe suite was decorated in moss and gold colored hues with accents of melon. The sitting room had a wood burning fire place and many hand crafted candles that had been lit for her. Chantal went in to the beautiful bathroom lit another candle and turned on the round jetted tub pouring in some foaming bath oil. It was 10PM local time and she didn't feel like having dinner. The suites featured a lovely bar with wine and various spirits. Crystal decanters held deep, smoky colored brandy, cognac and rum. Only the best brands in the European sector were provided by the hotel. Chantal poured herself a snifter of brandy and took it into the bath with her. She eased into the bubbles and lay back against the tub closing her eyes and relishing the feel of near hot water creeping up her neck relaxing her shoulder muscles. She sipped the brandy and felt its fiery warmth moving through her bringing a blush to her cheeks. Chantal pushed the music selection button on the wall beside her and 'Madame Butterfly' echoed through the suite. She sank deeply into her mind allowing herself to float with the rapture of the music. Suddenly she felt herself disengage from her body and move through the ceiling of the hotel continuing on and launching into the starlit sky. She rotated 360 degrees and looked way down at Vienna lit up with its characteristically soft lights below her. She could see the city centre and further Belvedere Palace reflecting pristinely off surrounding water against the deep night. A flock of birds moved with phantom wings past her and disappeared into the darkness. The quiet beauty of the evening held a mystery that lingered and enveloped her soul in the absence of a vibrant sun.

Aromatic tobacco began to fill Chantal's senses. She whirled around in the night sky and allowed herself to gently fall back into her body. Slowly opening here eyes the candle's flame met her gaze. She stared at its dance and became more aware of the tobacco scent now all around her as the music continued to play. Chantal arose from the warm water and dried herself off, dawning a Bordeaux colored chenille and satin robe. She released her hair from a large clip she had worn in the bath and entered the sitting room. A cloud of smoke floated above Zain's head as he sat semi reclined in an exquisitely carved chair upholstered in a design replica of the Lady and the Unicorn tapestries. Chantal was surprised to see him; obviously he possessed the unique talent for appearing in the most unexpected places. "Nice lodgings," he said with a grin as he puffed on his cigar.

"Would you like a drink?" Chantal offered.

"Sure."

Chantal walked over to the bar, "Cognac or Brandy?"

"Either is fine."

She poured a generous snifter of Brandy and brought it over to him. He swirled the amber colored liquid around inhaled the aroma and took a drink.

"I'm very curious as to what brings you all the way to Vienna," said Chantal.

Zain closed his eyes momentarily and listened to the opera that played. "Beautiful music," he said.

"Yes it's one of my favorites, Madame Butterfly."

"I know."

Chantal wondered if there was anything that he didn't know as she sat before him in her robe and bare feet realizing that he also would know every thought in her mind. She finally began to laugh and said, "I'm sorry, I…it's just that I have never known anyone like you and I'm used to at least a little more privacy."

"It's alright, sorry to disrupt your evening. Have you thought anymore about what I said?"

"Hmm?"

"About the choice."

Chantal rapidly searched her brain to remember what he was referring to then the memory of his last comment at Evergreen Village came back to her. "I'm not all together sure what I think of that last bit of information you gave me about having a choice to stay in this timeline or not. To be honest I have had too many other things on my mind like this presentation tomorrow to give what you said enough consideration."

Zain butted out his cigar and looked at Chantal. The soft lighting in the room and deep color of her robe accentuated the delicate pallor of her skin. Golden light from candles danced against the silky texture of her hair. She appeared as if she could smoothly slide into any time in history. "The Global Communications launch tomorrow will prove to be a vital instrument in the defense of your world by providing simultaneous, instant information relay to all sectors."

"It definitely has that application and many other benefits. We are all very excited by the prospects."

"It is only the beginning of a network that will grow to become an extension of mind over the next few centuries. You've already seen some of this technology used in the future," Zain stated casually.

"Yes, some of what I experienced was incredible."

Zain took a drink from his glass eyed Chantal and asked, "Would you like to see more?"

"What, now?"

"Is that a problem?"

Chantal paused and looked at the clock sitting on the fireplace noting the lateness of the hour. Her body was still on Pacific Standard Time and not tired. "I'll have to get dressed."

Zain stood up and approached her; he was at least a head taller than Chantal. His eyes had an uncanny intensity whenever he looked at her and she could feel his mind permeating hers. For a moment she looked deeply into them and felt as if she were falling into ageless personal history that had no ending. "You've lived a lot haven't you?" She whispered.

Zain merely smiled. "When you're dressed I'll meet you on board my ship.

It is cloaked and situated directly above the hotel; you should have no problem getting yourself there."

"Alright."

He turned from her, walked out onto the balcony of her suite and disappeared. Quickly Chantal threw on a pair of jeans and a sweater and then settled herself in a chair facing the fireplace. She allowed her mind to trance by staring into the flames growing brighter and more intense till she knew nothing but the fire. Energy circled up her spine, built up around the back of her neck and shot into her head pulsing forcefully. She focused all her mind on Zain's ship and the particular cabin that she had visited while the energy vortex within and around her began to grow more powerful. A magnetic pulling sensation towards her destination grew increasingly stronger till finally it momentarily overtook Chantal's whole being and in an instant she appeared on board Zain's ship. She blinked back into full consciousness and looked around.

"You made it," he said turning towards her from the viewing porthole.

"Well to be honest I have never teleported myself onto a space craft."

Novara walked into the cabin and greeted Chantal. She stood almost six feet tall with a deep complexion resembling someone from Polynesian descent, black hair that was tied and knotted atop her head and very dark eyes with a slight slant. "You are well?" She asked Chantal.

"Yes, excellent, thank you."

"This is Novara she is a medical science specialist and works with me often on various projects. She is responsible for helping you retrieve your memories from your time at Sacred Rose."

"Oh I see. Thank you," said Chantal. Novara smiled and began to busy herself at a grid console.

"Come on, there is something I want to show you," said Zain leading Chantal out of the main cabin. They followed a long corridor and entered a large odd shaped room that appeared completely empty. It had a very smooth grey colored floor and walls with no windows.

Chantal looked around the room not sure what the main attraction was supposed to be. "Am I missing something?"

"Watch," said Zain as he reached into the air, moved his hand and a grid like structure made of light appeared. It rotated and partially disappeared from view then reappeared when observed from a three dimensional perspective. "Let your mind adjust and just follow its complete rotation."

Chantal preceded to focus on the rotating structure till her brain flipped to a four dimensional perspective and with that a whole new dimension of the room opened up to her awareness. Criss crossed light filaments now glowed and turned through the room. "Wow," she said.

Zain began to move his fingers over the rotating structure that floated in front of him. As his fingers skimmed the edges of the grid beautiful colors and sound filled the room. Colorful birds appeared as if out of nowhere and flew towards Chantal then dissolved around her in a shimmering dance of sparkles. She could feel a warm vibration against her skin as this happened. He continued to manipulate the environment this way creating breathtaking music and visual displays. Gorgeous scents of various kinds filled the space and carried a heavenly frequency.

Chantal was stunned she had never experienced anything so beautiful. It made her quantum art software seem lifeless in comparison. A second rotating grid structure appeared and floated towards Chantal. "Try it," said Zain.

"What do I do?"

"This is a Sensory Holographic Navigator or what we sometimes call Virtual Nav. It responds to your though patterns the same way the reality matrix all around us does that you learned about at Sacred Rose. It is kind of like playing an instrument in that the touch of your mind carries an intent that makes the melody sublime. This principal is dimensionalized into multimedia instant expression."

Chantal closed her eyes and thought of snowflakes as she let her fingers drift over the edges of the Virtual Nav. Instantly the sound of chimes and a sprinkling of snow appeared in the room.

"Nice. The device works through touch of the hand and also can respond to pure thought from your mind." Zain demonstrated by focusing on the Virtual Nav lighting up the grid lines and filling the room with hundreds off fuchsia and orange colored roses accompanied by their exquisite scent. They looked very real and Chantal could feel their cool petals with her fingers. These looked familiar she thought to herself. "You can make objects as solid or transparent as you desire," he continued as the roses dissolved and turned into gauzy blue atmosphere that swirled around the room. "We can manifest anything from the matrix without devices but these are useful in constructing programs for educational and other purposes."

Chantal continued to work the Virtual Nav creating harp like string sounds with hundreds of iridescent butterflies moving in waves towards Zain and dissolving in a cascade of multi spectral sparkles that appeared to land in his hair. He smiled at her mischief and turned the sparkles into an ocean wave that headed towards Chantal's alarmed face appearing to crash upon her head but at the last minute dissolving into a beautiful rainbow and causing her to laugh. She quickly constructed a waterfall surrounded by beautiful flowers and plant life. "I wish I could go inside it."

"Why don't you."

Chantal looked at the waterfall and created a miniature of her self beneath the cascade of water. As soon as she did this she could literally feel the water upon her as she watched herself in the scene. In Humor she had dressed herself in a red bikini and a Hawaiian hula skirt. Zain appeared in the scene beside her and waved, Chantal laughed because he appeared in a brightly colored pair of shorts with large parakeets all over them. As she watched beneath the falls he took her hand and she could feel his in her palm. He leaned closer and ran his hand down to the small of her back Chantal all the while felt the sensation of slippery wetness on her skin. Her pulse increased and her mind began to swim as he pushed her with his body under the water and kissed her. In total surprise she felt the electric sensation of his mouth on hers beneath cascading water that ran down their faces. Chantal closed her eyes and allowed her self to experience his energy completely as the waterfall began to dissolve. Her own current mixed with his and she felt as if she was present with him in pure electrical essence beyond flesh. When she finally opened her eyes the waterfall scene was gone and replaced by a moonlit beach on the shores of the home she had visited in the future. Chantal touched her lips; a smile began to form as she looked across at Zain.

He smiled back, took a cigar out of his breast pocket and lit it. "Do you recognize this place?"

"Yes it's the seascape by the house in the future that I visited."

"Your house."

"Mine? You mean I own it?"

"Well, don't you?" he asked puffing on his cigar.

Chantal thought for a moment, "I guess I do own it. In my mind when I'm there I know it's my home but in my usual environment in this time I seldom think about it. That seems to be changing though and your presence makes it more real to me everyday. You are from the future aren't you?"

"Yes but I am not bound by any time."

"I believe I know what you mean. Once you time travel you live out of time."

"That's right."

"That gives one the power to change the past or the future the way we did whenever we want," said Chantal.

"Exactly. Everything you do in your current time will also change the future that you know. Even the demonstration I showed you this evening has created changes in your future if you want them."

"How?"

"Take a look; just use the Virtual Nav. Focus on yourself in the future here in this scene and watch what unfolds."

Chantal placed her hand against the grid of the Nav and connected in her mind to her presence at the house by the shore. Instantly she appeared in the circular abode and sat navigating what appeared to be virtual holographic programs. Each one opened into a detailed world of information about various planetary systems. Chantal watched herself input data and design some kind of links between the various worlds till a master schematic of intersecting information appeared. "I see but what exactly am I doing?"

"You are designing evolutionary platform programs for various quadrants of different universes. This strengthens the unification of diverse populations across many star systems and provides numerous benefits to life everywhere."

"Fascinating that's a task larger than my current mind could handle."

"I know but it is what you can evolve to take on once your decision is made."

Chantal turned to Zain, "you keep saying that I have a decision to make."

Chantal paced the room for a moment and gathered her thoughts. She realized that this was a thread unfolding from the work she had done in creating her current timeline. Clearly more potentials for her future were unfolding and Zain had appeared as a messenger helping her remember what she had created. "I know that I have a propensity towards leadership that is in my blood and that has influenced my choices," she said.

"Genetically speaking everyone on Earth has descended from several original races that came here and seeded humanity. Some people carry more of this DNA passed down by females as the royal bloodline that was linked to many of the Pharaohs of Egypt and later to King David and the lineage of Jesus. As you know this genetic line of succession was heavily suppressed by the Church throughout history but protected by groups like the Rosicrucians. It was also one of the reasons that religious groups were so afraid of women and have persecuted them throughout history. They literally twisted the historical information from Babylonian and Sumerian records to suggest that women were inferior temptresses and subordinate to men according to God. You are right in your current embodiment you carry this seed blood and your soul's record influences your potentials and choices." Zain continued, "in the timeline after the great cataclysms, a significant discovery of Atlantis records detailing the arrival of several advanced extraterrestrial groups on Earth and their influence on the development of Atlantis and Lemuria was unearthed in Antarctica. The artifacts at this site and the undeniable extensive libraries of knowledge that were found reduced all organized religions to institutions based on mythological fables that were sprinkled with truth often taken out of its original contextual accuracy. This was the milestone event that caused the disintegration of religions effectively ending thousands of years of their influence and control in the world. The discovery also contradicted most of the dates previously embraced by historians about the creation of man and civilization."

Chantal contemplated all they had discussed. She had personally experienced the struggles and achievements that forged her reality in 2020. Zain was right, on a deep level she did feel strongly attached to the beautiful life that unfolded around her everyday. Perhaps it was because of what it had taken to make it a reality and how progressive the world had become. Now restlessness overtook her that was her familiar calling card of change waiting to happen. She looked pensively at Zain and indulged in a humorous moment of blaming his presence for its arrival. She smiled covering her mouth seeing the gates of her mind opening to a host of possibilities. "Oh I'm feeling the momentum of personal evolution here," she said as her eyes flashed and she grinned at him. "Leave me till after the meeting and I will ponder the possibilities," Chantal requested.

"Are you dismissing yourself from *this* meeting?" He asked with mock seriousness.

"You have proven highly resourceful at finding me in the oddest of places. I am confident that you have not lost that ability and we will meet again soon," she replied simply. She stood across from him her arms folded across her chest and he approached her nonetheless placing a strategic kiss on her forehead.

"Ponder in joy," he said and watched as she disappeared from his presence.

FOURTEEN

At 2:15 AM Diana quietly rose, got dressed and packed a small bag. She took the stairs all the way down to the basement reaching the laboratory and opened the door with her keycard. Immediately she disconnected the security cameras and headed for the TII device. Already two more seats had been installed as the final modifications were nearing completion that would allow three people to cross time together. Diana shuddered at the thought and quickly got into the centre seat putting on the head gear and firing up the computer console. She began to focus on her destination immersing herself in the familiar frequency as the field began to form around her bathing her in light. Suddenly the device decelerated and the field wound down and dissipated. Diana looked up from her seat and saw Nicholas standing beside the TII staring at her. "Going somewhere?"

Diana had no reply knowing that her relationship to him and the Omega Group was now irreparable. In fact she realized that her very survival was tenuous.

"I have always lived by the conviction to trust no one and to rely solely on my own resources. Here you sit proving my reasoning to be flawless."

Diana was not surprised by his choice of words. "I can't participate in the Group's plans anymore; my experiences in the timeline that you would ultimately take over have changed me in ways that are beyond your understanding. There is such harmony and progress in this new world, unlike anything previously achieved by humanity. I can't bear to be a part of a plan that will literally take it all apart." Even as the words came out Diana knew that they would have no effect on Nicholas.

"Your inner conflicts about this operation are of no significance and we will complete our objectives. You will bring me and Colonel Stark through time tomorrow afternoon once all the modifications on the TII device are completed," Nicholas stated nonchalantly as he lifted Diana gently out of the seat to where she stood before him. "Fortunately your mind will be reformatted along with everyone else's eliminating any conflict within you so you see there is nothing to fear or resist," he said holding her hand. Diana tried to extract it from his grasp but he held firmly onto it. "I am going to have Dr. Rechter stay with you in your delicate mental state till our journey has been completed. I wouldn't want you to try anything foolish and hurt yourself."

Nicholas's extreme condescending attitude reducing her to child like ineptitude was his way of asserting his power over her and Diana realized there was nothing more she could do for the time being but acquiesce as he led her out of the laboratory and called for Dr. Rechter.

Back in her now locked room Diana sat on her cot and searched her mind for a way to dismantle the Groups plans. She was utterly horrified at the idea of having her mind restructured and would prefer death to becoming an obedient drone in The Omega Groups idea of a new world order. She knew that she had become a mere pawn now and once Nicholas shared with Colonel Stark the evening's events it would only increase the hostility that he harbored towards her. Nothing more could be done till they time traveled forward and once there she knew she had better come up with a solution or her mind would be scrambled along with everyone else's.

Diana lay back on the cot and let her mind drift to 2020 and for some reason Maya's face appeared. She felt the soothing frequency of that reality within her and allowed her vision to expand. Maya's face remained and Diana began to study it. She was not consciously aware of what she was doing but somehow the feeling of Maya's presence grew as she focused more intently on her face. Diana was a scientist and relied on technology with empirical data verifying all experiences that were anomalous. She did not have any training in the psychic realm but became aware of a growing connection to Maya in her mind. She decided to relax and explore this phenomenon further actually imagining herself inside Maya's brain. She concentrated with all her might and sent the words over and over, 'Omega Group is coming; mind tampering imminent, take precautions.' Diana continued sending the message till finally she fell into a restless sleep.

Maya tossed and turned in her bed then finally sat up. She picked up the phonecom and called home. "Lorne are you awake?" She asked upon hearing his sleepy voice.

Lorne rubbed his eyes and activated the phonecom visual display. "Maya, what is it are you alright?"

"Yeah I'm fine but something is wrong, very wrong. I think its Diana, I felt her inside my mind." Maya paused for a moment and collected her thoughts. "They're coming."

Lorne paused for a moment and comprehended what she was saying. "Are you sure?"

Maya closed her eyes and looked to the future. "Yes, I'm sure. There are two men accompanying Diana when they come through."

"Can you tell when?"

"Very soon, in fact anytime," Maya said with a distant look in her eyes.

"I'd better let Amit know right away."

"Ok, I'll call you later after the meeting. I love you."

"Love you too, bye." Lorne entered Amit's number and he appeared on the display sleepy, his thick hair in disarray but rapidly became alert hearing Lorne's disturbing news.

"The situation is more serious than we knew. We've been in touch with representatives from all sectors and apparently each one of them has experienced time storms. The suspect has appeared in and out of time world wide. Likely they have readied the technology to create massive mind erasure and reprogramming. I'll gather the Scientific Advisory Group immediately. Hopefully they have the local photon shielding device ready to implement. As for the rest of us we had better gather at CIV Central immediately."

"We'll meet you there," said Lorne and disconnected the call.

Chantal walked into the World CIV headquarters and met Maya who briefed her on her experience in the middle of the night. Chantal was not surprised and hoped that the other sectors had gotten their defense issues in order. Romy greeted them in the lobby. "Chantal!" he gently embraced her and Maya and gave them a kiss on each cheek.

"Good to see you Romy," she replied and they walked to the auditorium. IM's from all world sectors were gathered in the moments before the meeting began. Chantal looked over the agenda and noted that she was scheduled to present after the Asian and European sector members. "We're third," she said to Maya as they took their seats around the immense circular, elevated table and put on their translation devices. The first presentation was given by the head of World Security and Defense which updated all the IM's on the defense measures that were being taken world wide to protect citizens against the potential threat that Diana and her group posed. John Willowby had provided the schematics for his local sector photon shielding devices to all sector representatives and was heading the development of a global device that would be launched into space within two weeks time. Construction of the local devices had begun in all sectors but would not be completed for another two days.

Maya listened to the end of the defense update with trepidation. If the impressions she received in the middle of the night were correct then two days lag time in initiating shielding could be catastrophic for the other world sectors. At this point she chose not to alert anyone because she did not know the exact arrival time of the travelers and even if she did the shielding devices would not be ready for two days.

Romy Lindt rose and dazzled the group with a launch presentation featuring the results of a world wide coordinated effort of research and development of new technologies. This effort existed between various innovative minds and groups who were funded by the CIV in all sectors. Once the products were developed a portion of the profits returned to the research and development fund and in this way progress in new innovations was supported and continuous. One of the featured updates was progress in the quantum computing network that would be the platform for global communications. Cross linking of all and any technology run by computers had finally been achieved in an ultimate quantum network that connected all communication devices everywhere. This would provide greater security resources in each sector as this network could be used world wide. In addition anyone anywhere would be able to access global communications information and programming through any computer run device. All relevant information would be available through this system and could be accessed anywhere. SCC cards would be linked up to this network providing a greater range of information that citizens could now utilize. Separation would be effectually wiped out because every one could be reached at any time with any information.

"Illuminated Members please take out your mini phonecoms, Q palms or whatever other devices you are carrying and turn them on," Romy requested.

As everyone complied and took out whatever electronic device they were carrying a large, master holograph appeared in the centre of the room and came alive with a flock of white doves flying skyward and disappearing followed by the words Unity Network Launch. "Please observe your devices," instructed Romy.

Everyone looked at the display portion of their electronics and saw the same image appear as the master hologram. Cheer and applause followed as everyone witnessed the first world wide demonstration of the Unity Network. "This is Amazing!" Chantal said excitedly to Maya as she watched her Q palm display.

"The Unity Network is now officially on Line," announced Romy.

At the conclusion of the demonstration Romy introduced Maya and Chantal who would be presenting the Global Communications plan. Chantal loaded the audio visuals and Maya began presenting the first portion which dealt with the restructuring and amalgamation of all network stations to become extensions of the Unity Network. She also outlined the consolidated world news programming plan and the citizens' political forum that could be accessed through the Unity Network for voting purposes. All council decisions that the public currently voted to approve would be more accessible at any time through the new system with state of the art interactive features.

Chantal's part of the presentation came next with the cultural content for the year being outlined. An innovative blend of history, arts, science, technology and other educational areas from around the world would be accessible by everyone. The entertainment portions of the programming included film and other artistic projects from a wide variety of producers and artists. Unity Network featured a new language interface that translated broadcasts into any language in real time depending on the setting one had on their quantum devices. For the first time a blend of content from around the world would be seen everywhere uniting all sectors to build a common cultural expression world wide. The IM's responded enthusiastically towards the presentation and voted to approve the content that Chantal and Maya had suggested. The next step would be to broadcast the presentation to the public over the Unity Network and gather the results of the consensus.

A lunch break of one and a half hours was announced and the IM's began to rise and leave the auditorium. "Are you going to have something from the buffet?" Maya asked Chantal.

"I think I'm going to plate up and have a break in my room," replied Chantal.

"Ok," Maya smiled knowing Chantal preferred to spend time alone between meetings and other public events.

Chantal headed to the buffet room and picked up a beautiful gold etched china plate with a painted cameo in the centre. She selected some salad, herb rice and schnitzel with a glass of ginger ale and headed back to her hotel room.

She sat in front of the fire and enjoyed her meal, glancing out the window and watching drifting hazy clouds. Chantal loved when winter cloud formations became a satin sheen subtly lit as if from within by a hidden sun and stretched across a silvery sky. Her mind recalled how midnight darkness enveloped Vienna the previous night and harbored Zain's cloaked ship right above the Hotel. She recalled the incredible events that took place with him and all the options that had been discussed about her future. She looked down at her hand made of translucent, pale skin covering bluish veins and slender fingers and thought about the blood that ran through her. Unique genetics she possessed that held potentials yet to be fully unlocked. Chantal knew that exposure to different timelines and environments which changed the frequency a person was exposed to could cause the body to metamorphsize through the activation of its DNA in new ways. She contemplated what that would mean for her if she were to keep going and move forward five hundred years. What would the consciousness be like in five, ten or fifteen thousand years? Her mind projected out of her body down a long corridor of thought that seemingly had no end and she was soothed by the assurance of the unknown to provide limitless adventure.

Zain, all of a sudden she thought of him and touched her lips. She closed her eyes and remembered the sensation of water washing across her face, over her mouth locked beneath his. A tremor ran through her body as she recalled how the energy had moved between them powerfully. No one had ever affected her this way before and she knew that no one else ever would. His disarming directness and simplicity coupled with an underlying intensity produced a magnetism that she found difficult to resist. He was a mystery that she found herself wanting to solve into eternity and these thoughts were completely contrary to her usual indifferent attitude towards men. He always looked at her like he knew something that he was not revealing and Chantal longed to pierce that veil with her mind.

Chantal glanced at the clock and noted she had twenty minutes before the second half of the council session began. She closed her eyes and leaned back against the armchair listening to the fire roaring softly. Falling backwards into the void of her mind she reveled at the edge of unconsciousness and floated; stretching each minute that passed into a spiral that flew out of time. She fell deeper and landed softly in a bed of scarlet roses which sprang out of the depths of nothing and grazed her mind with soft fragrant petals. Chantal lingered there for an infinite moment and then opened her eyes with a knowing smile. She stood up refreshed her lipstick and headed back to the auditorium.

FiFTEEN

"Wake up my dear," said Dr. Rechter as he gently shook Diana's shoulders. You need to shower and get ready for your departure. All the modifications on the TII device have been completed to allow Mr. Sealy and Colonel Stark to accompany you."

Great, thought Diana to herself as the doctor left her to prepare. She sat up and cradled her head in her hands due to a throbbing headache that permeated her frontal and temporal lobes. Diana reached inside the bedside drawer next to her and pulled out two acetaminophen tablets swallowing them dry. She coughed as the stuck in her throat on the way down. She stumbled into the bathroom and turned on the shower somewhat curious at the absence of steam appearing from behind the glass door. "Oh don't tell me," she said aloud to herself. Diana put one hand under the icy running water. "Shit! This morning is getting grimmer by the minute." She took a deep breath, braced herself and jumped into the freezing shower letting out a yelp. She lathered herself as fast as possible her teeth chattering uncontrollably and shampooed her hair.

"Everything all right in there? I thought I heard something unusual" Dr. Rechter inquired.

"No everything is not all right the goddamn hot water is out again!" Diana informed him.

"Oh sorry to hear that my dear, we temporarily lost power during the preparations in the lab. It should warm up soon."

A lot of use 'soon' was she thought to herself as she got out of the shower and huddled in a towel for a few moments to regain some warmth. Diana reluctantly finished getting ready and met Dr. Rechter who escorted her to the laboratory. Nicholas and Colonel Stark were already there waiting for her and Dr. Ospov to arrive and neither of them acknowledged her when she walked in. "Where is Dr. Ospov?" Nicholas asked Dr. Rechter.

"He is on his way now with the MIP and the extra protective shield generators."

"Excellent."

Dr. Ospov walked in with a look of satisfaction on his face knowing that Nicholas would be pleased with the results of his work. "Everything is in perfect working order Sir. I have two extra personal shield generators ready for you and Colonel Stark to wear upon implementation of the MIP. These will effectively make you totally immune to the mind reprogramming," said Dr. Ospov as he handed the devices to Nicholas. "Simply pin them to your lapel and depress the blue button to activate the shield. It will stay activated until you depress the blue button again plus you can use it more than once." Next Dr. Ospov handed Nicholas an orb shaped metal object with a miniature key pad embedded in it. "This is the MIP initiation control used to commence the MIP. Simply key the code into the device and it will beam a signal to the nearest receiver cones that Diana has planted in all the world sectors. Like a chain reaction each cone will activate the next till all are simultaneously emitting the electromagnetic MIP sequence. When this is in effect the keypad on the control will glow red. Make sure you have activated your personal shields before commencing any of these procedures to protect yourselves from the MIP." The doctor took all three of them through a mock simulation of using the personal shields and initiating the MIP. Once the group was ready they each pinned one of the shield emitters to their chests and climbed into the TII. Diana put the head gear on and powered up the device. Nicholas discreetly reached over and ripped Diana's device off her shirt and put it in his pocket.

"You won't need this," he whispered in her ear.

Diana's blood ran cold. '*Bastard*,' she thought to herself. As the familiar hum of the field the device generated began and the tingling sensation filled Diana's body a surge of confidence filled her that she had never felt before. In that split second she realized that having taken this trip many times she had a distinct advantage over her undesirable travel companions and an idea possessed her in utter clarity. The time travel coordinates controlled by her mind were set for January 10th, 2020. Instead Diana fixated back to the New Years Eve party at CIV Central. At the threshold point just as Diana usually began to loose consciousness at the moment of entering the wormhole she dug her nails into her thigh hard enough to draw blood keeping her self lucid. She observed for the first time the beginning materialization of the destination she was focusing on. Just as it was becoming more solid and the party in full swing formed around them Diana literally turned a sharp right angle in her mind as she depressed the time jump button and focused with all her mental power on the coordinates of January 10th depressing the time jump button a second time on the TII console. A powerful surge filled her body and her cells screamed as they were ripped from the intense magnetic pull of one reality and thrown on to another. This time Diana lost consciousness.

Back at the 2020 New Years celebration at CIV Central Nicholas and Colonel Stark materialized in the middle of the party in the midst of stunned guests. "Oh God," said Nicholas as he and his travel companion faced the hushed crowd.

"Security!" screamed Maya. Quickly Colonel Stark grabbed a wine glass from one of the guests and smashed it against the wall effectively creating a menacing shard. He then reached for Jena who was standing a few feet from where the men materialized and held it against her throat. As security assembled and pushed the crowd back Nicholas and Colonel Stark backed towards the door. "Stay away or I'll slice open her throat!" said the Colonel. Amit arrived and watched in horror at what transpired. Diana stood nearby dressed in her formal gown. Her only conscious reality was the current evening of the party and she locked eyes with Colonel Stark wondering what he and Nicholas were doing here and how they got through without her. "What did you do you bitch!?" screamed Colonel Stark

Diana had no idea what he was raving about but obviously something was seriously awry. Two security agents apprehended her and led her out of the room. "Stay back! This man has no problem with taking the child's life, that is what he is trained to do so if you want her to stay alive I suggest you let us leave the building," said Nicholas.

John had entered the room and cried out for Jena totally distressed at what he was witnessing. The security agents had to restrain him to avoid anyone getting hurt. Nicholas opened the front door of the CIV and backed out with Colonel Stark who maintained the razor like edge of the glass shard against

Jena's throat. Outside Nicholas grabbed the valet parking attendant and demanded a car. The nervous young man looked to the security agents, "do as he says or they will kill the child," ordered Lorne.

"No wait!" said Amit. "Lorne we don't know why they're here, if we let them go we could be jeopardizing everyone's lives."

"If we don't he'll kill the child, I know it. Are you willing to stand by and watch that happen? They can't get far. We will apprehend them."

Amit had a really bad feeling about the option of letting these men drive away but admittedly he knew that Lorne was right, they would not hesitate in taking the girl's life. "Alright, let them go!"

The parking attendant arrived with a silver sedan and Colonel Stark pushed Jena inside the back. "If anyone follows us we will kill the girl. If you leave us she will be set free once we are out of your range," warned Nicholas.

Neither Lorne nor Amit believed him watching in utter frustration as the sedan pulled away.

Diana lay on the ground beneath a tree at Rainbow Park two miles west of CIV Central. Slowly she regained consciousness and sat up. Every fiber of her body ached as if she had run a week long marathon and her head was pounding with a migraine. As soon as she tried to stand up she vomited and had to sit back down again. Her hands shook as she opened up her travel bag and fumbled for pain medication and a small bottle of water. She took a dose and slowly sipped the water leaning back against the tree. This travel sickness was far worse than anything she had previously experienced likely because the adjustment her body had to make in transitioning out of one time coordinate into another at the last minute. It was a miracle that she had succeeded at all and a huge relief that neither Nicholas nor Colonel Stark were anywhere to be seen. She took a small pocket knife out of the bag and made a small incision into her palm extracting the small chip that allowed her to be located by the TII device. Her hand bled but her head hurt too much to feel the pain as she applied some antiseptic and a bandage. She knew that she should have gotten rid of the chip at New Years but had been too overwhelmed with fear to cut loose from the Omega Group. Diana sat against the tree and waited for the pain meds to become effective. The park was relatively empty except for an elderly man walking his dog. She shivered and pulled her jacket hood up against the crisp winter air. Slowly the pounding in her head began to recede and upon reaching a tolerably low level of pain she stood up and made her way towards CIV Central.

James phonecom sounded and the smiling face of Chantal greeted him.
"Hey there, how did your meeting go?" He asked.

"Fabulous!" Chantal replied. "I'll tell you all about it when I get back. Can you pick us up from the airport at six tonight?"

"Absolutely, I'll be there."

"Thanks bunches, bye!" She said and disconnected.

Richard walked into James's office with Lorne and Amit. James looked at their sober faces and could tell something urgent had transpired. "What's up?" He asked.

"The blond woman who appeared at the New Years party has just walked into the building. She wants to talk to us."

"Diana?"

"Yes," replied Amit. "I have security with her in the meeting room with the other IM's. We're all heading over there now."

"Ok, let's go," replied James and joined the group. When they walked into the meeting room, James looked at Diana. She appeared somewhat paler than he remembered and more frail. A fading bruise was evident on her forehead and her face showed the strain of stress. He noticed that her breathing was somewhat labored. She sat in a chair facing the group of IM's and began to speak once the remainder of them sat down.

"It is a miracle that I sit here before you in one piece and I have come to give you information about the intrusions into your current reality." Diana proceeded to tell the IM's the whole story from the beginning about the Omega Group and their plans to take over the current timeline in 2020 through radical mind restructuring.

"Why have you come here to give us this information?" Asked Amit.

Diana paused. There was no simple answer to that question. "Because I wouldn't be able to live with myself if I didn't. I can't explain it in rational terms, but every time I came here it changed me. You would know what I mean if you spent time around the Omega Group and the disastrous timeline they are stuck in. The contrast to life and consciousness here is shocking. These people are barbarians who care about nothing but power and control at any cost. It has become vitally important to me to disrupt their plans and preserve your way of life," she said and was suddenly wracked with coughing.

The IM's were silent for a moment pondering her words. "How do we know this is not some sort of trick to deceive us and why should we trust you?" Asked Samantha.

"Look," replied Diana tearing the bandage off her palm revealing the small open would. "I've removed the tracking chip that would allow them to retrieve me back in time. This was a one way trip for me, I can't go back. I'm at your mercy now. Is that proof enough?"

"Where are the others that you said wanted to come through with you on this trip?"

"During the transport I did something unprecedented. Instead of focusing on the coordinates to this present time I focused on the New Year's Eve party that took place here. Just as we were beginning to come through I sort of switched gears with my mind and interfaced the technology to pull myself out of that reality and appear into this at the last minute. My body is experiencing some extreme side effects of this maneuver but Colonel Stark and Nicholas Sealy did not appear with me when I arrived here. I am surmising that my plan worked and they're in your past at the party as we speak."

"Diana to the best of your ability can you describe exactly what you witnessed when you were beginning to materialize back in time at the party?" Asked Lorne.

Diana rubbed her temples, her headache was returning. "Everything happened so fast and I was straining to stay lucid at the peak of the most intense energetic surge a person can withstand but I'll do my best." She sat back for a moment and collected her thoughts bringing her back to the moment just as she dug her nails into her thigh. Her heart rate increased as she began to remember and her breathing became very shallow; "the room is materializing. I can see guests milling about and to my left Colonel Stark is beginning to materialize…he looks sort of phantom like. I can see Nicholas coming through now and realize this is the only moment I will have to change my mind…" Her voice trailed off and everyone watched as her body began to shake uncontrollably. "Oh god, no!" were Diana's last words before she disappeared from the meeting room.

"Shit! Where did she go?" Asked Lorne jumping to his feet.

John spoke up. "I'm not familiar with the exact nature of the TII device technology she said they used but it would appear that her mind still had a link to the past entry point in time to the New Year's party that became activated the moment she began to describe it."

"You mean she is there now? How do we know that her people have not retrieved her and that this isn't some sort of trap?" Asked Richard.

"We don't know anything for certain but I doubt that this is a trick of some sort. I believe her. If she removed the tracking chip from her palm then the logical conclusion is what I stated earlier. Somehow her mind is still linked through time to New Year's."

Samantha stood up, "if they succeed in implementing the MIP in our past how will that affect the timeline we are in now?" She asked.

John spoke up, "there are two potentials I am theorizing here that could occur. The first and most desirable is that in a parallel universe what ever happens to us stays as an alternate reality that would not affect us. The second and more alarming is that whatever occurs that night in our past changes the face of our current timeline and potentially our future in a drastic way. We don't have expertise in time travel yet so the outcome is uncertain at this point but I would say that the risks are very real."

Chantal and Maya watched the meeting through the Unity Network on board their flight home. "I agree with John, I'm certain that Diana appeared back at the party, what do you think, Chantal?"

"I think so too it makes sense," she replied. Chantal knew the only person that would have meaningful input to potentially aid this situation that she was aware of was Zain. She closed her eyes and focused on his face bringing his presence deeper and deeper into her mind. To her surprise she began to feel a response within her; tingling warmth spread inside her chest and moved into her head. 'I need to speak with you,' was the mental message she sent to him. A picture of Zain's ship clearly appeared in her mind. She opened her eyes and knew what she had to do. Chantal reached over and squeezed Maya's hand. "Maya, I have to do something and I need you to trust me and not ask questions right now. I want to go somewhere that will give us answers to this problem," she said.

"Now?"

"Yes. Please have James hold onto my bags and tell him I will return soon."

Maya studied Chantal's face to see what she was up to. She could read the eagerness and conviction Chantal had to proceed and a space ship appeared in Maya's mind. Ultimately she knew Chantal would go with or without her agreement so she just smiled and said, "I'll be waiting in suspense."

"Thanks Maya," Chantal replied with a quick embrace and got up to go to the on board washroom. Once there she sat on the toilet seat and did her best to relax in the cramped little room. She began to trance and focused on Zain's ship. About twenty minutes later Maya overheard an elderly lady complain to the flight attendant about the length of time someone was occupying one of the washrooms. She peeked around the corner and heard the attendant knock on the door and call out, "hello are you all right in there?" After receiving no response they used an emergency access device to open the door. "How odd, the room is empty.

How on earth did this door get locked from the inside with no one here?" Exclaimed the attendant.

Maya covered her mouth and muffled a laugh making a mental note to release the latch on airborne washrooms should she ever decide to teleport out of them.

SiXTEEN

Diana appeared in the middle of the New Year's Eve party at CIV Central with Colonel Stark and Nicholas. She watched as Colonel Stark held the glass shard to a little girl's throat and backed out of the building. Then her eyes met her alternate reality double and in an instant they both understood what was taking place. Security appeared confused at the presence of two of the same person and apprehended both of them. Diana felt something warm trickling down her cheek as she was put into a room with her other self and the door was locked. They could hear the chaotic movement of guests and security outside. Some people were beginning to become ill from the time storm that had been created by the intruders. "You're bleeding," said Diana to the aspect of herself that had appeared suddenly with Nicholas and Colonel Stark. She was somewhat distraught at the state of deterioration the other version of her self exhibited. Diana watched as the other touched her own face and witnessed blood running out of her left ear. She was obviously in a lot of pain as she sunk to the ground and shook violently gripping the sides of her head.

"I don't have a lot of time," the kneeling woman said to her with pleading eyes. "You must remove the tracking chip from your palm immediately unless you want to experience what's waiting for you if you return. Take a good look at me because this is what it looks ten days from now. I'm your future and I failed to do what I'm telling you to do soon enough. Do not plant the MIP cone. Destroy it." The woman fumbled with her bag and withdrew a small pocket knife. "Here, take the chip out with this, do it now!" She said handing the knife to Diana and with those words the alternate reality self began to cough up blood and fell unconscious onto the floor. Diana's body began to tremble. She watched helpless to do anything till the other began to dissolve from her reality and disappeared. All that was left that proved she had ever existed was her bag and a red puddle of blood on the floor at Diana's feet.

With trembling hands Diana picked up her pocketknife and opened her blade. She inhaled deeply and sliced through her palm carving out the tracking chip. It fell to the floor and she smashed it with her shoe. Her hand throbbed, bleeding and she sank into a chair relieved that she had prevented her own future demise from happening again. At the death of her other self the awareness of all the emotion this aspect had experienced were suddenly alive in her and a knowingness of what she had endured was recorded in her soul. It was as if the two Diana's had merged into one consciousness filled with strength and resolve that she had never experienced before changing her profoundly.

Amit walked into the room with two security officers. "Where's the other woman?" The first officer asked.

"She died and then disappeared, take a look at the blood on the floor that's from her," she replied still shaken by what she had witnessed.

"This is getting more bizarre by the moment," Amit mumbled to himself picking up the bag that had been left by the other Diana. He examined the contents as Lorne walked into the room.

"Where are the two men that appeared in your midst, have they been apprehended?" Asked Diana.

"Friends of yours?" said Lorne sarcastically. "They escaped holding a sharp object against the throat of a ten year old girl. Would you mind filling us in on where the hell you people are from and what you want? Are there doubles of them too or were you the only one who has a twin?" Lorne was beginning to loose his composure which happened rarely. John had succumbed to his emotions outside a few minutes prior and Lorne reassured and consoled him as best as he could but Jena's abduction had brought up anger in him.

"Take this and destroy it," said Diana handing him the MIP cone.

"What is it?" asked Amit.

"It's the last of a series of devices that have been planted in each sector of the world. The two men and I are from an alternate reality that is very bleak and troubled. We are part of the Omega Group which is comprised of some of the most powerful members of the former government and Illuminati who mean to take over your current timeline by radically restructuring your mind and memories. This in turn will change reality as you know it which is anchored by your mind and you will not even know it has occurred. Nicholas Sealy carries the MIP control which can start the mind altering sequence and then a chain reaction will occur setting off all the world wide devices. If this MIP cone is not planted they won't be able to set the program in motion because they will be out of range of the next devices planted outside of the North American sector," Diana explained.

"What if they travel to the next nearest sector?" Asked Amit.

"Then they will be able to initiate the sequence but this sector would remain unaffected unless they got a replacement MIP cone and brought it back here."

"Can you give us the locations of all the other cones that have been planted?" asked Lorne.

"Yes, if you can remove them then further risks can be avoided," she replied.

"Explain your double appearing with them," said Lorne.

"I'm not sure if I can. To tell you the truth I was as shocked to see them all appearing here as you were. This was not supposed to happen. I'm the only person that has been able to travel to this timeline. Others have tried and failed. I arrived here on my own a few days ago so somewhere in their plans something must have gone wrong to cause this unscheduled appearance. If I appeared with them it must have been from another point of observation in time. My double as you call her warned me before she died that she was my future demise if I did not abort my mission."

"Do you have any idea where the two men may have taken Jena?" Asked Amit.

"No I'm sorry but I don't know where they would go. They're not familiar with this time at all except for a map that has been created through my surveillance efforts here. With that they could choose to go anywhere."

"You are in a serious predicament because of your actions. Your willingness to cooperate however is appreciated under these circumstances and if you continue to do so you will be given special consideration. I would like you to debrief our scientific advisory group on all the details of the time travel and the mind restructuring technology. If we are to prevent further disaster then they will need to know everything you can tell them," Amit told Diana.

"I will give them all the information I have. I don't want these people to succeed with their plans. I genuinely am in awe at what you people have accomplished as a society and that to me is worth preserving." She looked away biting her lower lip. "I'm truly so sorry for all of this."

Amit gestured to one of the intelligence officers and said, "this is Francis. Get used to him because he is about to become your personal, full time chaperone. We will arrange a room for you at one of our CIV residences and he will be posting guard there. After you give us the locations of the MIP cones he will take you there to remain for the time being unless you are called to meet with any of us. You won't be restrained but Francis is armed," he emphasized with a stern look. "You can give him a list of any personal items you require and he will see that you get them. Do you have any questions?"

"No and I won't cause you any more trouble," Diana answered and sat with Lorne and Amit to provide the information that they requested.

Nicholas had switched cars at a local shopping centre parking lot, abandoning the silver sedan in favor of a sport utility vehicle. "What are we going to do with the girl Sir? Surely you weren't serious about releasing her," said Colonel Stark.

"That's what I like about you Stark, you know how I think. She's too valuable as insurance that we're untouchable."

"My thoughts exactly Sir," replied Colonel Stark as he drove gloating form the compliment. His hand kept reaching for the side of his neck and he felt hot itchy welts that had broken through his skin. He knew about the side effects that could occur from time travel but these had progressively worsened since his arrival. Nicholas did not appear to be suffering any ill effects thus far. He held the map and directed Colonel Stark to the edge of town where they could find an inconspicuous place to hide. They had a serious problem because they did not know if Diana had planted the last MIP cone in the North American Sector or not. Nicholas had seen her apprehended by the CIV's security people and new that the opportunity would be lost if she had not planted it earlier. If they activated the sequence and the cone was not present the procedure would not work. The only chance they had would be to travel to the next sector and initiate the MIP sequence there but the North American sector would be unaffected without the presence of a cone and that could cause disastrous complications. Nicholas needed a quiet place to think and some time to conceptualize and alternate plan.

In the back of the vehicle Jena rested her head against the seat in a deep trance. Completely unafraid of what was happening to her, she transmitted all of the details telepathically to the Shining Ones who where aware of the unfoldment of this alternate timeline that Nicholas and Colonel Stark had initiated. She felt the stirrings of Romanius connecting with her essence across time and allowed it to fill her entire being with love. Jena knew that if her life was threatened again she would have to act to preserve herself but that time had not arrived as of yet.

Chantal appeared on board Zain's ship and took a deep breath, stretching out her arms and bringing herself back to full conscious awareness of her surroundings. "I see you got my message. Welcome aboard," Zain said with a big smile.

"I see you got mine, thanks for the invitation," she replied taking in his appearance. He wore a very modern looking loosely fitted shirt and pants that appeared to me made of a fabric she had never seen before; dark in color and of a very light weight micro weave that skimmed over his beautiful form.

"You like my garments? I'll take you shopping sometime my mother knows all the best places."

Chantal grinned wondering what galaxy they would end up in and this was the first time he had ever mentioned his mother.

Zain came over and took Chantal's hand. "I know what's happened, come sit with me we need to talk."

Chantal sat with Zain on a long, curved seat next to an observation window. "Zain, who designed your ship?" Chantal asked changing the topic. "It's really beautiful."

"It was conceptualized and adapted from engineering used in the Pleadian system. These craft can travel at speeds exceeding light or fold space time in an instant. They also offer excellent cloaking and navigation technology that is highly efficient. In a few hundred years technologies from other star systems are shared with Earth which enables it to join a diverse galactic community in exploration."

"How fabulous!" Chantal exclaimed looking out the viewing area at the cosmos.

"Yes and you will likely see all of that but first we need to deal with a serious problem that has arisen that can potentially fragment your current timeline."

"You mean the appearance of the two men that Diana brought through with her back to New Year's Eve at CIV Central right?"

"Yes, they made it through and they've taken a hostage effectively avoiding capture and managing to escape."

"Who?"

"A child that you know by the name Jena."

"Oh god that's John Willowby's adopted daughter."

"Not quite."

Chantal furrowed her brow, "what do you mean?" She asked perplexed by his comment.

"Let's go to use the Virtual Nav and I'll show you," said Zain rising and leading Chantal out of the room. An opening appeared they stepped into the gray room and Zain activated the Nav. Part of the wall in the room dissolved revealing the star lit sky. "Let's keep our enchanting view," he said. "Here is a record of what took place since Nicholas Sealy and Colonel Stark appeared in your past at on New Year's Eve in a parallel universe," Zain continued looking at the holographic projection.

Chantal watched the events unfold on the holographic display ending in observing Jena in the back of a vehicle being driven by Colonel Stark. "We have this as recorded history now from the points of observation of all present and participating in the events as they took place. The Virtual Nav is programmed to access data recorded by conscious beings in whatever local universe the ship is present in."

The Nav then showed a close up of Jena and suddenly images of a tall, exotic being with pearlized, rainbow colored skin appeared. She had a strong but feminine form and unusual eyes that reflected light with a metallic sheen. "Wow, who is that?" Chantal asked.

"Beautiful isn't she? That's the girl's native form. Her name is Larina and she's from a race that would translate in your language as Tribe of the Rainbow Light. They are beings form the Central Universe that possess the most unique genetic characteristics that exist in any species; the ability to shape shift and adapt to any environment across the multiverse. They are the only beings that have the genetic signature that allows this to occur. As you know the abilities of highly evolved consciousness allows for the blending or unifying of that consciousness with any life form. That is how masters can see through the eyes of a bird or become the scent of a flower. Though our mind is free to become anything we are however limited at the level of the physical body to occupy only environments that produced and can support these bodies. Larina's race is not limited genetically the way the rest of us are. Where we can travel in our light body she can go and unfold her physical garment transformed genetically into the species that occupies that world. This allows for seamless integration into whatever planet they perform their duties on without being detected as an alien presence," explained Zain.

"I knew there was something odd about her. At the New Year's party she told me I would be needed to help protect the present and the future. I was surprised by her comment to say the least. Why is she here?" Asked Chantal.

"Her role was to ensure that memories regarding the construction of the photon shielding device that John Willowby had lost were retrieved and that the technology was implemented in your current timeline to ensure your people's safety. Upon completion of that her presence would no longer be required on Earth."

"We are about a day away from that being a reality. Will her abduction in the alternate timeline affect her ability to leave?"

"Yes, her consciousness will not be able to fully disengage Earth if a part of her is held in the parallel world. It's a complication that must also be resolved."

Chantal sighed and asked the question she dreaded, "so what else could go wrong?"

"Diana's presence in the parallel reality could provide an entry point for Nicholas and Colonel Stark into your current time."

"How? She removed the chip from her palm that gives her access to the TII device."

Zain paused and looked at Chantal and continued, "Once a person has been exposed to a specific technology that interfaces with her mind she can develop the ability to create the reality without the aid of the technology."

Chantal pondered the implications of what he said. "You mean she can time travel without the device? Does she realize this?"

"It would appear that she was beginning to on her last trip, wouldn't you say?"

Of course! Chantal thought. "Definitely, that must be how she unloaded her travel companions at the New Year's party and kept going to appear in my time," she replied.

"Exactly and it won't take her long to figure out what her double from the future did because after all the idea will come from the same mind."

"If Stark and Nicholas get their hands on her she could theoretically pull them forward to my time with her."

"It's a long shot but still a possible risk."

"They wouldn't know that she has the ability to do that, would they?" Asked Chantal.

"One thing I have learned is that sometimes the potential that seems least likely to manifest does so I've learned not to create a false sense of security by ignoring the more improbable scenarios," said Zain.

Novara walked into the room and handed Chantal and Zain two glasses full of a vivid green beverage. "I sensed that you would benefit from fortifying refreshment," she said.

They thanked her and she left the room. "I was getting thirsty and a little tired," said Chantal sipping the drink.

"Novara is very adept at creating an efficient and holistic on board environment. She adds value with her assistance without being in the way," said Zain.

"She's very beautiful and so tall," said Chantal.

He smiled, "yes the people of her race are all genetically strong and tall, their height reaching to eight feet among the men. Novara is from a planet called Axaritan on the other side of your galaxy."

"I've never met an extra terrestrial person before she is my first I guess," said Chantal.

"Second actually," said Zain casually.

Chantal looked at him wide eyed, "you?!"

He laughed deeply and replied, "yes but that's a story for another time. We have a more urgent matter to discuss."

"Fine, but I'm going to hold you to that."

Zain only smiled knowing that she would.

"So what could be more urgent than all the drama that has been unfolding in our troubled little reality?" Chantal asked taking a sip of her juice.

"Your involvement in a solution to it," he replied.

Chantal choked and sputtered green juice everywhere in response to his comment. "Jesus!" she said taking a handkerchief out of her jacket and wiping up the mess with it.

"Well he wasn't the one I had in mind for this assignment but if you turn this down…" Zain said looking out at the stars with his hand on his chin.

"Very funny," said Chantal composed once again. "I'm not planning to jump ship, just tell me what you have in mind."

He leaned his strong torso squarely towards her. "Have you ever teleported through time?"

Chantal thought for a moment, "not that I'm aware of. I have only time traveled by mind and in my astral body."

"Chantal I'm going to share a little more information with you," said Zain.

Finally, Chantal thought. She instinctively knew not to push Zain for more information than he had shared with her thus far but knew that he held back on a lot of things.

"I know that you are aware to some degree from your training at Sacred Rose the nature of service as it pertains to masters in the course of their evolution."

"What I have an understanding of from my own evolutionary experience is that as masters we naturally attract opportunities that allow us to take on greater responsibilities in the stewardship of life and that this can occur in a limitless variety of expression. We earn this through the evolution of mind and abilities that accompany that growth. It is not unlike the MDR system that allows our citizens to have greater input into governing decisions."

"Yes and since there are many degrees of mastership there is a history from those that have progressed before us since they ultimately leave a path to where they have gone. They are aware of us when we evolve and can welcome us into their consciousness if we desire and have made ourselves worthy."

Chantal was seeing images of beings surrounded by light with beautiful, serene faces emanating deep wisdom as Zane spoke. "I understand what you are saying but what does that have to do with me?" she asked.

"You have captured the attention of such beings and have been watched for some time now. There are qualities that you possess that interest them specifically your visionary abilities that provided much to work with in constructing your current timeline, your creative leadership and your painstaking assembly of past history that you developed into educational presentations for the youth of the new generation to know of the dire circumstances of Earth's recent past. There are benefits to this interest they have in you because opportunities for advancement in learning, evolution and service can manifest from mutual association."

Chantal took in everything Zain was telling her. She looked out at the midnight backdrop outside the ship suspending stars that reached beyond her vision. How many beings in the cosmos had experienced moments like she was having now knowing what she knew? Who had they been and who were they now? She wondered. "I can feel them," she said softly. I always have but in flashes of recognition as something familiar yet elusive to definition. Like you....I felt you before I actually met you," she said gazing peacefully into Zain's eyes.

"You know the saying, we're only a thought away," he said.

As they looked at one another it was as if a bridge of consciousness formed and Chantal could see it reached far into the future. It was a bridge made by two that would support the weight of earnest hearts crossing to greater continents of life. She wasn't completely sure what this meant yet but she observed it nonetheless. Hear pulse quickened and energy moved into her head. Something was happening to her and she looked at Zain in wonder.

"Just let it happen," he said.

She closed her eyes and surrendered to the surges of energy hitting her brain and a bright light appeared in her head. It was if someone shone a thousand watt light into her face and she began to feel herself floating. The three hundred and sixty degree vision she was familiar with began and suddenly faces swam in her inner vision of breathtakingly beautiful beings whose eminence was indescribable. As she observed them the most exquisite peace permeated every particle of her and in an instant holographically rich, detailed information was transmitted to her. The vision faded and slowly Chantal opened her eyes and looked at Zain. "I know what they want me to do," she said. "I have to go back to the past where the problems are occurring."

Zain studied her and she could tell he was very pleased. "Yes," he said.

"So I teleport back in time?"

"That is one way but there is a smoother procedure we can employ here," he said. "Remember you are already physically present there. What if you could bring to life in your conscious awareness all that has transpired over the past ten days to your mind on New Year's Eve, wouldn't that be simpler?"

Chantal could conceptualize where Zain was leading her in thought. "Yes! That would be much simpler, then there wouldn't have to be two of me and no one would know what I was doing."

"Exactly, it would be seamless."

"How do we do this…wait! I think I know," she said excitedly. "It's the way I experience the future…the same but backwards. I become myself in another time. But I've only experienced this as an out of body projection so far. I have to physically pull it off this time and actually be present in my body at the party as my future self from this time."

"We can help you with that here by using the Virtual Nav to create a set of coordinates for your mind to move into. It's how I teleport anywhere I desire through time. I choose and observe a coordinate, use it as a focal point and ride the light to appear there."

"But I'm not teleporting I…." Chantal began to protest till Zain put his arms around her and silenced her with a kiss. Chantal enveloped by the sudden warmth and scent of him forgot what she had been saying and surrendered to the electrical sensation of energy moving between them. When he released her from the embrace and before she could say anything Zain took her by the hand and brought up an image of her standing by the balcony at CIV Central on the Virtual Nav. In the scene they surveyed she wore her white dress with her hair pinned up just like she remembered. "I want you to memorize what you are looking at like a photograph in your mind. Take all the time you need to absorb the details as these are your destination coordinates," he said.

"Alright," replied Chantal as she studied the scene before her taking in the deep night sky, quiet bare trees of winter covered with a thin layer of glistening snow. Her hands were touching the white, marble balcony railing as she looked out. "I'm ready," she whispered.

A hovering, body contouring lounger appeared in the room and Zain instructed Chantal to lay on it. Novara came into the room and placed a device around Chantal's forehead and temples. "This consciousness tracking device will help you move into a deep state of delta and hold you there while you focus on your coordinates. As you do so focus on yourself at the party and merge as one. Your body will rest here and you in the deepest state of consciousness will be observing only that reality. Once you have become your self in the past the rest is easy because you will not need to do anything further in this time other than observe what is taking place in a parallel universe. It's just like having a lucid dream," said Zain.

"My self in the past will know all I know?

"Yes."

"What do I do while I'm there to correct the situation?" Asked Chantal.

"You will know what to do at the right time but there will be an opportunity to save a particular life. It will be your choice whether to do so or not."

There he goes being mysterious again, she thought.

"Remember you are connected through mind to others who know what is happening and to me. The answers will come when you need them and we will be able to watch your progress through the Virtual Nav," was all he offered.

Chantal did not feel exceedingly reassured by his reply but knew that she would not turn back. "Ok," she said. "Let's do it."

Novara programmed the Tracker around Chantal's head with a compatible sequence of brain wave patterns gradually moving her into delta. Chantal closed her eyes and many images flashed across the hologram as she settled her mind to prepare to focus. Novara and Zain watched as pictures of the CIV meeting, Chantal's light and other unrelated fragments of memory appeared. Then a scene of Zain kissing Chantal appeared on the Nav. Zain shifted his feet and glanced at Novara who did not look at him, continuing to observe the Nav but he noticed a faint smile on her face. Finally a solid picture of Chantal's coordinates took form in the holographic matrix and stabilized as she slid deeper and deeper into consciousness.

SEVENTEEN

Maya walked into the airport baggage claim area where James greeted her. "Where's Chantal?" he asked looking over her shoulder.

Maya sighed searching for the best words to explain Chantal's absence and not finding any blurted out, "Oh crap! You know Chantal James, she's gone."

"Gone? I'm almost afraid to ask, where has she gotten to this time?"

"Well I don't exactly know but she teleported off the plane latrine. She looked at me with those big eyes of hers, asked me to trust her and said she knew someone who could help with our current problems."

James was getting the picture. "Yes I know. She's very good at telling you nothing and somehow getting you to cooperate nonetheless." He had been treated to that experience on more than one occasion. "Amit is going to hate this if he finds out."

Maya's bags arrived and James picked them up and carried them out of the airport to his car.

"My advice; let's not say anything unless we have to," she said as they got in to the vehicle. "Perhaps she'll be back soon and there won't be any need."

"Right, I agree," replied James though he knew instinctively that Chantal would not be returning as soon as they might hope.

Maya smiled as they drove away, "who are we kidding?" She said and looked at James.

On New Year's eve Chantal touched the cold snow clinging to the CIV Central balcony railing as she stood outside in the crisp winter air. Her breath made swirling vapor that floated away from her face and dissolved into the night. She felt someone's eyes on her and turned squinting into the dark corners of the balcony. *I must be getting paranoid, no one else would be out here freezing his ass off*, she thought to herself and began to turn back towards the garden. A moist chill crept up her spine and she turned around and witnessed a vaporous ball forming in the air in front of her. "What the"...she began to say then watched the ball begin to glow. It floated towards her and in the centre to her surprise she saw her own face. As Chantal stood with her back pressed against the railing the approaching orb gently moved into her body. Exhilaration filled her as this happened and Chantal stood holding on to the railing, hear heart rate accelerating. Slowly her pulse returned to normal and she became light headed passively observing in her mind memories playing like a sped up movie of events that had occurred from the New Year's Eve party forward in time. When it was over Chantal regained full conscious awareness in the present and realized she had just watched ten days of her future unfold. It was an odd sensation because it was exactly like remembering but forward instead of past. The last scene she remembered was of her body lying on board Zain's ship dreaming the reality she was now experiencing! *What the mind is capable of never ceases to amaze me*, she thought to herself in wonderment. Feeling the chill of the air permeate her body thoroughly now Chantal reached for the French doors and opened them glancing up once knowing that Zain's ship occupied some coordinate deep in the night sky. "There you are!" said James grabbing Chantal by the arm as she stepped inside.

"I was just getting some air I had a headache coming on and..."

"Well you missed all the excitement. Jena's been taken hostage by two men who appeared out of nowhere in the middle of the party."

"What!?" Chantal said feigning surprise as best as she could.

"It looks like we know who the time travelers are but they used the girl to escape. Some of the guests are beginning to get ill. The whole party's turning into a nightmarish slice of chaos," said James as he led her out of the room to the security area at the back of the building. As they walked through the main room Chantal could see the intelligence team re—establishing order and escorting the guests out of the building. Diana, led by the arm of a tall intelligence agent, walked by Chantal and James her eyes momentarily locked with Chantal's. A flash went off in Chantal's brain and she experienced a premonition that she and Diana would meet again.

"You alright?" Asked James.

Chantal pulled herself away from watching Diana leave the building with her escort and looked at James. "I'm not sure…I got this strong sense about her and I meeting again soon. Sorry, no words can really describe it. I don't know what it means if anything."

"Well that's helpful," said James with a hint of sarcasm.

Chantal eyed him noticing he appeared to be loosing some of the patience he usually had. *Maybe he's just tired,* Chantal thought to herself.

James sighed and rubbed his forehead, "I'm sorry, I think all these strange events are getting to me. Look, why don't we get out of here. I have something for you and I want to talk."

Oh God not this again. Chantal knew he wanted to give her the bracelet and what the 'talk' would be about. "Look James, I can see you're not having a great evening and I apologize ahead of time but I'm about to make it worse. Please don't even think of talking to me about getting serious because I'm not interested. I love you James, you're a great friend but that's all I want."

James looked at Chantal with a stunned expression and could not think of anything to say.

"I'm really sorry." I have to get some air," Chantal said got her coat and walked out of the building. *What was wrong with everyone?* Chantal wondered. She felt agitation the way James appeared to have and noticed that the atmosphere in this time was different and laced with tension. It was more than just the evening's chaotic arrival of the intruding time travelers. Their presence in this reality had changed the feel of it. Chantal could almost perceive the minds of the Omega Group penetrating through time and couldn't wait to get out of here. She began to walk down the street away from CIV Central and saw a small figure standing at the end of the block. She stopped for a moment to get a better look at who it might be but only saw a young boy. She thought it was strange that a youngster would be out alone this late and approached him.

She opened her mouth to speak but before she got any words out he held out his hand and said, "come with me, it's important."

Chantal looked into his large, almost black eyes and saw sincerity there. She put her hand in his and as soon as she did they both disappeared. Moments later Romanius sat cradling his knees and watched Chantal as she surveyed her surroundings. They appeared to be in a miniature house of some sort, she noticed. Raw wooden walls surrounded them and miniature furniture; two lovely hand carved chairs and a table with a bowl of fruit in it. "We're in a tree house at my grandma's place. She's asleep. My name is Tristan but I think you know my true nature," he said extending his small hand in a handshake.

"Pleased to meet you Tristan," Chantal said with a warm smile as she shook his hand.

"In my home world I'm known as Romanius."

Suddenly Chantal knew who he was. The information just appeared in her mind. "You are Larina's friend?"

"Yes, we have to find her. She was supposed to be back already as her work here is complete," he replied.

Chantal could see the look of concern on his young face. "We'll find her," she said. "I know who has her."

"The men from the other time who want this reality for themselves."

"Yes, I see you know about that," said Chantal.

Romanius shrugged and replied, "all is there for everyone to know as you are aware."

"Have you gotten anything as to Jena's location?"

"I feel them on the move and they have not stayed anywhere long enough for me to determine exact coordinates. She's fine though."

"I doubt that they would hurt her she's too valuable as a safety shield for them," said Chantal.

Romanius gazed at her with a faint smile but intense expression in his eyes, "they would be foolish to lay a hand on her."

Chantal wondered what he meant and as she continued to meet his gaze a pressure began to form in her head, steadily getting more intense. "Ouch!" she exclaimed grabbing her temples and then the sensation stopped. She looked up at Romanius, "did you do that?"

We are peaceful lovers of life in all universes but have the capacity to defend ourselves if necessary. Larina can create a brain aneurism or any other type of sudden death in seconds," he replied.

He's not kidding, Chantal thought to herself still rubbing her head.

Romanius laughed like an ordinary mischievous boy and came over to Chantal. He gently placed his hands a few inches from her temples and radiated soothing energy into her. Instantly she felt as if sliding into bliss, all remaining tension dissolving. "Better?" He asked.

"Yes, thank you. Why did you bring me here?"

"We are here for the same reason."

"Yes, I suppose that's true. We can work together but I'm not just here to find Jena — I mean Larina. What these men want to do must be stopped."

"They will not succeed but can still cause a lot of damage in trying to. The MIP cones are being removed world wide. They will likely determine that their only chance to salvage their plan is to apprehend the woman who found this time. She is the only one who can travel between their world and this one bringing others through," said Romanius.

Chantal knew that she would at some point have to share information with Amit and his team but they would not be aware of their parallel existence that she came from and on top of that her working with extra terrestrials would be a lot to explain. She looked at Romanius and he appeared to know that she was troubled. "Go home and get some rest. I will find you when I know Larina's location."

"Alright," Chantal said with a sigh. She closed her eyes and within minutes she disappeared from the tree house and appeared back at her house. The lights were off and her cat ran up to greet her. Chantal picked him up, carried him on her shoulder to the bedroom and sat down on the bed. She looked around the room remarking that everything looked the same as usual but there was an indescribable difference in the feel of this time. This was her first experience time traveling to her past while experiencing it in the body and she wanted to preserve the wonder of this moment in her mind because she would be returning forward again.

Colonel Stark looked at himself in the washroom mirror and examined his neck. Large, red welts had grown in size and ran all the way down to his shoulders itching intensely. He looked at his bloodshot eyes and pale face. Nausea was beginning to take hold of him and he had already vomited several times since reaching the remote motel they had checked into under false names. He could not understand why he had been affected so severely by traveling to this time and Nicholas failed to show a single symptom. He had tried to lie down and rest but each time he almost drifted off to sleep disturbing images came to life in his mind from the past going all the way back to his college days. He and two of his friends had hired a stripper for their fraternity party and after her performance was over they lured her into a back room offering her more money for a private dance. Once there however, she was raped by them and beaten by him. They had all drank too much and when it was over blamed their inebriated state for triggering their behavior. The girl was highly distraught and her face was bruised. They tried to calm her and offered her a significant sum of money not to turn them in to the police threatening to find her and do worse if she pressed any charges. Grudgingly she accepted the money and left the party. No one ever found out what had happened and Colonel Stark had not thought about that night again since but every time he closed his eyes her bloody face hovered in his mind and he could hear her pleas for them to stop what they were doing. Worse still some of the atrocities he had committed while serving in the Persian Gulf War haunted him as well. Bodies of young soldiers he had killed with excessive cruelty floated into his consciousness. All of these images were accompanied by a foreboding feeling and lingering anxiety that made his nausea worse.

Nicholas could hear the toilet flush knowing that his travel companion's condition had not improved. Already circumstances provided ample frustration and Stark's deteriorated state did not help their current situation. They had locked the girl in the bedroom while Nicholas reviewed all their available options. He knew it was unlikely that the MIP cones were still in place since Diana was in custody and probably provided their location to the CIV. Driving to the next sector and attempting to activate the process would be futile. His most logical move would be to arrange an exchange of the girl for Diana who was needed in order for them to effectively move the other Omega Group members to the current timeline. His presence here might have enabled him to potentially bring them through but he knew he couldn't risk going back and not being able to return. He had a feeling that Stark would definitely not make it back because of his compromised physical condition but Nicholas had a unique genetic advantage that provided protection from adverse reaction to the time storm they had created. Nicholas twisted the gold signet ring around his index finger as he pondered his options. Perhaps he wouldn't need the other members of the Omega Group after all. Replacements here were plentiful provided the MIP could be performed. There was a way it could be done without his having to go back in time and then return to reset the cones. A last resort but logical since all humans he had created an alliance with on behalf of his people eventually proved to be unreliable. Clearly they had also ended up in the wrong time coordinates thanks to Diana's maneuver and out of principle he desired to correct that. The more he contemplated this last option the more determined Nicholas became to contact his people.

Colonel Stark stumbled out of the bathroom and went over to the window, looked out and then sat down looking somewhat relieved. "You alright?" asked Nicholas.

"I don't' know. Just this strange feeling I have that someone's out there watching and they're coming."

Nicholas studied him. He had noticed that over the last couple of hours since they had arrived at the motel Colonel Stark's behavior had become erratic. He constantly peered out the window looking nervous and agitated, perspiring profusely and this appeared more linked to his mental state than his malaise. Nicholas determined that if Stark became a liability he was completely expendable. "I want you to stay with the girl, I'm going out for a while," Said Nicholas rising and heading towards the front door.

Colonel Stark knew better than to question him. "Alright sir, will you be gone long?"

"Maybe an hour. Make sure you check on the girl."

"Yes sir."

Nicholas left the motel room and got into the car. He needed to find a quiet place where he could make contact and preceded to drive down a nearby abandoned road adjacent to a forested area where he pulled over. He got out of the car and walked into the woods instantly soothed by the scent of moss and live trees. Inhaling deeply he sat down against a tall fir, reached into his breast pocket and withdrew a slender, folded electronic headset. He placed a small, transparent circular chip inside it and put the headset on. Vibrations moved into his frontal and temporal lobes as the device hummed softly. Nicholas could feel the familiar sense of moving in consciousness to the presence of his people's ship. He entered the code numbers with his mind waited for clearance, heard the tone that indicated he had it and removed the headset. Nicholas looked up at the sky knowing they would arrive soon.

Colonel Stark unlocked the bedroom door where he left Jena and walked in. "How are you doing, do you need anything?" he asked.

Jena sat up on the bed and looked at him. He was obviously in poor physical condition himself, she noted. "No thank you, I don't need anything but you don't look too well yourself," she replied.

"Fine then," he replied and was about to leave.

"Wait," she said and when he looked back she met his gaze drawing him into her eyes. To Colonel Stark the effect was like being drawn into a narrow tunnel where all he could see was her face. "I can tell the pictures in your mind are getting worse. Even if your body gets better, your mind will not. You've done horrific things and they will possess your sanity, it's already happening. The vibration of this reality is not compatible with your consciousness, don't you know that? If you stay here you will lose your mind," said Jena.

Her words stunned him and a combination of shame, vulnerability and anger welled up in him at the thought of anyone knowing how his thoughts had betrayed him. "How do you know this?" he demanded, incredulous.

"It doesn't matter, but you are slowly going insane."

"That's crap! My mind is fine; there is nothing wrong with me!" Colonel Stark replied vehemently.

Jena continued to hold his gaze and said, "I have the ability to help you get better but the only chance you have to save your mind is if you change. You won't though because you enjoyed what you did to those people. In fact if they were here today you would do it again. As long as you get enjoyment out of violence and perversion you can never stay here and keep your sanity."

He backed out of the room and slammed the door behind him. His stomach was in knots again and he ran to the bathroom and vomited. When he finally came out he was badly shaken and now the macabre images in his mind played even when his eyes were open. Rage moved through him because he could not deny to himself that she was right about his indulgent, violent nature. It was something that he believed no one knew about him and the thought of a child holding that kind of power over him infuriated Stark. He wanted to go into that room and strangle the life out of her arrogant little face, silencing her forever. He clenched his fists and all kinds of scenarios that he could tell Nicholas about her death passed through his mind. *This girl is dangerous and for the sake of achieving our objectives she must die,* he rationalized. Surely Nicholas would agree once he knew the truth about her being able to read thoughts. Colonel Stark ripped an electrical cord out of the wall, wound it around his hands and slowly opened the bedroom door.

Chantal opened her eyes and sat up in her bed. She thought she had heard a sound coming from the living room and rose to see what it was. When she walked in Romanius stood in the centre of the room. "Hi, I have the coordinates for Larina's location. We must hurry though, a potentially dangerous situation is developing," he said.

"Let me throw some jeans on," said Chantal quickly returning to her bedroom. She came out again moments later dressed in black jeans and a t—shirt, grabbed her jacket and said, "Let's go."

Romanius held Chantal's hand as they teleported to room 32 at the Skyline Motel. She looked around at the shabby décor and her eyes fixed on the bedroom door from which muffled sounds escaped. Romanius looked at her and they approached the bedroom, slowly turning the handle. Once open they peered in and saw the Colonel on top of Jena with the electric cord pulled tightly around her neck. Before Romanius and Chantal could get to her he let go of the cord and grabbed his chest, falling backwards. Jena sat up and continued to concentrate with all her might on accelerating his heart rate effectively inducing a heart attack. Simultaneously Romanius began to create pressure on the Colonel's brain with his mind till blood began to run out of his ears and he fell over in the throes of his death. "His consciousness was corrupted and unsalvageable," said Jena as they all witnessed his slumped body.

Chantal went over and examined Jena's neck which now displayed red, raised marks where the cord had begun to cut into her skin. Romanius approached her and instantly she smiled. They pressed their faces together in an embrace and Chantal witnessed their wordless communication that could only be described as an electrically charged, moving field of animated mind between them. Romanius held his hand to her throat and in a few moments all signs of trauma to her flesh disappeared. "I have arranged for safe return to our world, there is nothing more we can do here that will not interfere more than is desirable," said Romanius.

"Our presence in the timeline you came from will effectively be erased and no one but you will have memory of us ever having been there," said Larina.

"What about John and your relationship to him?" Asked Chantal.

"It must be done this way. My presence in his life was an illusory memory implant. It will simply be erased and he will not suffer any emotional trauma."

"I understand," replied Chantal.

"Never underestimate your own power, you have much more than has yet been experienced," said Larina.

Chantal watched as colorful swirls of plasmic energy formed around Romanius and Larina creating more density of light around them. In this enveloping cocoon of energy she could see their forms change, grow taller and become breathtaking embodiments of dazzling colors overlaying long limbs and beautiful features. They both smiled at her just a second before a brilliant flash of light appeared in the room and then they were gone.

Wow, Chantal thought to herself, now alone in the motel room. She sat down for a moment to collect her thoughts. She had no idea where she was and knew that staying to confront Nicholas alone would not be the ideal option at this time. Her mind kept returning to the premonition she had about Diana and sensed that this is where her attention would best serve. Chantal knew that Diana was the key to all the time travel activity of the others to 2020. She decided that keeping her away from Nicholas and the Omega Group was the priority now. Somehow she needed to find a way to get to Diana without having to explain all these complications to the CIV who were unaware that Chantal had arrived from their future. She knew there was one person she trusted to help her with what she planned but first she would need to eat some humble pie.

EiGHTEEN

A large, black, rectangular space ship with rounded contours approached the location where Nicholas waited in the forest. It hovered directly above him and then emitted a spotlight of golden particles. He walked into the light and allowed it to suspend him in luminous density as he floated up towards the opening in the ship. His form entered the decontamination chamber where ultraviolet light emitting measured pulses washed over his body. A door slid open and Nicholas walked onto the main deck which was occupied by several beings dressed in garments fitted from a fabric that resembled shiny, leathery bat wings. This same substance was fashioned into tall boots and overcoats with collars that stood high around the neck against very pale skin contrasting dark hair and dark eyes of the beings. These were a renegade group of people descended from the Anunnaki race that called them selves the 'Rabum Kataru' legion which translated to 'Great Alliance.' The word 'alliance' was intended to signify their involvement with less evolved planetary consciousness but in reality, these beings sought to covertly influence the global economies and activities of such worlds through select, prominent individuals in power.

Commander Alal greeted Nicholas in their native language calling him by his real name as he entered, "welcome Amelatu," and motioned for him to sit in a curved, black chair. Two female members of the crew approached and activated the memory download that fed from his mind directly to a chip loaded into the headrest of the chair. Upon completion one of the women gave the chip to Alal who inserted it into a device that allowed him to view the contents in his mind instantly. Nicholas waited for him to finish and felt tension form around his forehead. Contacting his people was reserved for a time when the plans he was empowered to execute on Earth had failed, were unsalvageable and he required assistance. This was the first time such an event had occurred since his involvement in Earth's affairs which Amelatu primarily undertook in his previous role with the CIA. Members of the Rabum Kataru had kept contact with him over the years on an as needed basis but as long as he delivered on their objectives for maintaining control over key world resources and government activities they left him alone to do his job.

"Your decision to ask for intervention from us at his time is warranted and wise Amelatu," said Alal. "The situation on Earth has become unnecessarily complicated and needs to be simplified by us."

Amelatu realized what was transpiring as he had not asked for intervention and was hoping to receive some assistance and then resume command of overseeing the legion's covert operations on Earth. It now appeared that Alal planned to take over completely and that meant he would be making all the decisions.

Alal noticed the slight disappointment on Amelatu's face and said,

"We are family, Amelatu and will work together to achieve the same success that we have attained on this planet for thousands of years. There is nothing to be concerned about," said Alal putting his hand on Amelatu's shoulder. "This organization, the CIV they call themselves, are in their infancy of wielding global communications and electromagnetic technologies. So the air is finally clean and they have attained world peace. How long has it taken for such a small leap in consciousness to be achieved to where they are no longer living in their own cesspool of pollutants? They still need us to oversee and guide them through a carefully scheduled progress. If they advance to far and too fast another collapse in consciousness is inevitable because the personal power that they attain will corrupt them the way it always has. It is a drug Amelatu that has to be dispensed wisely among those that will align them selves with our higher vision otherwise it is a danger to their own human survival. This timeline in 2020 that you are so close to claiming is approaching the threshold of such a danger and we must intervene to re establish our alliance and control the rate of their progress."

"What do you have in mind Alal?" Asked Amelatu.

Alal smiled and addressed him, "we will accomplish complete mental reprogramming of all the citizens in the desired original timeline of our focus. That means Amelatu that you will become the head of the world CIV on Earth and all of the current IM's will serve our vision. We will insert you into the original timeline that Diana discovered and there a plan more brilliant than originally conceptualized by the Omega Group will unfold. Not only will all the minds belong to us but we will maintain guardianship of these minds indefinitely through a technology that you are ready to know about because of your exceptional loyalty to us. Come with me." Alal motioned Amelatu to follow him, passed out of the ship's main deck through a narrow corridor and into a small room. Inside Amelatu saw stacks of neatly organized vials containing a phosphorescent looking liquid. "Behold the future on Earth," said Alal as he motioned to all the vials in the room.

"What are these?"

"They hold the elixir of our engineered consciousness as potentials for all the people on Earth. Our ancient program that collectively we all share as one mind created by the most advanced of the Rabum Kataru upon our defection from the Shining Ones and their exclusive genetic and spiritual platform dictating life across the universes millions of years ago. This is the platform that has allowed an alternative model of consciousness to exist in many worlds that we have influenced across this universe where we reign supreme as one and only creator. It is our collective mind and not the so called "God" of the Shining Ones that is the source of evolution for the sentient beings on the worlds that we have inherited with our technological superiority. This is how you Amelatu and all the people from your home planet were freed from the program of the Shining Ones when we arrived hundreds of years ago. Souls under our care no longer need to reincarnate over and over in an insane pattern of so called learning only to return to more angst and adversity of their inferior cultures. Yes masters have emerged on Earth and elsewhere who have transcended the illusion of their reality and ascended to what the Shining Ones refer to as the 'Kingdom of the Father' but this is only an embarrassing handful while millions continue to suffer. We have afforded billions across the worlds we guard exponential growth technologically without the collapse of consciousness that the 'free will' model which the Shining Ones so stubbornly cling to inevitably produces. Ascension is not required by us in order to partake and become the consciousness of a powerful creator in the universe we the Rabum Kataru strive to give this right to all people when they are ready."

Amelatu picked up one of the vials and watched as tiny particles swirled in the light of the liquid. "Alal, please tell me more about the technology I am observing."

"In the beginning when a small group of us defected from the ranks of the Shining Ones they left us to create our own evolutionary platform but banned us from the arena of genetics. We could not create life forms based on DNA or the truce would cease. That is how we came to create the first Animatrons; silicone based beings that were animated by artificial intelligence. Souls will only inhabit genetically based life forms so to compensate for this we built programs based on the soul wisdom of us, the first defectors that became the core mind of the collective Rabum Kataru. We soon found a way around the rules of the Shining Ones to achieve what we had always wanted: our direct influence over the evolution of consciousness. What you are holding is a quantum pattern that is injected into the blood stream of organic beings, travels to a specific area of the brain and comes together in the form of an implant. This effectively overrides all connection to the program of spirit that the Shining Ones oversee and delivers the mind and soul of the individual to the collective creator mind of our legion. We then place the population on a consciousness evolution schedule that has already been achieved by others who have joined our collective mind. Because we are able to reduce emotional intensity in a being the soul is relieved from emotional conflict and is redirected through specific programming to desire nothing more than to be a part of our collective creator mind. Amelatu, only those most worthy who have proven themselves are finally given full disclosure about our true history as a species. I honor you today so that you may feel renewed enthusiasm about your role on Earth in this exciting time of transformation."

Amelatu pondered all that Alal had told him. He knew that he had always been a part of the legion's collective mind and that there was an ancient defection that had taken place long ago from the Shining Ones but the details of how their race had come to evolve to its current consciousness had not been revealed to him completely. Master programmers of the synthetic matrix fed infinite amounts of data to the collective creator mind through electromagnetic technology and this role was reserved for the Animatrons. Their function was enhanced by the lack of a soul which needs emotional experiences to survive because their only purpose is to continuously ensure the smooth dispensation of all programs to the collective mind. Amelatu new that ultimately Alal with the collective would be overseeing the dispensation of this technology to Earth's population but he felt reassured of his importance to the Rabum Kataru in his role on Earth since Alal had confided in him. He turned to Alal and took his hand. "My deepest thanks for your confidence in me, Alal. I will continue to do whatever is necessary to ensure the dispensation of this program on Earth."

"Excellent! You will now be prepared for your return to the proper coordinates in 2020. There is much data to download into your mind before we can send you back. Assistants are waiting with the information chips relevant to your mission in the data room and upon completing your orientation we will initiate a temporary rift in the electromagnetic field of the earth and insert a program that will effectively gather all of the citizens to health units where they will be inoculated against contaminants that they will believe were brought into their atmosphere by the 'time travelers.' All of the necessary vials will be teleported to all health units and self serve health outposts effectively ensuring the secure delivery of the population to our guardianship," said Alal.

"What of Diana and the Omega Group?" asked Amelatu.

"You are spoiling my surprise for you upon your return but that speaks to your keen intelligence. Diana will also be located and transported to the proper time coordinates for reprogramming. You can decide what role she will play in society to atone for her disruption of our plans. As far as the Omega Group surely you see that they have honorably served their purpose but were never meant to be integrated into this timeline, Amelatu. Come let us begin your preparations," said Alal and dismissed any further discussion on the matter of the group.

Chantal materialized in James's office effectively startling him and watched as he spilled coffee all over himself. "Jesus Christ!" James exclaimed.

"Sorry, but I had to see you," said Chantal in a hushed voice.

"That wasn't the impression you left me with last night."

Chantal could tell he was still sulking over the confrontation she had with him. "James I apologize for being so abrupt with you after the party but I'm going to tell you something that will help you to understand everything."

"The suspense is killing me."

It was obvious that this cynical side to him in this timeline had persisted and she hoped that she would still be able to reach the James she knew and cared about. "James you know I don't sugar coat things so I'm just going to tell you straight out that I have traveled back in time from our recent future."

He stopped and Chantal watched him study her face carefully. "Are you serious?"

"More serious than I have ever been in my life and I really need your help."

James sighed and sat on the edge of his desk. His intuition told him that Chantal was pulling him into some unorthodox situation and doing so on the heels of breaking his heart.

Chantal felt his reluctance and said, "we already had the conversation about the bracelet and our friendship. We worked things out amicably and I made the mistake of perceiving you as less real in this time because of that when you brought it up. I was insensitive and for that I'm truly sorry."

"Well you are clearly seeing me in a real enough light to be asking for my help now aren't you?" James retorted.

"Yes James now can you give me a break here and listen?"

"Alright."

"Things have gone terribly wrong in our future. Diana managed to open the way for the Omega Group to take over our reality by systematically erasing and reprogramming our memories with their technology. She diverted Nicholas and Colonel Stark away from the future time by making them arrive here instead of forward but she is still a dangerous link that Nicholas has to the future. I want you to help me get her out of here and back to our future so that he can't exploit her."

"That's why there was two of her?"

"Exactly, she came to warn us. Apparently she had a change of heart about going through with the Group's plans and briefed the CIV on everything prior to appearing here."

"Ok, I believe you. I can get you to where she is being held; it's the CIV Cooper Point property."

"Let's go," said Chantal. James took her hand and they disappeared from his office. They reappeared in the living room of the comfortable home to the surprise of the agent assigned to guarding Diana. He rose from his chair with a start and began to say, "what the…"

"It's alright Francis, there's been a change in the handling of the detained woman and I'm here to relieve you," said James.

"Amit never informed me of any changes," he said reaching for his communications device.

"That won't be necessary; he sent me and asked me to call him on my arrival. I'll need your device to do that please," said James with his hand out.

The agent looked unsure for a moment but knew better than to question an IM's authority. Reluctantly he handed the communication device to James and left the house.

"That was close," said Chantal.

"You're on your own now, hurry and get her out of here."

"Thanks James!" said Chantal embracing him and kissing his cheek. "See you in the future," she said and headed for the room where Diana was being detained. Chantal used her keycard to open the door and walked into the room.

Immediately Diana stood up somewhat surprised to see Chantal.

"I'm here to get you out of here now so please cooperate."

"What are you talking about?" Asked Diana

"You are a risk to the future timeline in 2020 that your double came from. We have to go forward to ensure that Nicholas cannot use you to gain access to that time. Take my hand," said Chantal holding out her palm. Diana instinctively knew that Chantal was right and grabbed it.

NiNETEEN

A moment of confusion arose as Diana materialized aboard Zain's ship in the Virtual Nav room to see Chantal reclined and seemingly fast asleep. All around her a grid made of light projected the image of the room where moments before she had been held by the CIV. Zain walked in with two beverages in tall glasses, "please take one and drink it. This will help you adjust to our on board environment," he said as he handed Diana one of the glasses. She looked at the bright blue liquid and decided to drink it. Instantly she felt her body relax and was filled with an uplifting euphoria. Zain tended to Chantal who had opened her eyes and removed the head gear. "Here, sip this slowly, it will refresh your body from the long rest it has experienced," he said handing Chantal the other glass as she sat up. Zain waited for the women to finish their beverages and Novara came in to collect their empty glasses and the head gear. "Welcome back Chantal," she said on her way out.

"Where are we?" asked Diana.

Zain smiled and answered her, "you are on board my space craft which is hovering above the CIV Central building cloaked as a holographic cloud. This is the timeline in 2020 that your double arrived from. Please watch the following and you will understand what has taken place."

Chantal and Diana watched the Virtual Nav play all of the events that had taken place since Chantal's departure to the past including the activities of Nicholas Sealy and the Rabum Kataru.

"Oh my god!" said Diana. Everyone knew that Nicholas had unusual connections but he's not from Earth. These people's minds are like living artificial intelligence."

"That's exactly what they are," said Zain. "They have taken over many worlds and are interested in executing control over Earth's population. Once people's minds are plugged into their artificial matrix of consciousness they become part of their collective mind with a stunted emotional body. They have developed staggering technology on the worlds they occupy and a strong sense of order but individuality no longer exists. Because of these self inflicted parameters they cannot evolve beyond a certain point and the soul's individuated expression is limited."

"This situation has gotten more complicated than apprehending a few renegade time travelers. "What are we going to do about this?" Asked Chantal.

Zain looked over at Diana and handed her a small, flat case. "It's time for you to return to Earth. This is a document created by Chantal that you will present to the CIV and a keycard to a small home where you will be able to live. They will allow you to remain without conflict because of your assistance."

"What's in the document?" asked Diana.

"Details about the Rabum Kataru and information about benevolent extra terrestrials who are in part responsible for the relocation of Earth's population to the present timeline several years ago. A meeting between the CIV and this group who I will refer to as the Shining Ones is possible. All that they will need to prepare is contained in this diskette. You will tell them Chantal will return shortly and is already in contact with these beings. Study the entire contents here and present it to the CIV as soon as we send you back."

Diana was stunned. She couldn't believe what Zain had said. "You trust me with this task after all I've done?"

"Zain is right and I agree Diana. You have done so much already; dying to prevent the Omega Group from taking over our reality. This opportunity you have earned not to mention that your science background qualifies you for the assignment. Isn't this what you have always wanted to do with your training; make a substantial contribution?" asked Chantal.

Tears ran down Diana's cheeks and she replied as she held the diskette tightly, "yes, thank you."

Novara entered the room and escorted Diana to a private chamber where she could study the material.

Chantal furrowed her brow, "what else is on that diskette anyway?"

Zain smiled and said, "I have much to tell you."

"Somehow I knew you were going to say that," she replied.

"We are going to attend a meeting with the Shining Ones but in order for you to join me we must make some preparations."

Chantal's mouth dropped open but she found no words.

"We both come from the same original universe but incarnated on different planets when we reached this one in the movement of our souls. My path took me to the Pleadian system where my personal journey and evolution began and you know your earth history from the orientation you received here. You have been able to access information from the greater cosmic mind that we all share as divine beings because of the evolution in consciousness you have achieved and how your brain functions. In this life you have evolved beyond all other lifetimes and thus you are creating a reality of important choices."

"What exactly are you talking about, the future in five hundred years?" Chantal asked as her heart continued to race and she began to feel her mind shift in the way it did just before something significant was about to happen. An answer to the question she had just asked appeared. It was far more than time travel, technology and the state of world affairs. All these things she had experienced and participated in creating a magnificent reality that Earth's citizens shared. She knew that the current problems that the CIV faced would not overwhelm them or compromise that reality. Too much had been accomplished to allow that to happen; she simply refused to observe such an option. This steadfastness in her vision had allowed a greater concept of her own future to bloom within her mind.

Chantal looked at Zain standing before her and took his hands, noticing the unbelievably smooth, warm skin. He always had a luminescence to him that was utterly beautiful but subtle. He smiled as she examined him and stepped back. "Watch," he said and Chantal stood witnessing the light of his spirit begin to increase and form a beautiful radiance all around him. Now his smile beamed so brightly she felt the impact in her soul. She could feel a vibration coming off of him that made her feel very light headed and euphoric.

"You're glowing like an angel," she teased and felt a surge of great joy in observing him this way. She looked at her own hand and noticed the clean energy of determination and love of herself that she exuded. Her heart began to beat faster as she took in all that was happening in the moment. Chantal closed her eyes and felt the rhythm of her energy field move and call her upwards to a greater potential than she had yet become. Like a thousand drums beating all at once this knowingness held her steadfast towards flight of her spirit in the ancient ways of transmutation. Tears flowed down her face but no words escaped her.

An indescribable power overtook her in that moment that she had never fully experienced before. Unaware of the brilliant flash she created in the room Chantal dissolved in pure ecstatic bliss accompanied by an unearthly sound reaching a state of pure conscious awareness in its nuclear brilliance. As pure mind she danced becoming star like bursts of energy that formed beautiful patterns in shimmering momentum. She rotated with mathematical precision and created astounding realities that defied common understanding. Following the thread of her creation she was able to experience what she created on multiple levels of conscious awareness that existed in dimensions where time was truly relative and passed at a highly accelerated rate. Her experience was a moment out of linear time but for her lasted like hours. She passed through worlds of fluid golden bodies and glittering realities filled with sound like hundreds of chimes in harmonic perfection. An ultra violet, geometrically laced garment she donned next as her mind swam in a familiar plane of consciousness that she had been initiated into years before and knew well.

She descended further and could begin to see the inside of Zain's ship distantly as she passed through the light realm and then hovered behind him as a plasmic phantom brushing the back of his neck with cool fingers. As he turned his head she rematerialized fully behind him holding an exotic looking black flower with azure and coral accents. The centre was violet with curious, iridescent moisture emitting a scent that began to fill the space between them. "I created this for you," said Chantal as she held the bloom out for Zain to take from her hand. "It is a new species of orchid that I'm calling 'midnight.' It reminds me of the first time you brought me on board your ship and showed me the Milky Way galaxy on New Year's Eve."

Zain looked at her eyes alight with understanding and took the flower inhaling its scent. It moved deeply into his mind and he knew that he would never forget it.

"Enjoy it because the way it is designed the centre only releases the scent at midnight for those who are awake and dreaming," said Chantal.

"Now you know," he said simply and smiled.

"You are the only one like me that I have met so far face to face prior to my transformation. Where I went I was gone a long time compared to the time flow we are experiencing now and I met others."

"That will grow and you will meet the Shining Ones mind to mind. There are many places I can show you that you may like to experience."

Although she had made much progress in her former consciousness at this moment her awareness was a thousand fold greater than ever before. Chantal could clearly hear Zain's thoughts in her mind now and he showed her images of places they could visit in the future; scenes from the most exotic and progressive worlds encompassing several universes. She knew some of these places from traveling in her dreams from her deepest, subconscious mind. Now she delighted in the prospect of experiencing them with Zain in form.

Suddenly all around them a grid matrix appeared a burst of violet butterflies with magenta bordered wings dotted by azure blue at the corners moved towards him and gently skimmed his face and hair in their passing. Soprano voices like nymphs from a distant forest accompanied the beating of their delicate wings as they dissolved from the room. In her ascended state Chantal's mind had become like the Virtual Nav technology and beamed at Zain from across the room. He came over to her and she noticed his eyes were moist.

James stood inside Chantal's office and ran his finger over the robust leaf of her favorite Orchid plant. He noticed the flower was beginning to wilt from dryness and turned the built in mister on that coated all the plants with much needed moisture. Instinctively James knew that Chantal was alright but wished that she had contacted the CIV by now. He missed her friendship and the workplace dynamic was not the same without her. Every member of the CIV added a richness of mind that created a unique, productive resonance in teamwork. Everyone felt the ripple of absence whenever one or more of the IM's was missing. James turned, left Chantal's office and walked straight into Diana with a start effectively trampling her foot.

"Ouch!" she exclaimed and stepped backwards.

"Sorry about that, I didn't see you." James took her by the shoulders and examined her appearance. Her pale, blond hair looked shiny and smooth, her complexion warm and lacking the sickly pallor and bruises that he remembered her having. "Wait a minute," he said, "you look much better then the last time we saw you. Diana, you made it back!"

"No, I died, but that's another story," she said with a smile. I was actually looking for you and am here on behalf of Chantal."

"Is she alight? No one has heard from her and I've been concerned."

"She's fine and has given me information to present to the CIV that will answer many questions and update you on some important developments. She has a final meeting to attend and then will return safely but didn't want to delay in getting this information to the CIV," said Diana.

"Alright, I'll ask Samantha to call an emergency meeting. Why don't you wait in my office till everyone is assembled," said James as he led her down the hall.

All the CIV members arrived in the meeting room and Diana began her address. "Illuminated Members I am here on behalf of Chantal Colombe and have much to tell you. In addition I have important information that I have brought directly from her on a data diskette for your review in preparation for a meeting that will be requested between the CIV and representatives from an ancient extra terrestrial race that are the founding fathers of civilizations across many universes including ours. They are in part responsible for the relocation of your population to the current timeline. The relevant details are all contained here," she said handing it to Richard. "Before its review I will update you on the events that have taken place over the past two days," she continued. The last time I saw you I disappeared from this very meeting room and appeared in a parallel universe; the one we had been discussing at the CIV New Year's Party. There Colonel Stark and Nicholas Sealy appeared and changed the whole timeline. They were meant to appear here as you know and my maneuver with the TII device placed them there instead. Unfortunately my body was so traumatized by the last appearance back to that time that it died. What you are witnessing now is my return from your past in that original form but having absorbed the memories of my future self. In effect I have had the bizarre experience of death and mind transference mingled with time travel."

IM's around the room spoke to one another in hushed tones. Everyone noticed Diana's obviously radical improvement in appearance and well being. The change was simply too drastic to have fabricated and the general tone in the room was one of acceptance of her story.

"What is the status of the Omega Group's plans, do you have relevant information about that?" Asked Amit.

"Yes and what timeline are they currently operating in?" Added Richard.

Diana paused and collected her thoughts, knowing that part of that information was on the diskette and in order for her answer to be absorbed properly she had to choose her words carefully. "We know that they now have access again to the current timeline. Colonel Stark is dead but Nicholas is in contact with his people."

"The Omega Group?" asked James.

"No, I'm afraid the news I have to give you is worse than that. The Group's plans to take over the current timeline failed due to my appearance in the past. I effectively briefed you on the location of all the MIP cones; a technology used to reprogram memories of the Earth's population. This prevented Nicholas from being able to implement the procedure and gained us some time. We believe that out of the desperation of the situation he abandoned his plan to transport the rest of the Omega Group members here and contacted the Rabum Kataru Legion; a group of renegade Annunaki extra terrestrial beings linked to Earth's history. This group has had long standing covert influence over governments, religions and shadow organizations for thousands of years. Because in this timeline citizens of Earth are approaching technological power that comes close to theirs they desire to secure control over your progress and development. They live in a delusion of superiority effectively placing themselves as potential guardians of your consciousness by plugging everyone into an artificial intelligence matrix. They believe that without this intervention you will destroy yourselves with your own technology because technological development can out pace the development of the mind that creates it. The details on this group are on the Diskette as well as the representatives of the benevolent Race referred to as the Shining Ones that desire a meeting with the World CIV," said Diana pausing to let that last bit of information to fully register in the minds of the IM's.

James rubbed his jaw and looked over at Amit and Lorne. "Rather a fantastic tale you bring us Diana," he said.

"Most of this information is new to me. Chantal and a confidential advisor of hers who is linked to the Shining Ones hold the key to all this information. She is still with him and together they created the briefing on the diskette I brought you. You really have no time or means to verify what I am presenting here because of the critical risk posed to your International security so please review this meeting and what I have brought with the most open mind possible for the sake of the world."

Amit frowned at James who knew exactly what Amit was thinking and shook his head. He knew Chantal's obsession with truth sometimes got her into unique situations that in the end benefited the CIV but Amit was not fond of her lack of disclosure in how she handled things sometimes. This was proving to be one of those 'unique' situations he realized as he rubbed his brow in frustration.

"What I am most shocked at is the condescending attitude of this Rabum Kataru. We have the most progressive society that the Earth has ever experienced and it is an outrage that this group arrogantly intends to declare themselves as so called 'guardians' when in fact this is obviously a control ploy of at best an immature, overblown fanatical consciousness," said Richard.

"Absolutely, and unfortunately they have succeeded to do exactly that on other planets. I have nothing further at this time to share with you and leave you with the remaining information if there are no more questions," Diana concluded.

"Thank you Diana, would you mind stepping out of the room for a moment while we review your brief?" Asked James.

"Certainly," she replied and left the room closing the doors behind her.

James turned to the group and said, "I'm going to suggest that we keep an open line to Diana as a potential future resource and arrange for some security clearance."

"He's right. I will speak to her and make the necessary arrangements," said Amit.

"Why not invite her to watch the rest of the information with us. Obviously she has already seen it," suggested Lorne.

Amit stood up and addressed the IM's, "let's break for a short lunch and resume in an hour."

"Fine, I'll talk to Diana and bring her back to the meeting then," said James and stepped out of the room.

He approached Diana who had seated herself in the hallway and took her hands in his squeezing them with warmth, "thank you for all you have done, your contribution is so important right now."

Diana smiled a bit awkwardly and looked at him. "I hope it's enough to get us all through this."

"The IM's are breaking for lunch but would like you to join us in reviewing the document you brought back with you and to remain as a resource if we need you for any more information regarding the issue at hand."

"Certainly, I'd be happy to."

"Do you have a place to stay?"

"Yes it was arranged by Chantal and her friend. I have a keycard to a small house in the area."

"Good. After viewing the diskette Amit wants to meet with you about some security issues," said James.

"Of course," replied Diana.

"I' going to drive up to the Village to grab a quick bite before we view the information this afternoon would you like to join me?"

"That would be nice," she said with a smile and left the CIV building with him.

James pulled up to Abraxas Tavern and stepped inside holding the door open for Diana. They sat down at a quiet table in the corner of the dining area away from other patrons.

"Good afternoon to you James," said Cherrie, one of the usual lunch shift servers as she handed them menus. "We have a scrumptious lunch special today; beef dip with wild greens salad and a cup of mixed, creamy mushroom soup."

"Sounds great, let's have two of those, with iced tea if that meets your approval Diana."

"Fine," she replied.

James looked at Diana sitting across from him and said, "it's pretty amazing all that you've been through not to mention death."

Diana choked on her tea and started to laugh.

"Was it something I said?" Asked James innocently.

"Well that isn't quite what I am used to in terms of casual lunch conversation but is in fact how directly I usually approach a subject and it is funny to hear someone be as comfortably blunt as I usually am."

"I guess you're right. You know we're all like that at the CIV we just speak our minds."

"It's very refreshing and quite a contrast to what I've been used to dealing with the Omega Group. With them it was hard to tell how much cover up or ulterior motive was present in anything they said. We were all like that; supposedly working together for our cause but all covering our asses in case betrayal or deception came from other members."

"That's very honest of you to admit."

"It was a horrible way to live and I'm relieved to have extracted myself from that life," said Diana.

James admired her level of candor and intelligence. She was an exceptionally attractive woman with a science background and clearly gifted at group communication skills. She definitely had strong leadership qualities and sensed she once had a ruthless ambition. Images from her past flashed in his mind and the coldness of her former consciousness chilled him. He realized just how much she had changed in a short time.

"What's the matter?" She asked noticing his changed expression.

James played with his napkin for a moment and decided to be candid. "You're a different person than who you used to be, it's just really obvious."

Diana's lower lip trembled momentarily till she bit down on it controlling her emotions. "No power is worth wiping out a civilization for and when you rob a person of their mind and in essence feed them whatever illusory truth you want without them desiring it that is in effect what you are doing. I had that kind of power and used it in the past timeline where I came from. The results were highly unstable because of the low frequency of thought the population was placed in. Easier to control that way was the rationale we used. I just can't do it ever again. It's too bad that the Rabum Kataru Legion depend on such technology to maintain control over vast numbers of people."

"Well that's not going to happen here," James replied firmly.

"You're damned right it's not." Diana looked at him with an edgy determination that contrasted her pale blond hair and apricot complexion. Here blue eyes turned icy and he knew she meant what she said from the core of her being. "I've been through too much to see this place go down the toilet because of excessive arrogance and hunger for power. I've had more than I can stomach and this is going to end."

James took her hand and squeezed it. "If we stick together we can all overcome this risk and hold an even greater value for the life we created here."

Diana's face relaxed and she held on to his hand remarking that she could not remember the last time anyone had touched her with such warmth. She had gotten used to living isolated and always on guard, never really trusting anyone and only realized in that moment how alien human contact of this nature had become to her.

James watched her response to his friendliness and realized he was witnessing a deeper thaw of this woman who sat before him.

"So you want to know what it was like to die?" She said with a grin casually retracting her hand.

Caught off guard James hesitated not sure if she was serious but decided to take a chance, "sure give me all the grisly details," he replied with boyish enthusiasm. Just then Cherrie brought their lunch special over and served them.

Diana laughed and her eyes sparkled as she told her story: "I use humor to have an acceptance of what happened to me because it was truly horrible. I mean imagine yourself appearing in your past from the future, wheezing and coughing up blood all over the place, pale, bruised with internal bleeding and all to deliver a cryptic message the gist of it being; *clean up your act or this is what you have to look forward to.* Then you watch yourself keel over and disintegrate into nothing."

"That experience would change anyone," said James solemnly biting into his sandwich.

"Yes but I'm hear to talk about it and no longer the person who created it. Maybe that's why I'm not scared about the future. I already died and that experience toughened me in ways that are now intrinsic to my nature. Also I fine tuned operating the TII device with my mind by actually changing the technology on a quantum level with the power of thought. It made me realize that no matter how much our technology advances it is vital to maintain an ethical mind interface option because then you maintain control of the technology instead of becoming overly reliant upon it."

"That's exactly the principle we are endeavoring to embrace with our science team. I think it would be very beneficial to us if you worked with them in the future on some level after this is all over. I'll have to broach the idea with the other IM's so I'm not promising anything but I have a feeling that they would be receptive."

"That would be amazing, thank you James," replied Diana. She pondered the possibilities while they finished up their meal with genuine hope for an opportunity to serve the CIV. Cherrie returned with the bill which James paid promptly and left the Tavern with Diana and headed back to the CIV building.

TWENTY

Zain held Chantal's hand and said, "there is a place I want to take you to that you will know."

She smiled and squeezed the hand that held hers.

Chantal and Zain moved like a living holograph whose eyes were windows to forever. Through these anything they wanted to observe appeared and they could engage that reality. Images of a building came alive and immediately Chantal recognized it. Instantly they created and traveled through a wormhole, gaining heaviness and form in layers till Chantal they rematerialized at the beautiful house that she had visited in her out of body experiences in the year 2505. A heavenly scent permeated the air and she noticed a cut crystal vase overflowing with Spanish red roses. Gorgeous orchids lined the windows and the ethereal music she remembered played softly through the house. In daylight the place looked different with the walls reflecting light like smooth marble lit by a clear sky above them coming through the domed ceiling. The contrast of the colorful flowers against the alabaster background accented their life force; permeating the room like a cherished blessing. Chantal kicked off her shoes and stepped onto the floor made of a curious substance that resembled lucite. It felt warm beneath her feet and gently lit up wherever she stepped. She touched the walls and light emitted from them and as it did she observed a matrix of light within them.

She remembered this and called forth the central room holograph of the fire. It appeared in brilliant, violet flames and she stared into it. Zain moved behind her and subtly wrapped his arms around her waist cradling her against him.

"This fire burns pure and bright, I love loosing myself in it as I look into it. It is like my spirit that can never be extinguished," she said tracing her fingers over Zain's hands. "You burn clean like that without consuming me so I can fly and that is why I feel so right with you. I have never experienced that before with another, such naked honesty in love."

Zain's lips kissed the side of her neck and she felt his sincerity move through her as her eyes transfixed on the fire; all elements of the moment merged into a sacred bond between them.

Chantal lay against Zain in the large oval shaped bed covered with a green hued sheet of a fabric that resembled raw silk. His arm wrapped around her waist and held her close, his face pressed against her hair. Her eyes were closed and she floated in the charged current of their lovemaking still feeling a gentle energy moving along her torso and up her spine. Brilliant color bursts in her head had subsided and the expanse of the void suffused her consciousness as she lay in peaceful stillness. Suddenly still wrapped in the sheet Zain picked her up and carried her down the hall to the solarium room that he had created for her. In the centre was a recreation of a miniature hot spring with steam rising from it. The sheet dropped away from her and he slid her into the warm water with him. Chantal looked through half open eyes at Zain as vapor swirled between them. Their minds were joined now in perfect telepathy and the richness of a moment described by many words in linear time could flash to the mind in seconds. Knowing him so little yet so deeply lived like a mysterious paradox in her being. She slid over to him and wrapped her arms around him kissing the wetness of his lips as in her nakedness her breasts pressed against his chest in a contradictory innocence. Exotic flowers sprung from the soil around the edge of the spring as vapor carried their scent. Zain picked one and placed it behind Chantal's ear. He kissed her again and just as she melted into him he said, "are you ready for a change of scenery?"

"What?"

And without further delay they transported to the mother ship Lycos precisely on schedule to attend a meeting with the Shining Ones.

Chantal blinked twice, adjusting to the abrupt change of venue and sat at a large, translucent table next to Zain dressed in a micro nit suit. He beamed mischievously at her and she knew that she had better get accustomed to his oddities in creating overlapping experiences.

Across from them sat five beings; four men and one woman all with incredible faces filled with such reverence that she was utterly mesmerized by them all. Ancient these beings were and to sit in their presence was a moment she never wanted to forget. They smiled at her and instantly a grid arose from the table that connected at geometric points on the walls around them. Collectively all seven of them moved from the consciousness of their bodies to a state of awareness where they viewed in rapid sequence multiple timeline potentials unfolding in their field of observation relevant to the unfolding events on earth. Together they pinpointed the best reentry of Chantal into the current timeline of 2020 and created a pattern of potential events that would culminate in the meeting between the Shining Ones and certain world CIV representatives. In the next moment Chantal was back in the hot spring with Zain with the meeting recorded in her memory.

Zain shared with her some of the endeavors he was involved with in different realities. She noted the ones of interest to her as she scanned the information. Something in Chantal drew her to move through the grid with her consciousness and examine the Rabum Kataru's interference into Earth's reality where she new developments. All of the population on the planet was moving to health units to receive inoculations of some sort. Upon further examination she understood what she had seen. "Oh my God," she said looking at Zain. She touched his hand instantly pulling him into her vision.

"This is it," he said. "Their plan to enact the mental reprogramming with quantum pattern technology." They have used it on other planets with success. The difference is that they have moved up the ultimate agenda to integrate the human species into their collective mind which is the door that this technology provides. Chantal, we cannot waste any time. You must return to the CIV immediately and warn them. I will alert the Shining Ones of the change in your reentry point."

"Alright," she replied and prepared to appear back at the CIV Building.

Amelatu left the data room with a slight buzzing sensation still lingering in his head from all the information that he had been downloaded with for hours. "Amelatu! I see you have completed the data orientation," said Alal as he greeted and led him back to the main deck of the ship. "The inoculation sequence has been programmed into the 2020 timeline and within the hour citizens all over the Earth will gather to receive the injections over a three hour period. All of the vials have been teleported to the necessary locations and now we wait for the masses to move and can synchronize the program form our vessel when the implantation of the population is complete. You may watch the progress at the viewing station with me Amelatu and when everything is ready we will transport you back to Earth as the head of the World CIV organization in Vienna. There is a ten acre property that will be yours along with control over key businesses around the world that dispense vital resources to the population. All this was already in the orientation I presume?"

"Yes, assets, properties, all the relevant earth based information as well as new background and history of all CIV IM's and other citizens of relevance to our mission. I am thankful you added full disclosure on monitoring and adjusting the quantum pattern from the ship's programming centre as I find this information fascinating," replied Amelatu.

Alal smiled broadly, "oh there is much for you to learn about how the programs work on multiple levels. I am happy that this is an area of interest for you because that ensures your continued orientation of these matters. I will set up a regular schedule for your enhancement of knowing this science and one day you may wish to contribute to the programming model for Earth."

Amelatu had hoped to be involved on a much broader level than just the Earth program but he knew that if Alal continued to be pleased with his performance that opportunity would arrive in time. He followed Alal to the viewing station to watch the progression of the initiated events.

James walked into the CIV building with Diana and they headed to the health station on the main floor for their inoculation. A line had already formed as the other IM's chatted and each received their booster in the arm. Diana watched as James rolled up his sleeve and a tiny syringe shot a pressure vial of phosphorescent, greenish liquid efficiently into him with such a small needle that no visible puncture could be seen on the flesh. He rolled his sleeve back down, smiled and said to her, "your turn, enjoy!"

Diana held her arm out for her injection and though she knew it was necessary she could not remember what possible contaminants had been brought through with her arrival here. The gap in memory made a mental alarm go off in her mind and instinctively, being the last in line to receive the injection she pushed her blue, suede purse against it and quickly followed James back towards the meeting room. Something was not right. She had engineered enough programs to know how smooth the interface could be with the mind; a thought implanted that you were sure was your own but in fact was a memory implant. She stopped and examined the memory; *the world would be receiving this inoculation against potentially hazardous contamination from the time travelers.* Diana felt a chill rising up her back as her suspicion grew that this was a way for someone to access the bodies of every human on the planet for programming. She looked at her purse and saw the glowing stain that had formed on the leather which appeared to be evaporating leaving behind a curious residue. She touched it with her finger. "Silicone," she said to herself as she entered the meeting. Unsure of what to do she sat down and watched for any effects that the IM's would possibly display. They had all received the injection so if she was correct in her deduction and they had received some sort of mind tampering serum likely there was an initiation sequence that was being followed by Nicholas and the Rabum Kataru. Diana was not familiar with the nature of the technology they were using but the silicone residue on her purse suggested a programmable serum.

Samantha was about to load the diskette into the holographic projector when suddenly a flash filled the room. Everyone paused and looked over to the source of it and inadvertently looked upon the form of Chantal that had just appeared in the meeting room. She beamed a huge smile at the IM's and said, "you cannot imagine how happy I am to see all of you!"

Everyone looked at her; she appeared so radiant and beautiful, the same but different with an ethereal glow about her that was difficult to put into words. Her hair appeared longer which was odd because she had only been gone a few days. Silently the IM's registered the vibrational change in her but no one said anything.

"I came to alert you about immediate implementation of the mind reprogramming that has been initiated as I speak. You have all received a memory implant that will direct you to receive an inoculation against potential contaminants that were supposedly brought by the time travelers. This is a lie and a false memory but a way for the Rabum Kataru to implant you with a mind control chip that assembles itself at the base of the brain once the serum has been injected into your body," said Chantal.

"We all just received the inoculation at the health station, said Amit. Chantal could see growing alarm among the IM's.

"I never took the shot," said Diana. I just had a feeling something was not right when I could not remember anything about a contaminant being brought through when I traveled here from the parallel timeline. My instincts told me that this was a perfect way for Nicholas to implement the mind reprogramming in an alternate way after the MIP technology failed to be initiated. I am the only one here that has not been inoculated."

"Good, said Chantal but the rest of the world is in the process of receiving the injections and we must stop this."

"I will alert the World CIV immediately of the developments and warn them not to take the inoculations," said Amit rising from his chair.

"Amit if the council is in agreement I am planning to arrive there shortly to update them in person that the Rabum Kataru plan to initiate the mind reprogramming simultaneously on everyone. I was hoping that any IM's with teleportation skills accompany me to deliver the details of what has happened in person."

"I think that Chantal's suggestion is the best course of action. Maya, Lorne and Julio would be of benefit to accompany her if all agree," suggested Richard.

James hesitated because he wanted to help her but something told him to stay behind and keep contact with Diana.

"I'm fine with that and will take care of security issues on the home front," said Amit.

"Whatever you do don't alert the public. I think it is wise if the Rabum Kataru is kept unaware that their plan has been discovered; we're not sure how they may retaliate if they find out what we know. All the CIV buildings world wide are protected with cloaking shields as arranged by my contact so information about what goes on inside cannot be accessed by the Rabum Kataru."

"Sounds like the most cautious approach, I agree with Chantal," said Richard.

"I have no problem with that," concurred Amit.

John Willowby stood up and addressed the group, "I suspect that in order to initiate the mental reprogramming they will still be using some form of electromagnetic technology to do this however the shielding device is likely not going to be effective against brain implant activation without serious revisions. I doubt that we have time for that but will consult with the science team as soon as possible."

"He's right," said Diana.

"I may be able to disable these chips," said Chantal as she approached James. "Don't mind being my first guinea pig do you?" She said as she examined the back of his head.

"What do you think you're doing?" He asked a bit nervous of her poking around his brain. He was not aware of her having any medical or scientific training on the deactivation of brain chips.

Chantal read his mind. "A lot has changed since you saw me last just trust me."

James sighed and thought to himself, *not those words again.*

Chantal used her new ability to look at his brain within his biological light matrix and saw the location of the chip. The technology worked on high frequency light impulses so she reasoned that if she directed an isolated, short range blast of gamma radiation with her mind and overload it she would likely disable it from receiving any further light impulses carrying programs. From the burst of energy Chantal saw the implant dissolve completely.

"Ok, I've disabled it. I can disable the rest of them quickly before I depart to Vienna." she said as the other IM's waited in turn to have their implants removed.

"How did you do that?" Asked James.

"With my mind. Explanations will have to wait for later. Let's just say that I have developed some new abilities since you last saw me." Chantal replied with a smile as she continued to disable the other chips.

"Wait," Diana interjected. "It would be helpful to have a subject that had one of the active implants so that we could run some tests to determine the nature of the technology we are facing in the general population."

Chantal paused and realized the possible benefits of what Diana had suggested. "Ok then we need someone to volunteer to remain infected with one of the chips," she said looking at the remaining IM's whose chips had not yet been deactivated.

Richard spoke up, "I'll do it everyone else please go ahead and allow Chantal to complete the removal."

"Richard, are you sure you want to keep that thing inside your head? God knows when the activation of the mind reprogramming will be initiated but I feel it is coming soon if we don't do something," said Maya with concern.

"I have confidence that the science team will be able to determine the nature of what is being used in the serum quickly as we already have similar technology that we use ourselves. Chantal, the key to how you are deactivating these would obviously be helpful for me to relay so they can put this thing in my head out of commission when the tests are complete," he replied.

"A short burst of precisely targeted gamma radiation will do it instantly," she answered as she resumed deactivation of the other IM's chips. They expressed profound relief and thanked her. Chantal gathered her things, "I'm ready," she said and the other IM's who would accompany her to Vienna joined her. Together they focused on a coordinate setting their arrival destination in the reception area of the CIV world headquarters and disappeared. Moments later the marble floor grew more solid beneath their feet and footsteps echoed behind where the small group had appeared.

Yvette St.Jaques greeted them a little startled by their sudden appearance, "Mon Dieu! Mademoiselle Colombe, Monsieur Manderas welcome! This is an unexpected surprise, may I be of assistance?"

Chantal embraced Yvette and asked her to locate Romy Lindt.

"You can find him in the records room, come let me take you there," said Yvette and the four IM's followed her up the grand, winding staircase to the floor that housed international and local documents and records. She opened large, green carved doors and led them into the room. "Monsieur Lindt, Chantal Colombe is here to see you with other Illuminated Members."

Romy turned away from his computer and took off his reading glasses. "Chantal! What a pleasant surprise, you look absolutely radiant. I see you have brought some of your North American sector comrades," said Romy as he embraced her and Maya then warmly shook Lorne and Julio's hands.

"Romy, I'm afraid we are here on a rather urgent matter. We need to update you on some alarming developments regarding the planned take over of our current timeline. You must stop the IM's from taking their inoculations. These are a ploy by an enemy group to reprogram the minds of every citizen on the planet."

Romy looked at the four of them with agitation forming across his brow, "Chantal almost everyone here has had the inoculations. The population is in the process of proceeding to health units everywhere. I'm not sure what you want us to do about the situation. This sounds like international disaster in progress." He paused for a moment and continued, "we should alert the public to stop the inoculation process…"

"No, that could be dangerous. We have no idea what measures the group that is responsible for this may take if they find out we are aware of their plan," said Lorne.

"What group is responsible? And what about the photon shielding device? We have it functioning can't we use it to protect the population?" Asked Romy.

"An extra terrestrial renegade group called the Rabum Kataru legion who has been involved with supporting corrupt governments and secret organizations on Earth for thousands of years is responsible," replied Maya.

"Because the technology they are using is an advanced, implant that is delivered through the serum and collects at the base of the brain our shielding device would likely fail without some modifications. The science of the implants they are using here is currently being examined to gain more understanding of it in order to create defensive measures," said Chantal. "I have however successfully disabled all of the chips that our local IM's were implanted."

"Disable mine, please!" said Romy.

Chantal performed the procedure on Romy and watched his face relax a little. "The rest of the world is about an hour away from completing the inoculation process," said Maya. "We must find a solution to this problem before they initiate the mind reprogramming."

"There is no point alerting all other CIV headquarters world wide at this point. We simply risk creating a panic button somewhere that could backfire. Somehow the whole planetary population must be dealt with in one blow to neutralize these chips," said Romy.

"I agree, that is the best option we have to deal with this threat most effectively," replied Chantal. "Something we have not mentioned yet Romy is that Nicholas Sealy plans to arrive here at World CIV headquarters to become its new head sometime after the reprogramming is complete."

"Perhaps we should let them think they have succeeded and greet the bastard with a different version of a welcoming committee than he has in mind," suggested Julio. "It would be poetic justice if he got to experience his own creation of a parallel universe and know what it is like to have his mind messed with."

Lorne and Maya smiled at Julio's suggestion. "I think it is safe to say that we would all like to get our hands on this perpetrator," said Lorne.

"Even so that doesn't solve the bigger problem of this Rabum Kataru legion's aggressive meddling in Earth's affairs. We have no defensive measures against such a power," said Romy.

Yvette opened the doors to the records room and was about to enter. "What can I do for you Yvette?" Asked Romy, quickly walking over to her.

"Oh, Monsieur Lindt I am sorry to disturb you but Madame Kraussen requested some copies of agriculture development budgets."

"Fine, please go ahead and get what you need," replied Romy.

Yvette could see tension in his face and the mood surrounding the other IM's made her realize realized she had obviously walked in at an inopportune moment. Hurriedly she gathered the data she needed and quietly left the room.

"Sorry about that interruption, I think it best if we move this meeting to my office where we won't be disturbed."

"Sure," said Lorne as Romy headed for the doors.

"Just a minute," said Chantal. "I would like to return to my contact that has helped me to stay abreast of the situation we are dealing with to discuss some viable options for ending this problem. I think I may know of a way to disable all the chips without alerting the Rabum Kataru."

"Chantal, at this point do whatever you can to help rectify this mess," said Romy with some exasperation.

The other IM's nodded in agreement and Julio added with some humor, "don't leave us here too long I'm supposed to shop for Lisa's birthday; it's tomorrow and I don't have a gift yet."

Chantal smiled. "I'll be back in no time," she said and disappeared.

TWENTY ONE

Mesmerized by the content of the data diskette the IM's looked upon the face of Zain as he divulged the details of the Earth's citizen's relocation in time on the last part of the presentation. Information about the highly advanced extra terrestrial effort interfaced with select people form Earth finally answered the long standing question about how everyone had arrived at this progressive timeline. Renewed enthusiasm to preserve true sovereignty that the population enjoyed for the first time in the history of mankind bloomed in the hearts and minds of every CIV member. All looked forward to the opportunity to meet with representatives from the Shining Ones which would herald a conscious alliance of minds across space time to preserve what had been meticulously created for Earth. Zain indicated that contact would shortly be made by them at the appropriate time and the presentation was over.

John stood next to Atlan Fleming, the brain chip expert of the CIV science group as he presented his findings after running select tests on Richard Lonesbay. "Interesting technology. It is not unlike what we currently use except that it has pre set pointers to manipulation of the lower seals of the human energy field. This is totally contrary to the aims of our brain chip programs to support a higher level of consciousness but not surprising as a strategy of mind control on baser levels."

After the CIV had convened their meeting Diana was invited to observe the disclosure of information about the Rabum Kataru's mind control devices in case she could add any input from her own experiences in that field.

"What this means is that the programmers can hyper stimulate the sexual, power and emotional centers of an individual to the point that rational discernment is far more challenging to maintain. A citizen made to juggling between these dynamics for a prolonged period of time could suffer the deterioration of higher goals and aspirations. We witnessed this on going problem brought about by a limited cultural model prior to the great cataclysms. The environment suffered and world economies dwindled while the population remained plugged in to survival mindset tempered by low grade entertainment and social activity. Anyone with success from original ideas was labeled as a genius while the rest of the population consumed in droves the products that these anomalous people created. Economic hardship curtailed the natural propensity to create from individual inspiration and physical well being suffered along with a crippled spirit in the majority of people on some level. The outlets then sought by the individuals of our past became anything that provided emotional stimulation mostly through the sensory experience of the body to counteract the stress of an unbalanced life. The select who did not plug into that popular mindset often resorted to intellectual pursuits that fed them knowledge but hardly any actualized that as experience and merely gathered facts to rise above the seeming mediocrity of society. This in turn also failed to truly nourish the spirit as we now know knowledge alone cannot catalyze evolution of mind. It is the integration and living of that knowledge that creates the newness and inspiration necessary to birth what used to be called genius and is simply what we now recognize as mindful brilliance that every citizen is capable of."

Richard walked out of the test room rubbing his head. "Good god am I glad that ordeal is over. I have never had the pleasure of experiencing a Napoleon complex combined with strange food cravings and an urge to prowl the neighborhood for available women," he said and began to laugh. "To put it mildly Atlan put me through the rigors of fully testing the range of the implant programming options. I also experienced the desire for an anti depressant medication to take the edge off of the fear, anxiety and futility I began to experience. An intense euphoria was also successful induced in me but this was of a nature that lacked the higher state of consciousness I am accustomed to and I found it boring. Frightening to see what is possible with this technology. I did however have some success overwriting the incoming programs with my mind. I used focused intent to change what was arriving in my consciousness to what I wanted to experience in stead as my state of mind. It feels like swimming against a current but after a while the effects of the program are less powerful as consciousness uses the brain to change them. I am however truly grateful that the chip was finally removed from my head and am driven to ensure that no one else ever has to experience what I did in that room."

"I am very familiar with the themes of this type of program. By inducing subtle levels of these states in people it can erode their enthusiasm for life enough that they cease to question what the authority of the sectors is implementing in terms of government activity. They simply follow any directive from leaders like sheep believing that they are cared for and helpless to evoke change on a grander scale," said Diana. "This is the consciousness that the Omega Group relied on to function in power and that Nicholas was initially interested in re creating here."

Atlan handed Richard a data disk with relevant information about the engineering of the brain chips. "This has all the particulars about the design of these chips for the CIV to review. They are silicone based nano tubes that form and collect cohesively into an organized chip at the base of the neocortex. The design in fact is similar to what we use but ours are carbon based and engineered to accommodate higher frequency learning interface."

Richard took the data and escorted Diana out of the lab. "Now we wait to hear from Chantal and the rest of the teleportation team from the World CIV headquarters as to the next steps in deactivating this technology in the general population," he said as they walked to his car. They got in and drove back to CIV Central to await further developments and share the research information about the brain implant with the other IM's.

Diana felt the warmth of sunlight against her face as she got out of Richard's car and her heels clicked against the stone steps that led up to the CIV building. He went in and she told him she wanted to get some air. Unusually mild weather prevailed today she noticed and it hinted of spring that would not arrive for a few months yet. She stood outside the door for a few moments inhaling the clean air and knowing that everyday she breathed in this time she would never take it for granted. In the other world that she came from the pollution was thick and a chemical odor had always prevailed. Diana closed her eyes and felt a peace permeate her being that in spite of recent events grew stronger within her everyday. Such a simple feeling but worth more than all the wealth a person could hold. So many conflicts she had witnessed between people who would never know this as desire for it is inevitably lost in the lust for power. Diana looked down at the stained purse she still carried and marveled at the evidence of scheming minds. *Would people who created this serum ever know peace without having control over another life?* She wondered. *I have changed so much, what makes me different?* She knew she used to be like them and if she could change then anything was possible.

Diana turned and entered the building proceeding to James's office. He welcomed her in and she sat down sharing with him the results of Richard's tests and the conclusions that had been drawn by Atlan from the science group.

"Not surprising at all. This is the same kind of lower consciousness garbage that we faced in the old timeline we came from for the last century as you know," said James. "We may not have been implanted with devices that amplified and fed it but it came at society from everywhere; the media and World Wide Web, depressed economies, crappy entertainment, you name it. The single thing that makes this society so sustainable is the boom of personal expression in all kinds of innovations that span across all facets of life. Everyone is given an equal opportunity to contribute value to our way of life; this is drastically different than anything lived on this planet in the past perhaps as far back as the Egyptian Dynasties."

"I certainly notice the way that your government operates is more akin to stewardship than a body of elected representatives supposedly ruling democratically with side doors to hidden agendas that ensure more control over the population than they were authorized by the people to have. How many decades did the world endure of that type of leadership?" said Diana emphatically.

"Too many and thankfully that type of rulership is just a mediocre memory at this point," replied James. I don't care what Nicholas Sealy and his alliance thinks they can do here. There is no way anyone in this time will tolerate going backwards to living a daily life of planetary instability. The Rabum Kataru need to accept that people here are not blind sheep to be fed a program of control but are an accomplished society that has found a balance between mind and spirit that is evident even in the way we apply technology. That single concern; the enlightened use of technology is what the CIV recognizes as one of our most important mandates because of civilizations in our past history that destroyed them selves by abusing it."

Diana knew that James was right and the irony of the Rabum Kataru using the cover of concern for Earth's citizen's safety in becoming an advancing society and facing technological prowess was either conveniently dismissed by them or they just didn't care and wanted control. No one knew much about them and the data diskette that Chantal and Zain had sent was the first brief that gave an overview of the Rabum Kataru and their objectives regarding Earth's affairs.

"I'm not surprised that these beings became tangled in affairs of Earth from our past because man's consciousness through the ages included a violent, competitive nature and the consumption of resources without much regard for the environment. Tyranny begets tyranny so in all fairness one frequency of mass mind attracts another. Also the mind set of our earlier population in regards to extra terrestrial life was mostly fearful and that trend translated into pop culture. This attitude continued through the twenty first century with story lines featuring malevolent aliens wanting to take over the world still being produced as films. The special effects of this type of entertainment improved over the years but the quality of the themes still had not evolved much beyond sci fi B movies created in the 1930's. Why on earth would more enlightened groups of extra terrestrial life contact us en mass with that kind of attitude prevailing?"

"Obviously that's why contact that did occur with benevolent beings was often limited to individuals who were more open minded," said Diana.

"Meeting with minds like the Shining Ones is an opportunity we have earned as a collective and will definitely evolve our consciousness regarding potentials for space exploration and collaboration with other species of life in the Universe. What really interests me is to learn more about who's out there and how we can share information for mutual benefit," said James as he leaned back in his chair with his hands behind his head staring up at the ceiling.

"Just imagine the interface of mind with technology that they must have in different galaxies in advanced societies. What is being embraced by the CIV has the potential to grow into great models like that," said Diana. They both sat silent in their musings till James rose from his chair. "I'm going to run next door for a coffee, please stay if you like. Care for one?"

"Sure, black for me," she replied.

James left his office and as he walked down the corridor he wondered if Chantal had made any progress in Vienna.

Chantal had left the CIV World headquarters building and sat in the adjacent garden gazebo to collect her thoughts. A small bird flew in and landed beside her on the bench. "Well hello there," she said as it looked intently at her with its dark eyes and fluffed its feathers. She opened her hand and manifested seed which she held out for it. Without any hesitation it hopped into her palm and proceeded to eat from her hand glancing at her every once in a while. *You are a welcome sight,* she thought enjoying the movement of nature in the stillness of winter. As the last of the seed was consumed it flew away and she was alone once more. Something nagged at her and she was not quite ready to return to meet with Zain to examine options for disabling the implants in the population. She moved her mind through the matrix and reviewed the history of Amelatu's movement prior to his contacting the Rabum Kataru. A scene of him sitting in the forest appeared and she read his thoughts noting some reservations he had about making contact with the ship. *Curious consciousness. He is one with his collective people yet he exhibits a desire for his individual expression in commanding the Earth based efforts,* she noted. In learning about the Rabum Kataru Chantal knew that very little individual expression was encouraged in their population. In order to stay loyal to them he would have had to keep this tendency in check. She also noticed that he felt a sense of failure from his plans to initiate the MRP being stopped and that making the contact had indeed been a last resort. Chantal pondered his inner motivations for a moment and then searched through his past for his origins. To her surprise she learned that he was not born on their home planet but in fact had been taken into the Rabum Kataru's collective at the age of nine from another world that they had integrated into their consciousness via the same technology they wanted to use on Earth's population.

Chantal examined the life of Amelatu prior to the take over of his world. The people there resembled Novara in stature and coloring except their skin was lighter. Other than more exotic looking surroundings the way of life had not been dissimilar to Earth's in 2020 and she saw scenes of him with his family partaking in a variety of activities normal for a boy of his age. Chantal was aware that his memory of his childhood prior to the intervention by the Rabum Kataru had been erased as was customary. This she realized was highly useful information. Possibilities raced through her mind and a single idea stood out that was risky but could potentially alter the course of events favorably.

Chantal set her mind on the coordinates of space time where Amelatu sat leaning against a tree in the forest. She appeared behind him and gently touched his arm. He lunged at her and Chantal disappeared reappearing about ten feet above his head casually reclined in a tree branch. "I just want to talk so relax, I don't have any troops with me," she said from above.

Amelatu eyed Chantal feigning disinterest about how she had gotten herself up there and she could see in his face strategy endeavoring to form. "What do you want?" he finally asked with a defiant tone.

"Your willingness to look at Earth's affairs from a different perspective."

He laughed. "What is this, the CIV sending an emissary of peace to negotiate?"

"Hardly. I am prepared to take your life if necessary and can do so with my mind in less than a heart beat," she replied. Your friend Colonel Stark is dead and the child is free." Chantal let her words sink into his mind knowing that he would wonder how that happened. She decided to let him ponder if she had anything to do with it.

The sting of her words slightly registered on his face and then he said nonchalantly, "harming me would only bring the wrath of my people upon you."

"Perhaps but I think it would likely send a message that we are not such easy prey to steal minds from. Surely they have invested much in you and your future, are you not of value to them?"

Nicholas hesitated in answering and Chantal moved swiftly from the tree and materialized behind him. "Just what *is* your value to the Rabum Kataru, Amelatau?" Chantal asked with almost a whisper.

Amelatu reeled around and looked down into her face. He was taller by a head and his frame huge in comparison to hers. Her eyes had no fear and held his awaiting an answer. She knew his true name and likely more but he had no idea what or how. He could easily physically overtake her but she was fast and he hesitated to act because he could see the conviction in her face. Amelatu relaxed his stance and looked at her with arrogance, "I ask you again what is it you want from me?"

"Simply to reconsider your actions and stop pursuing the mind erasure and reprogramming of Earth's citizens. I do have information to share with you that will likely alter how you see all of this," Chantal replied.

"Even if you succeeded to stop me my people are another matter and they are many."

"I know you came here to contact them because of your failure to succeed with your plans. I also know that they will in effect remove you from power in implementing the program you intended and try to take it over. Is that what you wanted to be reduced in importance down here? I came from the recent future where all of this has already taken place and I watched you go through the motions of it."

He had no idea how she had gotten all her information but her story was potentially a fabrication, he reasoned.

"Are you so sure I'm making all this up, Amelatu? What if it is the truth?"

She reads my thoughts, he realized.

"Are you or your people even aware of the caliber of intelligence you are dealing with on Earth in this timeline? We don't advertise our abilities we just live them quietly and are prepared to protect our way of life and I think you are getting the picture that we are more than equipped to do that with pure mind," she said. It had just happened; Chantal decided to let Nicholas think that everyone on Earth had her level of development and why not? Eventually they would; the time lag was a mere technicality. "No, I could take your life but what I really want is for you to go ahead and contact your people and let them know the truth about what they are dealing with down here."

Amelatu looked at her and she was right; there had been no mention from anyone in the legion about the level of personal development these people seemingly had. Diana had not found out about it and if they lived their adeptness quietly then clearly his group had missed vitally important information that could thwart their mission.

"Amelatu, do you remember anything before the age of nine?" Asked Chantal.

"Of course, I have memories of my whole life," he replied.

"Really. How long has the world you came from been part of the Rabum Kataru's collective consciousness?"

"What relevance does this have? We were always a part of the collective for as long as I can remember," he replied somewhat irritated by her question.

"I want to show you something," she said and unfolded a holographic grid that played scenes from his childhood for him. Amelatu watched himself run through forests with other children not unlike the one they were now in but the foliage was in hues of blue because the sun on his home planet was a blue star. His father had been a talented engineer and his mother so loving of him and his brother who he saw for the first time. His soul registered these memories like a man who wakes from a deep sleep and that adventurous, happy boy that he watched he remembered being. *What became of this brother?* He wondered.

"Amelatu, the Rabum Kataru took over the minds of your home planet when you were nine years old. They replaced all your memories exactly the same way they want to on Earth. There are members of your family still there but none remember anything of their original life anymore. The value that the truth of one's origins has is at stake for my people. It is partly from this that our individuality is born in each life. I wanted you to know what this really means because you experienced its loss," said Chantal.

"One of the most exquisite qualities of our society is that we no longer live in judgment of others," Chantal continued. "Diana has been accepted into our world and opportunities for an exemplary life are opening for her. You have a brilliant mind and there is no reason why you cannot integrate into our world if you are pure of consciousness and so desire. All people are divine beings on a course of evolution. Regardless what occurs Amelatu I will never forget your face when you remembered your childhood because in my mind I hold that I saw as your true nature."

Amelatu was silent and his body relaxed more than he ever remembered experiencing. He looked at Chantal and saw such compassion that made no sense considering the threat he posed to her world yet her sincerity was far beyond a façade. "Now look at the coming events and see a future timeline that you can now choose to embrace or change," she said as the holographic pictures played out the events that ensued once he contacted his people.

As she had said Amelatu watched Alal ingeniously extract him from true power over the events on Earth. The bait of future involvement in learning more about their secret technologies would be presented to him and the mind erasure was still the ultimate goal but now assimilation into their collective would be part of the plan. No where in the orientation that he would receive existed information about Earth's people's adept minds. His own worked fast and he knew he had some choices to contemplate. Vitally Alal would need to know the risks he was taking on in his ignorance of the level of consciousness that had been achieved by these people. Amelatu knew that Chantal would let him return to meet with the Rabum Kataru as he intended. There was little point in engaging the take over now and the tumultuous movement of his emotions after viewing his lost childhood had dampened his enthusiasm for pursuing his goals with his people. Furthermore, Chantal had displayed technology purely form her mind that he had never experienced before. He had no idea what else she was capable of. He needed some time alone to think and make a decision.

"There are several options. You could go to them and proceed with what awaits according to what you witnessed here and see if you can prevent the inoculation process from being implemented or tell them the truth about us and convince them that their efforts are futile. I will leave you now but you will remember all that has taken place here," she said and dematerialized from the forest.

Amelatu felt the stillness all around him alone amongst the trees. His mind reviewed his life and memories form childhood. All the children he remembered were oriented in a learning program that had been selected for them by the governing body of the Rabum Kataru and no one questioned it. Several factors were considered in deciding what role each person would play in their society and an examination of genetic propensity largely played a part in what role each child was prepared to assume as adults. Nicholas being large in stature, quick of mind and good with problem solving had been groomed from a young age to take on a role in the legion's strategic planning and initiatives. He had advanced quickly by proving his adeptness in these areas also demonstrating leadership. Skills that Amelatu possessed lead up to the decision Alal had made to send him to Earth where he became a CIA operative and advanced in its ranks. From his post he had the ideal position to influence certain government figures in ways that the Rabum Kataru encouraged. In particular he had influenced diverting monies away from NASA's activities towards military spending that the CIA directly benefited from especially in their foreign country activities. This helped create political situations where access to resources like oil, natural gas, minerals, etc which were vital to the economies of the world became negotiable and more controllable. His ties to secret organizations like the Illuminati who often funded major elections and the families who ran the Federal Reserve provided a network power that the Rabum Kataru indirectly influenced through Amelatu and others like him from their legion.

Amelatu thought about how easy it had been to keep world citizens ignorant about billions of dollars spent on space programs like NASA to seemingly promote the exploration of space while secretly they already had access to anti gravity technology and more in covert projects that the public knew nothing about. Meanwhile space shuttle launches continued in spite of the known risks to astronauts piloting the archaically designed craft. The only bailout system on the shuttles was the same that B—17 bomber pilots had in World War Two. No one had any idea about their time travel capability either and the only threads of truth that existed for the public to be informed came from independent, radical thinkers who did their best to make the information available through whatever means they had. Clearly attempting to limit the consciousness of more enlightened people in the current timeline could backfire. An invaluable insight entered his mind that he would remember in his future.

Amelatu stood on the bridge of the Rabum Kataru's ship with Alal now watching the last of the population on earth receiving their inoculations. Chantal's words played back in his mind and he knew that somehow the process though seemingly successful would be halted by her and the CIV. To complicate matters his people had not been able to access any data from world wide CIV branches due to security shielding that each building had apparently activated. After failing to disable it and meeting with other superiors Alal had agreed to send Amelatu down to rectify the problem. He would have to gain access into World CIV headquarters to ensure that the inoculations had been received by all IM's. The plan was risky because the Rabum Kataru wanted him to apprehend a key member and confirm that the process was complete. At that point the activation of the chips would commence and the programming agenda that had meticulously been prepared for all world sectors would be implemented.

Each citizen's personal history would be blended with memories of a different government structure and world economy and any conflicting past erased. CIV members world wide had individual programs that they would be fed to become active members of an altered political structure that had been created by the Rabum Kataru. Release of technology to the general population would be scaled back and more control over world resources and monies would be reinstated. Many other changes were included that would give more power back to the governing bodies over the activities of the citizens. Amelatu was aware of all this as it was the same program that he and the Omega Group had intended to implement through Diana's efforts. It had now been updated to include the merger into the Rabum Kataru's collective mind and all would recognize the legion as the founding fathers of 'true liberty of mind' on Earth. After some deliberation Amelatu had decided that the simplest course of action was to be transported to Earth and simply allow their plan to fail. By then they would learn about the level of mind they had attempted to interfere with which would explain their failure. Alal's determination to see their plan through to completion would possibly complicate the situation but Amelatu hoped that he would see the futility of attempting to control the events of the current timeline on Earth.

Inrashad approached them with Amelatu's supply case, "all is ready for your departure and transport Amelatu." He gave a short bow to Alal, collected his carrying case and proceeded to the transport chamber.

TWENTY TWO

Chantal stood on board Zain's ship and they examined all the current data on the situation with the Rabum Kataru. "Your idea to expose Amulet's true past to him was brilliant and is having the desired effect on his consciousness. Zain flashed a picture of Chantal hanging off a tree on the Virtual Nav and said, "I'm thinking of framing that. Amelatu has not left the legion's ship and I've picked up through the matrix is that he is in a different frequency of thought about his involvement with the plans to reprogram the population. They have not been able to penetrate the shielding we have provided around all the CIV centers and this is causing delays in the activation of the brain chips. We have managed to create a window of time to determine the best course of action to disable the chips en mass for the general population," said Zain.

"Excellent! Finally some progress in unraveling the complications this timeline has faced," replied Chantal with some relief.

"I have a trip planned for us," he said.

"Oh, where?"

"One of my favorite places to do business and share information; planet called Ixon 528 in the Star Chaser Nebula. There is a place called the Orbiting Mind Institute that houses technological systems developed to interface with the matrix around planetary systems. There you will find viable options for technological applications that will help solve the current problem on Earth," he said entering the appropriate coordinate in the navigation system and the ship geared up to fold space time.

Moments later light entered the observation window of the ship and Chantal looked upon a lavender sky created by a blue sun feeding the atmosphere. Below elongated, pale colored buildings with rounded roof tops some hundreds of stories high reached towards them. Zain's ship glided towards a curved structure that was lower to the ground but large; spanning at least an acre of land. A bridge connected it to a series of smaller buildings which were different sizes and Zain explained that these housed different research and development sectors of Orbiting Mind Institute. Immaculate landscaping bordered the complex in hues of blue foliage that Chantal had never seen before due to the color of the planets sun. They teleported to the main floor of the Institute and Chantal looked outside from huge, curved windows. She could see adjacent to the main entrance people appearing and disappearing from a platform prior to entering or after leaving the centre. She scanned the matrix and found these to be teleportation pads that existed throughout the cities as a basic form of transport. Chantal loved the energy of this place. It had a highly organized feel but an incredible lightness of being prevailed. She observed beings of all different coloring and stature milling through the building; a tall, exotic looking woman with blue skin and hair walked by Chantal. She was accompanied by another female who was dark skinned. Their hair was styled in manners she had never seen before and their clothing was similar to the fashions and fabrics Zain wore and had supplied her with.

"Let's go upstairs, they're ready for us," said Zain gently taking hold of Chantal's arm. They teleported to the fifth floor and walked into a large, circular room where several people worked at various stations. A beautiful female with blue skin and midnight colored hair with turquoise accents framing an oval face approached them. Chantal looked into her deep navy colored eyes and smiled shaking her hand. She greeted them in her native language which Chantal was able to understand as the information she relayed appeared in her brain. "I am Nadira, good to see you again Zain."

Zain introduced Chantal and briefly described the nature of matrix interface programs they were looking for. Nadira proceeded to present the most recent planetary grid access data links. Several options for mass planetary program deactivation interested Chantal as she watched the simulations unfold all around her. Some targeted select locations and set a sequence of events to unfold on a precise schedule that created a domino effect culminating in a desired objective. Chantal was particularly intrigued by one system that isolated all planetary citizens within the grid and simultaneously allowed one to execute a mass program. *That would be the simplest and most efficient solution to mass deactivation of the chips,* she reasoned. Zain agreed and once they made their selection Nadira prepared the data crystal and sealed it. "Here, all is ready. Will you be needing anything else?" She asked handing the item to Zain.

"Thank you this is all we require but I would love to show Chantal your facilities as this is her first time visiting."

"Please go ahead, stay as long as you like." she replied and returned to her work.

"Nadira has been a part of this design group for many years now and the work they do here has vast applications that are exported within the local universe and sometimes purchased by visitors like us from elsewhere. She specializes in planetary grid system interface technology and others here create space travel grid navigation systems similar to the one I use for my ship. They observed these being designed at several work stations and paused near a console where a tall silver haired designer was immersed in his work. "This is Virdek he's kind of the 'mad scientist' of the lot. Any problems with systems failure or glitches in the programs usually end up adopted by him. He treats them as wayward children that he tames into technological brilliance through sheer determination," Zain whispered as they stood behind him and watched. Zain cleared his throat, "having problems with the Haldeck 232 system again?"

Virdek turned away from his work and greeted Zain and Chantal with a smile then proceeded to launch into the merits of the current system he was working on. "Great improvements, nothing like the old program at all. I have perfected the coordinate calculations to be the most precise ever attained. The problems that the Odessik fleet had with this system are now obsolete."

"What sort of problems did they experience?" asked Chantal.

"Only skipping vital points along the matrix lines that transported the crew to the wrong galaxy," said Zain with a smirk.

"That only happened once…perhaps twice and the system was being run by fleet students who had not perfected their mind interface," said Virdek. Mainly the problems lay in less precise coordinate calculations of a minor nature which has now been fully rectified. As soon as the flight tests are complete we will reintroduce this redesigned navigation system as the as the Paladius 300 and it will be well received."

"I will spread the word about your new innovations Virdek," said Zain and prepared to depart with Chantal.

"Your navigation system, was it designed somewhere in the Pleiades?" Asked Chantal.

"My ship was built there but I had my father supply the navigation system. He is a design engineer of the highest achievement on a planet in the Crab Nebula known for specializing in space engineering."

This was the first time he had mentioned his father and Chantal wondered what his mother was like. "You will meet her later when we join her for dinner," he said reading her thoughts. "First we have another shopping trip to make," Zain said with a hint of mystery and they appeared in front of a large building that looked both ancient and exotic in architecture. It appeared as if constructed from carved stone yet unlike any that Chantal had seen before. Its vaulted, cathedral like roof reached up into a sky grazed with white clouds through which the sun infused the remaining sky with deeper shades of lavender. Carvings resembling knotted tree branches trimmed the buildings borders, appearing like phantom emanations that had arisen from stone. "Breathtaking," said Chantal as she and Zain walked into the Merchants' Pavilion. Before them stood three levels of shops providing an eclectic array of items and they proceeded to the second floor.

Zain led Chantal into a store that featured garments made of a variety of light weight fabrics in styles that were comfortable, functional but form skimming in a complimentary fashion. Chantal walked upon a lit floor made of a translucent substance with inlaid geometric patterns as she looked through the merchandise. Since they were to dine with Zain's mother she decided to purchase something to wear, which she realized was part of the reason he had brought her there. Chantal held a pair of silky textured but opaque pants that were form fitted almost like tights in a deep cherry color and a top that had a fine but raw textured gold knit skimming the collarbone and shoulders with a matching cherry fitted bustier that crossed the breasts in a straight line and was tailored at the waist. "I found something to wear for tonight," she said. Zain took the items and proceeded with a retinal scan to finalize their purchase.

Chantal and Zain strolled through the other floors and she witnessed innovation from the minds of masters that manifested unique items for the local population to delight in and purchase. All proceeds were fed back to the community to fund the advancement of children's minds in a variety of creative projects. Chantal stopped in front of a store that featured spirits and tobacco from all over the local universe. She stepped inside and saw richly colored liquids in beautiful bottles some resembling cut crystal that refracted light in opalescent hues. She picked up such a container filled with a deep purple substance topped with a lid that housed a large, dark blue colored stone. Pondering the contents Chantal found that it was a type of wine made from an indigenous fruit similar to the grape but with a more intense concentration of flavor. "Zain this looks exquisite, have you tried it before?"

He took the bottle in his hands and examined it. "I have had this variety of wine but not this label. It was crafted from the mind of Romitus, an ancient and rather mysterious master that no one has ever seen but who dreams all these elixirs for the enjoyment of those who consume them. Let's try it," he said and held on to the bottle as Chantal continued to browse. She came upon a transparent case housing many tobacco products and cast her eyes upon beautiful carved pipes and cigarette boxes. An array of cigars and slender cigarettes in a variety of colors spanned the contents of the case. So inspiring to see a quality of products that had obviously been meticulously created; to look upon them gave a rich impression of the anonymous being who had cast them into existence. Zain and Chantal left the store and headed downstairs.

A crowd gathered around the courtyard that spanned the centre of the Merchant's Pavilion. Chantal heard music that reminded her of lilies that hung from their stems heavy with scent and morning dew. Rich sound moved through the air as she approached the edge of the crowd and looked upon a dazzling display of photonically emitted colors and geometries creating virtual art. She paused with Zain and looked upon the moving holographs spellbound by the effect the frequency had upon her. Chantal's energy field responded in sync with the undulations of art and sound she observed. Her heart centre opened and the energy moved along her spine. Zain held her hand and her lids began to drop as the energy moved within her. Some one beside her sent a blast of energy from her mind that Chantal felt and she observed how it animated the photonic light; a burst of patterns emerged and floated upwards creating an 'awe' in the crowd. The music curved and exploded in unison with the visuals and Chantal felt the impact as thundering ecstatic waves of energy moving through her head and lifting her to a state of consciousness where all dissolved but her divinity. Drifting back from a bliss Chantal looked at the lovely creature beside her; a woman with chocolate skin and curled hair tinged with copper. Her eyes held such an enlightened state that illuminated her bronze eyes and Chantal loved the gift of mind that she had contributed to the visual art. A beautiful man across from them had captured her eye and unabashedly held the woman's gaze. He was fair in comparison, tall and adorned with hair that grazed his shoulders with waves of gold. Her eyes did not flinch from intrusion but interest registered on her face. He moved his mind into the holograph and it shone rose, geometric emanations that moved towards her and she closed her eyes absorbing the creation of his mind. Chantal saw streams of energy moving around the woman's head and out her third eye. Slowly she opened her eyes and looked at the young man who held her gaze; a look of recognition formed across her brow for she clearly enjoyed his frequency. The dark skinned master engaged the photonic art form once more for a mesmerizing moment and completely took it over creating a red orange sunset that was unseen on this planet. A sky of orange and coral rose bathed the spectators in warm radiance and symbols of gold entered her suitor's forehead. Chantal peeked at what the woman had created for him and saw images of lush gardens infused with blooms of unspeakable beauty. Life thundered in the visions she sent punctuated by children's laughter and the movement of wise women who cared for their families and dreamed of rains that would quench thirst of robust crops that they tended. A tear moved down Chantal's face as she realized the humble beginnings that the beautiful master beside her had come from. No small feat a mother that could focus ardently enough to bring rain that ensured her family was fed. This dedication of love had clearly inspired the daughter to seek her own greatness and her story was being imparted to the man standing across from her in naked truthfulness.

Chantal looked over at him completely caught up in the innocence of a moment between two strangers. She held her breath and waited with those of the crowd who had caught on to the subtleties of the communication between two sublime beings. Steps echoed through the courtyard as the young man walked over to the exotic woman with copper hair. He held out his hand and said, "honor me with a walk to where the trees commune." She smiled at him flashing her amazing eyes and took hold of his hand graciously walking out of the plaza with her new acquaintance.

Chantal and Zain teleported to the facility where his mother waved from across the room already seated at a table by the window. The entire enclosure was constructed of a see through crystal substance that allowed the patrons to view marine life engaging its natural habitat. Colorful schools of fish swam around the complex and consumed feed that funneled out to the water attracting a variety of species. An intricate coral structure grown over many years created a natural sculpture that was visible outside the window near the table Chantal and Zain sat down at. His mother greeted them and looked at Chantal with luminous dark eyes that held something of Zain but different; her own wisdom from a unique life animated them. She shook her hand firmly and introduced herself, "I'm Zara and very pleased to finally meet you. Zain handed her a bouquet of violet clustered flowers mixed with large, white blooms as he reached over and kissed her cheek. She handed him a package of data crystals, "these are from your father. Some interesting material on them that he designed recently."

He took one out of its package and held it between his fingers instantly downloading the patterned design into his mind. "Thanks, I look forward to examining the rest later," he said. A virtual server floated over to their table and manifested their menu rings; the day's seafood feature plus many other delicious looking entrees instantly appeared in their minds with full descriptions as each person held the ring in the palm of his hands and ran a finger around it. They all decided on the featured item and a bottle of Zara's favorite wine. "The data archive for children's' studies is almost complete now at Orbiting Minds," said Zara.

"We were just there today acquiring a program for Chantal," replied Zain.

"Ah yes, I am aware of the recent events that have been transpiring on Earth. Your people have their challenges right now dealing with all the interference."

"I have a plan to assist them with eradicating the potential for interference by the Rabum Kataru. Thankfully Orbiting Minds has provided a resource that will be used to disable the invasive technology that the legion is attempting to wield on Earth. With all the changes that have occurred in our society's evolution we have enjoyed such peace and put resources towards growth and expansion. We were unprepared for the nature of meddling that has taken place since we moved away from conflict amongst our nations."

"It is unusual to have a peaceful society that has accomplished harmony to be harassed by a lesser consciousness and unlikely that they would succeed. In the end a lesson about such interference will be experienced by these beings that is long overdue. There have been pockets of aggressive groups pilfering the resources of other simple cultures but usually this type of activity is stopped by the universal council of the Shining Ones. Zain has had experience on such a planet when he was very young," said Zara.

Chantal looked at Zain and scanned what she knew about him; oddly she could not see much about him in his youth.

"He has a few stories that likely he has not shared with you," she said with a smile.

Zain looked over at his mother and clearly she had taken a liking to Chantal if *that* subject had been brought up. She looked back at him with an expression he knew well and he laughed. "My mother cherishes my learning that gave me great understanding and compassion for less evolved societies that still engage in warfare and are locked in conflict. I do have a story if you are interested though it is not something I would have brought up as casual dinner conversation."

"Absolutely I'm greatly interested," said Chantal sitting up. "Please tell your story."

"When I was about seventeen years old I had an exchange with my father that would culminate into a pivotal experience changing me forever. To put it bluntly I was completely ignorant to the reality of those who took unfair advantage of other worlds resources and lived in conflict amongst themselves. I looked upon them with disinterest because the strife which they created for themselves was unpleasant for me to observe. I found nothing inspiring in their mindset that would warrant my attention at the time. My father was unimpressed with my attitude to say the least and petitioned my mother to support giving me an orientation that would immerse me in needed learning to garner greater understanding."

Steaming dinner entrees suddenly appeared before them all and a tray filled with their wine selection and glasses floated over hovering next to the table. Zain ignored the virtual server option and opened the wine pouring a generous measure for everyone. As he spoke holographic images appeared and illustrated his story. *My father had introduced me to an initiative by the Shining Ones whose objective is to help stabilize and replenish ecologically less abundant planets' resources. I had accompanied teams of specialists who use grid interface technology and create transportable domes housing mini eco systems that are suitable potentials for adoption by target planets. Once there we finalized the program that was accepted by governing representatives of the population and implemented the technology. The last mission of this nature that I participated in occurred on an arid planet in our local galaxy that was populated by a race of beings that are somewhat shy in nature towards outsiders but keenly observant and organized. Having faced natural adversity from harsh planetary conditions their nature was 'thick skinned' and not overly demonstrative.*

Zain continued thoughtfully as he enjoyed his dinner. *When we arrived and some of them toured the inside of the dome it was the first time that the Romalians experienced a truly abundant environment that would become a reality for their world. In their own way they appeared quietly overwhelmed at what we brought to their parched planet. An abundance of plant life, food crops, fish and animal stock that would provide sustenance would be integrated into their ecosystem once we initiated the grid interface program. Temperate zones would be created where enough cloud cover was maintained ensuring ideal environments for thriving habitats. They requested no changes and we began to implement the programming. Our team dispersed to key areas across the planet where each of us would oversee the habitats and monitor progress making necessary adjustments to the grid interface. We would also engage the local population to provide training on maintaining the habitats over a two month period. I was assigned to an area that was nestled against a mountain range where the new climate conditions were ideally supported. Unique to the area we also found access to underground caverns of incredible beauty. What the planet lacked in surface living conditions its womb housed grottos with walls made of a crystalline substance that refracted light with a golden sheen. In addition to dwellings tucked within the mountains some of these had been converted into living areas that people used to have relief from the high temperatures above ground. The local authority provided me with a subterranean abode that was a self contained, miniature grotto with a hot spring in the centre and a rest palette that had been carved out of the wall itself. It had been fitted with a hand stitched mattress filled with desert blooms of a variety that resembled crushed velvet when dried. The setting was far more primitive than I was accustomed to but so incredibly beautiful that I found a new appreciation for being cradled within the earth of this strange planet that accepted me and provided such a peaceful abode."*

"Its breath taking!" said Chantal as she viewed Zain's exotic lodgings. He appeared younger, not quite filled out yet and his hair hung past his shoulders. Chantal smiled seeing him in his youth for the first time and memorized him from his past.

Zain reached beneath the table and held her hand as he continued the story. "The first few days everyone observed the program in effect producing the new habitat zone; in miles of desert expanse moving air currents produced a cocoon of moisture that filtered out the hot sun. The humid climate now nourished lush vegetation and food crops we created. Waterfalls sprang from mountain cliffs that overhung the valley and flowed down a stream that became the local water supply. Wild fowl, rabbits and a species of wild boar roamed the area which provided a more varied diet than dessert cacti, root vegetables and lizards. The Romalians prepared a feast in my honor and to celebrate the abundance that now flowed to them. That memorable night a setting red sun lit the peach sky with an orange fire creating a liquid, solar mirage on the horizon. Songs of local birds whose call haunted the night desert echoed distantly through the mountains as we dined beneath unique heavens on this plane."

Chantal and her mother, who had seen all this before but never tired of its beauty, watched quietly at the visuals as the story unfolded.

A local female named Shara sat beside me with a plate of food and quietly ate whilst unabashedly examining me. We watched children run, play and engage their families and then she was upon me with unspoken local wisdom.

"You will leave us with this paradise that we only glimpsed in our dreams. When the ships of our adversaries arrive to collect the titanium from our mines and find these changes you will be gone. As you know they are not kind to our people. Who can predict what they will do when they find us so abundant."

Her words were an undeniable truth that would haunt me for days till I lived the actual experience of what she had spoken. That night of festivities and seeing the locals more relaxed than they had ever been stayed in my mind because it was the only time that I saw them so happy once the raids began again.

Zain paused and looked into his wine glass lost in memories for a moment that he did not animate. *The ships they used to raid the Romalians were dark, silent and used basic laser technology to blast into the titanium quarries with calibrated coordinates that would provide the greatest yield of product per trip. They then had a team that rapidly collected the alloy and usually left without engaging the locals unless they got in the way. Due to lack of weapons or defenses the Romalians experienced several episodes of demise when they tried to protect their mines. The Urak race was frail, tall with large eyes but had the advantage of technology which easily overpowered those who had none. They learned to stay out of the way when the raids took place and hid till their adversaries had taken what they wanted and left. Several days after I arrived I felt the tremors move through the underground where I lay on my palette. I woke instantly and headed outside surprised that none of the locals had risen to investigate the cause of the explosion. After making some rounds I found out what I already mentioned; a raid on the mines about a mile away was taking place and no one bothered to do anything because of the risks. I hesitated because the reality of how ludicrous the situation was registered in me. No advanced society would tolerate such an invasion. I decided to stay out of the matter because our mission was to set up the habitats and not engage in conflict; that was left to the Shining Ones to act on and we had not received instructions to intervene. About four hours after we heard the disturbance the Urak's ships began to appear over the habitat zone. I was transmitting data to the rest of my grid interface group in the grotto when I heard screams and commotion coming from above. I hurried outside and witnessed a massacre of the locals which put me in a state of shock: I had never seen such casual slaughter taking place and I retreated underground to contact the head of our group.* Zain stopped the holograph not wanting to share the details of what had happened but Chantal could read the impact that it had on him.

I was stunned, my instructions were to do nothing and they would relay the information to the Shining Ones who were aware of the problems and had intervened on behalf of these people before. Apparently the Uraks had stayed away for a while and then arrogantly defied warnings slyly planning their raids when the intervention groups were engaged elsewhere. When I surfaced again the Shining Ones had sent assistance to aid with the wounded and casualties. The habitat had been disturbed and I was asked to stay on at this location a little longer to initiate repairs to the program. Many of the friends I had dined with had died and a few of the children were orphaned but taken in by others from the area. I was angry because I felt like I had sat idle, no one urgently responded and lives were senselessly lost. Long I contemplated what had occurred because if the Uraks returned I knew I would not be able to sit by again and watch them take advantage of the locals or worse if the intervention group did not deal with the problem in time. I initiated the first clandestine move of my life and contacted a mischievous friend from the training academy that young masters attend in the Pleadian system. He was known for undertaking risky ventures that were not advised by his mentors but usually garnered him success because of his persistent nature. I contacted him and asked him to take on an unusual assignment for which I made a clever barter. I pledged to introduce him to a female childhood friend of mine who he shyly admired but had hesitated approaching. Intrigued with the potential he agreed to assist me in raiding my father's program archive and transporting something I required. With some maneuvering he found exactly what I needed that would provide a measure of defense should the Romalians be raided again by the Uraks.

"A few days later Shara appeared in my resting place and she said, "you have accomplished much restoration of the habitat in a short period of time but what is the point if our people continue to be attacked?"

I told her that I had taken measures to protect the habitat and that it would not happen again so long as I was responsible for ensuring its success. She looked intently at me and I could see in her eyes a knowingness that was odd because I did not tell her the nature of what I had arranged. She was different from the other locals in a way that reminded me of the adept minded I had grown up with but much more subtly. She simply smiled and left my presence. About two weeks passed and the work I had accomplished with the Romalians reestablished serenity and hope amongst them. We successfully created their agricultural model and helped them to learn skills required to begin to manage their given areas. At the end of a busy day I stood on a plateau that I used to climb upon to view the setting sun and have a glass of wine alone. From there I could see the expanse of the habitat, the movement of *local life reflection of rubies created by the last rays hitting the deep colored stream. It was in such peace that paradoxically the ships stealthily approached at the edge of the area. No one below had noticed them yet and I instantly appeared back at the grotto to contact my superior. The reply was that he would report the incident and advised me to move as many as possible to a safe place within the mountains. I decided to activate the grid defense device my father had designed to disable the Uraks' ships through the control matrix that we ran the habitat program through. An explosion sounded as one of them hit the side of the mountain and the Romalians had begun to surface from their dwellings to see what had happened. Two others were also grounded with all weapons disabled. The Urak crews had begun to emerge from the ships, disoriented and completely taken by surprise and vulnerable because they were now disarmed. Taking advantage of the moment I gathered a group of Romalians and we apprehended the Uraks and took them to a holding area in the underground. Some of the Romalians had boarded the two downed ships and were exploring. They had begun to remove various items and objected strongly when I asked that they be left alone for the intervention group to remove. A young boy ran away with an armful of the ship's contents before I could grab him. The rest also insisted on helping themselves to whatever they wanted rationalizing their entitlement due to their planet's resources being pilfered by the Uraks for so long. Some complications had begun since we had guidelines about the sharing of advanced technologies with less knowledgeable societies. This is where I began to encounter a stubborn side of these people and had difficulty reasoning with them on the issue. Thankfully they had agreed to leave the Uraks in peace till they were removed from their custody by the intervention group. I knew that once they arrived anything that was not suitable for the Romalians to keep would be confiscated.*

I asked Shara to help me find the small boy who had successfully gathered the largest 'loot' from the ship. She laughed when I told her what had happened and told me to look for him in the east underground area where groups of children built elaborate hiding places. I entered the caverns with a lumi torch and searched the area. No children played there having been kept with their parents during the attempted Urak invasion so the area was quiet. I felt a presence as I neared the far end of an area were clay had been molded into tunnels that I barely squeezed through leading into another section of the caves. I successfully managed to pull my haunches out of the tunnel and into the opening where a wide eyed child sat amongst his treasures. 'It's alright don't be scared,' I said as I approached him. I sat down beside him and casually began to examine the ship's contents that he had stolen. The main concern was a sonic detonator that he had taken along with some communication devices.

"What does it matter if I take anything of theirs? They are thieves and murderers," he said defiantly.

I explained to him in simple terms the way my people approach sharing of things that are unknown to societies and that was the main reason he could not keep all he had taken.

"Where are your people when the raids happen and they arrive too late? The Uraks are skinny and weak but have all this stuff that can destroy anything and hurt us. It doesn't make sense we cannot keep things that could to help us fight them."

I took his small hand in mine; his light brown, textured skin was smooth to the touch and I looked into his large, slanted eyes. We are working to share as much as we can with many worlds who want to advance but first they must learn about what they are given. Some of these things that you took are dangerous if you don't know how to use them. Technology is never a replacement for your mind which is far more powerful than any of these things. In my world I am learning to use my mind greater than any device. That is a secret gift all beings everywhere are given.

"How do you do that?" he asked as now I had piqued his curiosity.

There are beings from other worlds which can help your people learn and once the habitats are stable if those who govern you agree we can bring them to your planet and set up education centers. You can begin on your own by knowing the source of all life that created you is the same that lives in your beautiful red sun, the striped lizards you race with your friends, the stars. When that beautiful red disk rises in the morning sky and shines overhead it is just like the place you came from that shines for you. Just close your eyes and reach as deep as you can inside yourself and you will find it. When you do this often something magical starts to happen; you get its attention and it turns its light brighter and brighter till one day it brings you home.

He sat and pondered my words for a moment and said,"what is home like?"

You become a life giver with your mind brighter than any sun ever created. You never die and can create worlds, become anything you want.

A moment of realization dawned for that child as he looked at the things he had taken. The words I had spoken became his treasures and the material things though intriguing had lost their appeal. I did not realize as we left the cave that day what an impression I had made because that child became a highly influential leader to his people and still lives today five hundred years later.

Help did arrive once the situation was contained and this time the Uraks did not return due in part to my intervention. My father did not greatly appreciate my tactic to acquire the defense interface but he admired my courage to act in order to protect the Romalians while the habitat was under my care. The intervention group did *manage to confiscate items taken from the Urak's ship and eventually provided some technological and educational programs to the planetary governing body. Shara bid me goodbye on my last day and revealed to me her true identity; she was Larina and my father had asked her to keep an eye on me during my assignment. Simply put she was to remove me from the planet if my life was in jeopardy. Before departing she unfolded her magnificent, true form and held out her hands. Aquamarine palms held my hands and her arms colored by serpentine lines of different hues that ran up along her shoulders, neck and face from which changeable metallic eyes blessed me. Her race exalting the diversity of mind and life everywhere is a love that transcends and cannot be spoken but only experienced. To become the expression of the Creator's love for it's progeny in the diversity of countless species is a unique phenomenon to behold. Larina's mind is a mystery that I contemplated for many years and inspired me to deepen my love for all worlds that hold consciousness in its diverse expression as life unfolding.*

Zain ended his story and Chantal sat holding his last words in her mind as they paid their bill and left.

TWENTY THREE

Amelatu transported to an area just outside the CIV World headquarters and made his way to the grounds where the garden gazebo stood. He entered and sat down leaning against the lacquered wooden wall and gazed at the conference centre across from the gardens.

Inside CIV representatives from all sectors gathered to attend the world meeting with the Shining Ones. Romy gathered data through the Unity Network about the world wide inoculation process and a security report. Micro nano satellite and laser technology transferred condensed data with unprecedented speed and efficiency. Some of these satellite fixtures in space could be held in the palm of the hand reducing cost of production substantially yet they had many applications. Several companies that produced them in the European, Asian and North American sectors had created advanced satellite applications that eliminated pollution, stabilized weather increasing crop yields world wide and provided earth change detection. The science of plate tectonics and studying volcanic activity through innovative satellite detection and management by lasers had greatly reduced natural disasters.

"The photon shielding device is in operation in all sectors via satellite interface. So far over eighty five percent of the population has received the inoculation," said Romy as he finished downloading the data. Maya, Lorne and Romy gathered with the others in the circular meeting room for an event that was unusual in its format. A great ship hovered above them that would transmit the communication through a living grid projection far advanced compared to the current holographic technology the CIV used. Once assembled the members dimmed the lights and reviewed the data disk that Diana had brought to headquarters in Olympia. Upon completion the IM's dimmed the lights and waited for the contact to begin. The room began to fill with oscillating particle light projections that formed into blue beings who animated the presentation. As the atmosphere became ultraviolet glimmer the blue forms would move in flashes of lines that then unfolded into moving thought projections packed with information that directly interfaced the minds of the IM's. They watched as visuals moved through the room weaving a model for the expansion of the newly developed Unity Network global communications platform. A quantum brain chip database program that would be accessed by all containing not only the latest innovations from Earth but also installments of experiential knowledge from local and other universes was shown first. These would be downloaded from the network by the mind and then a wormhole would appear and if the viewer had calibrated his frequency correctly he would be able to access cosmic mind to experience more. Children's education modules would be included that teachers world wide would be able to access for home and classroom learning enhancement. A wormhole appeared and moved in front of various IM's who were processing the data in their minds and then experienced the wormhole opening in their consciousness to simulate the process.

Next the science portion of the presentation unfolded with an anti gravity technology update that featured engine innovation and space flight concepts that current scientific development could incorporate into future designs. These would not be added to the network but the science and engineering experts viewing this would have the knowledge to use the provided information as inspiration to evolve their concepts. All technological and scientific material that was developed however would also be available through the Unity Network for others to access once data was available to post.

Once space travel was developed over the years opportunities to visit other star systems within the local universe would be made available through a collaborative alliance with other civilizations. The atmosphere changed to gold shimmer and the blue beings now turned to liquid golden forms that animated rotating models of advanced cities and exotic natural environments. Completely mesmerized the IM's experienced a heightened state of consciousness that allowed an experiential glimpse into highly enlightened worlds that they would one day visit. Earth's society would greatly benefit from exposure to such diversity and evolve greater in its own uniqueness.

As the presentation inside the conference centre continued Amelatu contemplated his options as he sat inside the gazebo. This marked the first time in his life that he had no formal plan to dispense on a mission as he had abandoned instructions given to him by Alal. He hoped that Chantal and the CIV had halted the inoculation process in time to prevent the Rabum Kataru from succeeding with the mind reprogramming. With his head against the wall he observed the setting sun which cast rose tones behind the conference centre. The planet's atmosphere here appeared clear and smelled sweet like on his world; a refreshing change compared with the other timeline that the Omega group resided in. Oddly he had little remorse about leaving behind his associates there. The scientists were the only ones he truly had any respect for because they had a love for their work that went beyond lust for power. Like all the members they too had become corrupt because of their alliance with the Omega Group but at their core they cared most about inventive progress and that was in line with what he admired most about his own people. The rest of the Omega Group comprised of highly competitive individuals who had their own secrets and he trusted none of them. He thought about Diana and the way he had treated her. She had been like the rest of them but yet had found this current timeline and her experience had clearly changed her gradually; he had chosen not to observe that at the time. He wondered what had happened to her and if the CIV intelligence unit had her in custody.

As Amelatu sat deep in his thoughts a beam of rose colored light surrounded the gazebo. At first he thought that the setting sun was the source but then realized that it was emanating all around and from above him. Something resembling gold dust began to enter the gazebo and a pinpoint of deep blue light approached him, then washed over his form. He felt a lifting sensation in his chest and a feeling of expansion in his head. A strong presence filled the gazebo and he began to receive images that wove into a communiqué. The first thing Amelatu noticed was that his conscious connection to the Rabum Kataru's collective mind was being blocked and he suddenly became self aware in a way that was new. He was being given a choice to stay on Earth or to be transported back to his people's ship. If he stayed he had to agree to be permanently disconnected from his collective.

His home planet vastly changed appeared in his mind and the last part of the message indicated that he would be contacted again in time. He was given pause to make his choice and his history with his people ran through his mind for it was all he had known till Chantal had given him a glimpse into his forgotten past. The loss of his former identity began to take hold and before he could change his mind he indicated that he would accept the terms of the agreement and stay on Earth for the time being. An unanticipated peace washed over him when the disconnection occurred and the blue light continued to fill him with a radiant feeling of expansion.

As the light finally receded he opened his eyes and saw Chantal approaching the gazebo. She entered and sat next to him. Instantly she became aware of the events that had just taken place and smiled at Amelatu. "I will take you to Olympia where you will have a place to stay for the time being if you like," she said.

"What happened in there?" He asked indicating the conference centre.

"An unprecedented meeting between the world CIV representatives and the race of beings that helped to make this current timeline possible," she answered.

"Then what I experienced must be connected with that event because I was not familiar with whoever contacted me."

Chantal could see the change in Amelatu; his eyes seemed brighter and he lacked his usual defensive posture. "I am glad that you chose to abandon your involvement in the Rabum Kataru's plans."

"Have you found a way to contain the situation on Earth?"

"Yes, I have secured the means to end the interference by the Rabum Kataru," she replied without sharing any of the details with him.

"What happened to Diana?" he asked.

"She is safe and has assisted us greatly. She is with our science team as we speak back in Olympia."

"Let us depart now," she said taking his hand and filling his field with an increased vibration allowing him to adjust more slowly before teleporting out of the gazebo.

Back at the abode by the shore Zain sat in front of the violet fire projection and switched it to a live grid interface with the Shining Ones. He allowed his body to dissolve and entered the grid lines with his consciousness moving to the coordinates of contact. He unfolded his form in golden lines of light and joined many other beings within the matrix. A moving geometry hovered at the centre of the grid, rotating and changing shape as each being engaged it. The issue of the Rabum Kataru's empire of colonies and continued pursuit of power in the conversion of peoples into their collective was no longer being tolerated by the Shining Ones. For thousands of years their experiment of direct interference with an individual's sovereign right to his spiritual heritage had plagued many tumultuous worlds and now a peaceful and progressive civilization had become their latest target on Earth. The issue at hand had become not only initiating measures to stop the cycle of enslavement but how to handle the colonies themselves; some had been recently converted and others had long histories of belonging to the legion. Having completely disconnected from cosmic mind they were not preservable unless they wanted to abandon their own creation of separate mind. This option had always been available to the Rabum Kataru but none had chosen it and the race continued to be a menace.

Each member attending the meeting in sequence viewed potential strategies by engaging the universal geometric viewing structure; it was a highly advanced form of living mind where others could review each other's ideas. After everyone had a chance to have input decisions were made as to an overall approach that would solve the multiple issues at hand. The Rabum Kataru's Legion would be destroyed and the surviving colonies disconnected from their artificial collective mind. Memories prior to being converted into the collective would be restored as a result and assistance in stabilizing the free worlds would be provided in whatever manner necessary. Advances in technology that sustained balanced eco systems and learning that was progressive in nature over time would be available for them to access from a new, integrated state of consciousness from cosmic mind. Some of the potentials viewed offered the chance at an evolution towards highly progressive societies that differed from the original state that the colonized planets had lived in. The model for reintegration and stabilization of these various races would be fine tuned in subsequent meetings.

Upon his return Zain contemplated the progress that had been achieved in the meeting with the Shining Ones in his mind one option stood out that he wanted to explore further on his own. Not an easy task to reintegrate such a diversity of races into life while endeavoring to preserve what would be left of their original expression. Of great importance across all enlightened societies was the sovereign expression of the individual. He decided to contact his mother who had a long history in creating experiential education platforms for many diverse cultures and Larina who was the most seamless mind he knew at capturing the essence of any race. Zain located both of them and invited them to his place of contemplation.

Zara appeared with a container of data crystals and a big smile because she adored her work with a passion. She reviewed the construct that he had been pondering and pulled several options from what she brought. Larina moved into the room as a flash that traveled through the grid interface and unfolded her exotic form. She winked at Zain, handed him a bottle of wine and greeted Zara. Three humanoid and two alternate groups of peoples comprised the potential colonies that could be resurrected. Larina had only ventured to two of these cultures a few thousand years prior to the assimilation of these people into the Rabum Kataru's collective. One had been an interesting group of delicate, green skinned beings with dark, slanted eyes who lived in beautiful natural environments. At the time peace had reigned upon their world but later conflict between a more aggressive group of their race had escalated into planetary disharmony. Zain began to activate the programs his mother had brought and Larina projected a virtual version of herself as one of these beings into each one. They viewed one where she appeared tall, willowy, almost elfin looking and displays of a rich array of plants that provided thousands of uses when manufactured. The nature of their planets housed organic growth that had high concentrations of nutrients, medicinal properties and countless other benefits. This was one of the prize resources that the Rabum Kataru had acquired seven hundred years earlier. Zara had selected a program that could be adapted to restore the original mind of this race, its fruitful industries and progressive development of consciousness.

Next they viewed a group who was known primarily for technological advancement that had led to instability of their eco system prior to their integration into the Legion's collective. Zara had found an option that would provide some experiential learning that herald the beginning of interfacing mind with technology similarly to what Earth citizens experienced in 2020. Opportunity to lighten the mind set of these individuals through the program Larina suggested revealed a potentially joyous and light hearted society that contrasted their serious competitive nature of the past. This would likely result in a completely different technological development that would support their natural environment.

Zain and his guests reviewed remaining options for the other three colonies and upon completion everyone agreed on the suggested plans. He sent the package of information through the grid interface to the Shining Ones with confidence that they would also be pleased with the ideas.

Chantal and Romy met with the World CIV IM's after the meeting with the Shining Ones ended. Indications that they would be disarming the Rabum Kataru to prevent further disturbance in Earth's affairs was the last piece of information that the IM's had garnered from the meeting. Chantal explained the planetary grid system interface technology that would provide mass deactivation of the Rabum Kataru's brain chips. They had no current application on Earth that she could run the interface from and would return shortly to Zain's ship where the sequence could be initiated. No one knew exactly when the Shining Ones would initiate their plans to deal with the Rabum Kataru so Chantal's grid interface option provided extra insurance of the population's safety. The group of IM's thanked her for her persistence in finding a viable solution to enact mass deactivation and bid her leave. Lorne, Maya and Julio met her on her way out of the building and she exchanged warm embraces. Everyone felt great relief that soon the threat that the Rabum Kataru posed would end. "Now get out of here and buy your child her birthday gift," she said to Julio and left the building.

Back on Zain's ship she could not find him and asked Novara to locate him over the Virtual Nav and request his presence. Chantal searched for him with her mind and kept seeing a matrix with flashing lines and finally Zain appeared in their abode kissing his mother on the cheek. Shortly he walked onto the deck where Chantal waited for him and they embraced. She remarked on the delicious scent of wine he had on his breath and he told her about his meeting with Zara and Larina. With great anticipation Chantal and Zain activated the grid system interface and opened a holographic view of Earth. They could see people in their daily activities in different sectors all over the planet and once every person was located by the program a flash of light appeared over the holographic projection indicating successful deactivation of all the implants. "All is well again and thankfully not many even knew that there was a risk so life has not been greatly disturbed," said Chantal.

"Measures to put an end to the legion are being finalized as we speak," replied Zain.

"You know with all that has happened I have not yet had a chance to resign from the CIV. I need some time to contemplate how I want to finalize my departure from my work and wrap up my life on Earth. I am going to spend some time alone at our place now," she said and departed.

Amelatu sat with Diana at the dinner table in the CIV Cooper Point property and served up Italian pasta dishes which he had ordered from a local restaurant. She had been staying there for the time being and Chantal had set Amelatu up in the opposite wing of the house temporarily. The residence was stocked with the best wine that the IM's used to entertain out of town visitors at the house. He opened a bottle of well aged Bordeaux and poured it into crystal goblets embossed with the CIV emblem. The dinner ware was trimmed with the same symbol and etched with gold. CIV Central shone from across Puget Sound; its lights dancing on the water which provided a beautiful view. The dinner was Amelatu's way of making peace with her after the tumultuous history they shared. She scooped garlic prawn sauce over her linguine and studied her dinner companion not quite knowing what to expect from his invitation to share this meal; this was probably the most unusual dinner date she ever had, she thought to herself.

Neither of them excelled at casual conversation but both had relaxed in their demeanor substantially due to their mutual metamorphosis. She noticed the absence of tightness around his jaw and stern look that he usually wore. In his eyes she saw a new lightening of his being. Diana could not help but smile at him and said, "this meal is wonderful thank you for your kind invitation."

"I heard from Chantal that you were integrating into life here and wanted a chance to mend things between us before I moved on," he said simply.

Diana wondered what had caused his transformation but decided not to ask and let him share what he wanted. "I am smitten with the CIV's science group I must admit and have been spending much time there."

"Is there an opportunity for you to stay on and serve the CIV in some way?" He asked as he spooned up a generous portion of pasta onto his plate.

"Nothing definitive but James Edwards, one of the IM's I've befriended here is looking into possibilities on my behalf. How about you, Amelatu any plans you care to share?"

He sat in silence for a moment and collected his thoughts. "I am awaiting further communication about some options but I doubt that I will stay here on Earth. That is all I know for now."

A brilliant, blinding light resembling a nuclear blast filled the night sky and startled them both. Pensively they approached the window shielding their eyes and watched the slowly subsiding light. In his being Amelatu had felt a moment of dread when the light first flashed and then it ebbed away; he knew he had witnessed the demise of the Rabum Kataru's ship that had hovered near Earth and likely the rest of the legion as well. It was as if a last thread that had connected his mind to his former reality burned away. His appetite gone he felt the need to be alone yet *for what?* He decided to make himself stay and begin a new life without looking back.

"What *was* that?" Diana asked.

"I suspect the end of any further threat to your planet," he answered pouring more wine.

She looked to the sky; pockets of light gently receded but still lit the night sky to azure. "What of your people, do you think…" her voice trailed off and she looked into Amelatu's face.

"That is no longer my concern. I was removed from the collective mind by the Shining Ones not long ago," he replied and took a long drink of wine. Please, sit and enjoy the rest of your meal; I'm sure we are safe here," he said.

Knowing Amelatu did not want to discuss the subject further Diana sat down and picked up her glass, "let's drink to new beginnings for both of us." They toasted and finished their meal in a lighter mood.

James rang the door and Diana answered showing him inside; Amelatu had retired to his wing of the residence after dinner. "I wanted to make sure you were alright and let you know that everything is ok after tonight's episode in the sky," he said.

"Was the Rabum Kataru's ship destroyed? That's what Amelatu felt certain had happened."

"We think it has to do with activities of the Shining Ones and likely that's what's happened."

"I'm fine, I had a nice dinner and was just relaxing before retiring," said Diana.

"How about a walk? It is a beautiful night."

"Sure let me get my coat," she answered and James waited for her.

They left the premises and walked down to the beach. My mind has not stopped since the meeting in Vienna; our local IM's who attended gave us the highlights and I have been getting up to speed on all the latest additions to the Unity Network. Fascinating content, have you had a chance to experience some of it?" asked James.

"Not yet, I was working with Atlan in the lab getting updated on your technological platform for mind chip applications that you currently use to download knowledge. I was fitted with mine today but have not yet sampled the experiential programs," she answered.

"We can look at some when we get back if you like."

"I had not planned on that but why not?" Dian answered pulling her coat around her tighter as a cool winter gust blew against her face.

"Here," said James removing his scarf and placing it around Diana's hair. "This should help."

"She began to laugh as the wind blew and tied it under her chin. I feel like I'm eight again; my mother used to do this to me and I hated it."

"Sorry, I didn't meant to bring back any unwanted childhood memories," he yelled through a blast of cold air that hit his face.

Diana began to laugh harder as they attempted to walk against a wind that increased its strength.

"Perhaps we should turn back…" he began to say grabbing hold of her hand. They began to run back down the beach and James tripped over a rock and fell into the water inevitably pulling Diana in with him. She shrieked from the ice cold sea drenching her and James pulled her out as his scarf washed up onto the shore and collected sea foam. "Well that's had it," he said pointing to it and through chattering teeth she faintly laughed again as they quickly headed for the house. Once inside James ran a hot bath for Diana and left a pile of plush towels in the bathroom. "This should restore you, I'm sorry for this mess," he said as his coat dripped all over the floor.

"Oh shut up," she said and grabbed him by the collar effectively wringing more water out of it as she planted a wet kiss on his lips, then abruptly turned and entered the bathroom closing the door in his face. James was left standing in a puddle and a euphoric feeling suffusing his being; *a most paradoxical experience I am having here,* he thought to himself and headed to another room where he could find a change of clothes.

Diana tied up her hair and climbed into a steaming mound of bubbles. The heat warmed her instantly and she lay back, relieved to regain normal body temperature. She felt oddly exhilarated by the entire evening and had obviously developed a fondness for James, she realized. After a while he knocked on the door, "I'm leaving some clothes by the door for you; I don't know your size but they are Chantal's and you appear to be close in build."

"Ok thanks!" she said as she reached behind the door and grabbed the garments. Diana put on the violet turtleneck sweater and black slacks which fit adequately and combed out her hair. Her face glowed from the hot bath and joy she felt as she left the bathroom. She heard noise from the kitchen and walked in just as James finished preparing two cappuccinos for them.

"Here, enjoy a coffee with me. We can toast to warmth," he said handing one to her. "We can have these in the study where we can access Unity Network." They left the kitchen and Diana sat by the fire with their coffee while James turned on the quantum Q and searched for the new content.

Knowing Diana loved traveling between worlds he chose something the he knew she would enjoy. "Here, put on your program activator and we can proceed. I selected something I haven't experienced before but caught my eye that I think you will find interesting also. They both sat back in their chairs and waited for the download to begin. A planet in the Crab Nebula that specialized in advanced space engineering appeared in their mind's eye and they were taken on a virtual tour of various ships including the inside of some models. They both chose to appear in a round version that was made of an alloy which appeared crystalline when powered up; it would glow brightly and change hues before folding space. The entire structure was powered by mind and commands would prompt whatever on board environment or requirements were desired. Diana and James interfaced the program and were able to enjoy an operations and flight simulation. Each traveled to designate star systems that were made available by the navigation feature to allow a first glimpse at other worlds that one day people from Earth would be able to visit. The programs over time would orient potential travelers about the nature of life in other star systems and galaxies and included a component that allowed one to experience some of the frequencies of mind that represented the societies. At that point a wormhole would appear and enhance a heightened trance that would allow people to calibrate the mind over time to the other cultures they observed remotely.

James found himself hovering in the Void as his vibrational frequency climbed and felt totally weightless; his bliss was so great that he stayed in that state till Diana disconnected from the feed and moved from her chair. At that moment a light flashed and his consciousness returned to the room. He removed the activator and stood up. "Wait," he said as she was about to leave the room.

"I didn't want to disturb you."

He took her hand and looked at her. "We've had an interesting evening and I just..." James had no words to finish his sentence; he simply moved her close to him and kissed her. She returned it and they stayed like that for a while, locked in an embrace that was both sensual and explorative as they felt each other's presence.

TWENTY FOUR

People everywhere wondered at the awesome light that filled the night sky so suddenly over the North American sector and watched it recede creating a halo effect. The stars no longer as visible receded into the background of thought of those below. Heightened peace permeated the air and a great enthusiasm had begun to resonate amongst those who had experienced some of the new content placed on the Unity Network as a gift from the Shining Ones. Change had ignited from recent events and like a spark that would grow began to effuse 2020 in an evolution of mind and spirit again. Julio held his daughter's hand as they strolled down Hearts Lane in Evergreen Village; he had just purchased her birthday gift after their dinner outing to celebrate her tenth year of life. Richard saw them approach as he departed the local Tailor. "Any idea who scheduled the fireworks?" He asked.

"I called Amit and he has no idea what has caused this but we suspect this has to do with activities of the Shining Ones," he replied.

"That would explain things."

"Defense is gathering satellite data to determine the source of the event. If there is anything of concern in their findings Amit will contact everyone."

"Daddy, there is a glowing man inside my mind and he is showing me something."

Julio and Richard stopped and looked at Lisa who had her eyes closed and a big smile on her face. "What do you see my angel?" Asked Julio.

"Many people celebrating and happy but some of them are not from here. They have brought gifts that I haven't seen before. I can't describe them I just know what it means. Jena was there with them smiling at me."

Julio looked at Richard and said, "no matter how brilliant I become my daughter never ceases to shower me with blessings that inevitably leave me humble."

She looked thoughtful and said, "some day I will meet other children from worlds that are different but we kids are all the same."

"Ok, but promise to let me tag along, I would love to meet those kids too," said Julio.

"Ok dad," she said and gave him a big hug.

At three o'clock Amelatu woke up to strong vibrations moving through his body and a light passing over his face. He lay still while pictures began to form in his mind. He saw himself moving through a sequence of possibilities where he became actively involved with his former people who were now free in mind the way he had been freed by the Shining Ones. The colonies appeared to be in the flux of change and opportunity for him to reintegrate into a chosen society was being presented. Because of his choice to voluntarily disconnect from his former collective and his experience with diverse groups the Shining Ones were showing him potentials for expanding his gifts in leadership. When the communiqué ended Amelatu's mind raced with the possibilities for his future. He really had no idea what opportunities would present themselves but now he had more than enough to craft a new life. For hours he examined different options of where he would ultimately reside upon his leaving Earth and he finally decided to reunite with his home planet and possibly expand his activities to some of the other worlds as well. He drifted back into a deep sleep and did not awaken again till late morning.

Chantal floated above her rest area and virtual flowers from her mind moved through and around her as she bathed in their scent. She floated higher and light filled the room enveloping her form. In this state she projected her mind through windows that led to worlds of experiences she contemplated having in her near future. Some included higher, non physical learning and some were places she had a great curiosity about visiting where minds like hers created every moment both individually and collectively. She observed many such places and fell in love with the diversity of expression enlightened beings constructed realities with. Endless the possibilities and choice was her key that unlocked whatever she wanted.

Zain appeared at their abode and his eyes filled with a dancing mirage of Chantal's fading dreams that had filled their space. He sat in a large chair and lit a cigar observing them and decided to participate by creating within the remnants something new. These he sent back to Chantal who received them to her delight laced with the scent of tobacco. She would build upon these thought constructs and sent them back to Zain. For a while they engaged from a distance this way till a glittering, ruby colored door hovered before him and then a golden key circled his head slowly. He reached out to touch it with his light body and as the ruby door opened, he flew through it and saw Chantal all aglow smiling at him. She pointed at a vortex that she had created and moved through it quickly leaving him behind. Smiling he followed her and shed his light body for a finer frequency that oscillated in liquid gold. There he found her again and they danced as one to the sound of a million chimes at such a high pitch that varied with their movement in the cosmos of her mind's creation. Through her third eye she sent a construct that unfolded into living geometries that they became as they descended into slower, violet blue flashes appearing in the new reality. There the dance resumed and electric light moved through tiny pathways of their lattice bodies. Small, morphing shapes combined into larger structures that they flew through and rippled to the touch with a glow. After a while they slowly descended back through the levels and hovered together in the light plane of their abode before descending completely into their more solid forms.

Amit awoke early as usual and caught a peach extravaganza of sunrise that filled him with joy and renewal for his day at CIV headquarters. Forgetting to comb his hair he drove down the freeway and grabbed a steamed milk on his way to work. Results from the satellite scan showed that a massive explosion had taken place in space that had resulted in the previous night's anomalous sky. No debris was recorded; whatever exploded appeared to simply vaporize and calm had returned. They would continue to monitor the area around Earth's orbit but no further activity of unusual nature was observed. Amit heard James and Romy on the phonecom raving about the new content on Unity Network; feedback from the public had poured in non stop and the system was nearing overload processing it fast enough to relay in coherence to CIV members world wide. He peeked in on Maya knowing that she would be thrilled and observed her with flushed cheeks working wildly to amass data. He decided to leave her in peace and proceeded to his office.

Chantal loaded her car with gifts for all the IM's that she had purchased and headed for her workplace. On her way she met John at a stoplight and waved to him. "I'm just leaving the lab with new data created from inspiration the science group brainstormed all night after playing with some of the new chip material. None of us could sleep so we decided to work and came up with something extra ordinary; new anti—gravity models that can be applied to the automotive industry."

"Sounds exciting see you at the office," she replied as the light changed and she drove on. Once there she took all the gifts into the meeting room and arranged them around the table where everyone would convene shortly. Chantal made one last trip to her car and picked up the pet carrier with Morocco in it. She went back inside the building and headed for James' office. "Hi," she said and walked in. "I hope I'm not disturbing you but I need a really big favor."

"Hey, how are you?" He said greeting her with a warm embrace.

"Never better but you are the first to officially hear that I am resigning from the CIV today."

"Wow, that's a shocker."

"Well, now that everything is resolved and you are all safe again it's time for me to make my journey elsewhere."

He knew that she had been involved 'elsewhere' a lot lately and that explained her moving on. "I understand. Care to share your future plans?"

"God, if you only knew; infinite possibilities I have contemplated and am crafting a fabulous life. I also am involved with someone extraordinary and very happy," she said wanting him to know the truth.

"I seem to have stepped into something of a similar nature that looks promising."

"Have you now?" She had not looked in on James and his news came as a surprise. "Any one I know?"

He pondered his answer for a moment and replied, "I want to give this a go for a while first before I say anymore about it."

This was definitely new for James as he usually confided openly most important events in his life. "I understand and am really happy for you."

"What's he doing here?" He asked bending down and taking Morocco out of the pet carrier. The cat started to purr as James scratched him behind the ear.

"Well I know you have a fondness for him and I haven't been around enough to give him proper company that he has grown so accustomed to.

Lately whenever I return he has been a bit sad faced and I was hoping that you would welcome this furry friend into your life."

James laughed. "So you are gracing me with your favorite friend. Truly a blessing and yes I'll adopt him. He's likely to get fat though since I tend to spoil everyone I care about."

"He's already fat which you will experience when he pounces on your stomach during your most luxurious moments of rest. Then you'll think twice about fattening him any more."

James touched his firm abdominal muscles and said, "I think I'm fit to provide an ample springboard for the little fellow, not to worry."

"Thank you, I really appreciate you doing this. Have you seen Diana today?" she asked as she turned to leave his office.

"Yes, she was in to see Richard this morning and is officially being welcomed to join the science group which she has fallen in love with. He is planning to announce it this afternoon at our meeting."

"Fantastic! Now *that* is great news."

"Try her in the lounge I have a feeling she might be there."

"Ok thanks," said Chantal and headed over there to find Diana. She found her reclining with her eyes closed smoking a long cigarette.

"Hello," said Chantal greeting her.

"Ah the mystery IM returns," she replied sitting up.

"Mystery IM?"

"Don't you know that's what they call you around here."

"I suppose I've earned that. How are you I have heard only exciting things to do with your involvement here."

Diana smiled the most radiant smile Chantal had ever seen on her face. "I am fantabulous if there is such a word."

"Well your day is about to get better," she said taking her keys out of her purse.

"I am resigning from the CIV today and wrapping things up here in Olympia. I want you to have these; they're the keys to my house and car; I won't need them where I'm going."

"Are you serious?"

"Extremely," she answered with a grin.

"I don't know what to say, my god thank you. I was going to look for a place because I did not want to overstay my welcome at the CIV residence...."

"Well now you have one. It is furnished but do what you like with it. I will have everything transferred in your name by days end. James knows where it is and will take you there."

Diana embraced Chantal and said simply, "thank you."

At the meeting Chantal presented her gifts and bid everyone goodbye, not sure when she would see them again and was excused from giving formal notice that would have required her to stay on longer. Samantha Rogers had been assisting Maya with Global Communications and had always been interested in Chantal's portfolio. She had aided Chantal greatly in that regard over the past couple of years and everyone knew that she would be a wonderful replacement as IM of Education and Cultural Evolution. At the meeting Chantal noticed the way Diana and James stole glances at each other and it was obvious to her who his mystery lady was. An odd pairing likely to succeed and Chantal could see how the two of them would compliment each other.

She left the building and turned to look at the entrance one last time. Naked trees surrounded it and would grow new leaves soon; the courtyard always bloomed with the most profuse colors that the landscapers changed each year creating an inviting place to sit between hours of daily work. Chantal blew a kiss blessing the place where she found so much joy over the years, turned and left Earth totally free of all attachments and possessions.

A clear sky created a vibrant, blue backdrop over Evergreen Village as citizens conducted daily commerce and strolled through the area. Matthew Vanderhoof walked into his tailor shop and put down the crumpled, brown bag containing a bruised sandwich which he had dropped on the street on his way back to work. He ran a hand through his graying hair and opened a box of raw silk, Greco vanilla colored fabric. He had ordered it over the Network and if arrived within a day. He stared at it remembering a moment he had experienced after his inward journey during a 'Creative Paths' sample application meditation. He had hovered into a sunlit room that reminded him of the Mediterranean basin and visions of an innovative spring line of business clothing had flashed in his mind. A completely different array of cloth would be required to craft his creations; hence ten boxes filled the back space of his work area containing a most unusual inventory. His wife who took care of the accounting had asked for an explanation as to why he had spent more than double the spring budget. Unable to provide an answer he promised to take her to dinner and reassured her that business would triple for them in the approaching season.

Matthew worked through the afternoon arranging rolls of fabric, assisting various customers as they stopped in to pick up orders and have fittings done.

Richard Lonesbay walked in for his three o'clock appointment to be fitted for a new suit. Matthew was at least a head shorter than Richard, stout and usually wore his favorite assortment of dated Italian cashmere sweaters with slacks. He dressed humbly but had genius at crafting the most beautiful garments for his clients. Richard was a long standing client and had Matthew sew all of his clothing for him. "I have some new ideas I want to experiment with today," he said with a thick, Nordic accent.

Richard being somewhat conservative in dress and used to having a standard issue of suits all in the same style did not fully register Matthew's intent. He was somewhat surprised when the industrious little tailor began draping raw silks and a new, light weight, exotic fabric in deep plum over him. "You were not kidding when you said 'experiment,'" said Richard a little unsure about Matthew's selection.

The tailor just smiled and kept working; he had such a long history of enthralling his customers it never crossed his mind that his eclectic, new line would not be as eagerly purchased as all the rest of his designs. "Don't worry; you will love what I am creating for you as always."

Richard remained silent as Mathew matched several beautiful, pale colors of raw silk that would serve as shirts with two fabrics; the plum that was a new kind of weave featuring tiny braided pattern through the body and a rich, moss green, thick cotton with a slight sheen. The selections looked stunning against Richard's medium complexion and silver hair. "The new designs have no collars, just a square line at the neck and the jacket flows with a loose but tailored fit. The fabric is very light weight but supremely durable and the weave has a slight give to it that moves with you." Matthew showed Richard his drawings which the conservative IM could not help but greatly admire.

"You realize what is going to happen if I wear your new designs; I will become the fashion icon at the CIV, everyone will be in here ordering these," said Richard as he smoothed his beard.

"Well you are a little old to be my top model but I will accept the advertising benefits nonetheless."

"Alright, Matthew carry on with your creations and call me when the suits are ready," said Richard. His wife had wanted him to update his wardrobe and likely would be overjoyed with his new look, he thought to himself half smiling as he left the store.

Nearby at the park a family stood on a little bridge above the duck pond; colored lights had begun to appear in the air before them. Swirls of plasma in rose and violet moved and orb shaped forms danced in front of the children who laughed and squealed in delight. A little girl reached out to touch one and within the luminous globe shapes began to appear. "Look mama, a starfish! We were learning about the oceans at school today," she exclaimed. They watched as different objects manifested within the orb before it floated away and disappeared. A toddler ran down the gravel path chasing a rose colored orb and lost her pink hair band while her mother ran after her laughing. The child's fine, golden locks bounced around her face as she reached with all her might to touch the phenomenon that out paced her. She finally stopped and watched with enchanted eyes as it floated away.

James left headed down the CIV building steps carrying Morocco in the pet carrier and stopped suddenly; he blinked a few times and looked at the air in front of him. A fine mist had formed a few feet away and swirled in a circular motion. Curious he approached it and reached out with his fingers. As soon as he touched it an opening appeared and particles of light began to form into space craft and images that he had experienced the previous night while running the download off Unity Network. Now new pictures appeared and finally a woman's face smiled at him before the plasmic apparition faded away. He did not recognize the being whose face had appeared but he just knew that she was from one of the places he had observed elsewhere. James experienced a longing to visit some of these other worlds and looked forward to a time when through the endeavors of the space program this would be made possible. On the other hand he also contemplated the nature of Chantal's mobility through space time; she had increased her level of supernatural abilities of late. As he walked to his car he decided to download a Master's Series experiential training program that Sacred Rose Mystery School had recently developed for the public. Some of the IM's had tried them and said that they had intense experiences that heightened their consciousness. Bi— location and teleportation required an individual to attain an increase in frequency threshold that would result in a combination of levitation and remoteness of mind. This could provide one to experience movement of mass through time.

Diana ran out of the building after James, "wait!" she called. "I need directions to Chantal's house. She left me the keys when she left."

"Sure, I can give you a ride if you like but first I want to stop at my place which is on the way and drop off her cat which I inherited today."

"He's cute," she replied stroking his head with her fingers between the bars of the container. James drove up to his house and dropped the cat off then continued to Chantal's house with Diana. When they arrived James noticed that the whole place had been redecorated; he had no idea when Chantal had found the time to do all this or even hire someone but it was like stepping into a completely different house. Gone were her favorite antiques and rich colors; instead she had decorated the place with retro items from the 50's mixed with ultra modern pieces. The kitchen had retro, powder pink appliances with black counter tops and black tile floor trimmed with fine, pink borders. James turned hanging halogen lights on that emitted a rose light. The thread from which they hung glowed with the same. Throughout the entire place she had combined most eclectic colors and designs. The work area had been wall papered with brushed silver and all the furniture made of a semi—transparent material that had opalescence to it. Diana was obviously enthralled with the place as she walked through it. She sat at the work station and touched the table. "Wow, I had no idea Chantal had this kind of taste."

"Actually, neither did I. A few days ago this place was totally different; all antiques and bohemian style."

"You're kidding."

"No, I haven't a clue when she found the time to do all this. It's amazing."

"This décor is me. I don't know how she knew but I could not have chosen better. I feel like this is my home, totally." Diana noticed a round, Wine colored box on the table and lifted the slender, shiny lid. Inside and array of cigarettes had been provided. The first layer had long ones all silver filter to tip. The others were an array of colors including black with a fine, gold band around them. Oil floated around one side of the edge of the box encased within a built in, arced removable lighter. The other side had a built in ash receptacle. "Oh god, this will not bode well for my love of smoking. I was going to quit, forget that now these are too amazing to pass up."

"Chantal told me something once that made rational sense; she said that there is a way to consume any product mindfully so that the power of your intent moves within the body and causes the substance to deliver a desired result. This works with foods, beverages and even things like tobacco. She would say simply know that well being occurs when you smoke, the lungs are strengthened and you simply do not observe any toxins. This way you master effects on your body with your mind and never have to avoid anything that you want to enjoy. There is a great program on developing the power of intent in higher vibrations of mind that I can loan you. I experimented with it on beverages and had much increased energy through the day," said James.

"Sounds interesting. I'd like to pick up some groceries and try the new kitchen out. Want to stay for dinner?" Sure, I'll go with you then I can get cat food and whatever else I need to take care of my new furry buddy." James and Diana locked up the house and proceeded to the local grocer to make their purchases.

Upon their return James helped Diana to stock her pantry and prepared a speedy steak marinade. "Beer does the trick in half the time; these should be ready to grill in about two hours. Care for some wine while we wait?"

"Absolutely. Let me put some music on. Do you like Jazz? I perused the network and purchased a bunch this afternoon on my lunch break."

"Sure, anything."

Diana selected some classic tunes by Louis Armstrong and lit a cigarette in the living room. She reclined on the sofa with her feet up while James finished in the Kitchen. He brought their wine in and sat with her for a moment. "Want a drag?" she asked handing him her cigarette.

"Well I don't smoke but oh what the heck," he said and took an inhale. The unexpected hit to his lungs made him pause and he began to cough through a manufactured smile."

Diana smirked and lit another leaving him with his. "It's ok put it out if you want."

"Just a minute I'm about to master this and then that will be the end of my smoking foray," he said and with concerted focus took another puff creating smoke rings. "There, my school backyard shady past has surfaced. I ventured and tried one of these with a friend who had raided his mother's purse at age eleven. We hid beneath some stairs at day's end and took our first puff."

"Did the two of you develop a habit?" She asked playfully.

"No, he said. When I got home my mother lectured me while I brushed my teeth vigorously to cleanse my breath before my father got home."

As the two of them drank their wine and a favorite song of Diana's came on. They began to dance close in the centre of the living room, warm from the drink and ambiance that they created. Diana closed her eyes and leaned against James's' shoulder and when she opened them again she saw something extraordinary; a holograph of The All Stars playing in what appeared be a Cuban nightclub had formed. "James, look!"

He turned and saw what she was pointing to. It was faint to him at first but then he also saw the hologram forming in the air. They both watched the scene and then after a while it faded. It was as if they had moved in the moment of their dance so richly into the period when the music had been created that somehow a window had formed into another dimension. "This is like the quantum brain applications coming to life and the second time I experienced unusual phenomenon today," James said and told Diana about what he had seen leaving the CIV building earlier in the day before she caught up to him.

"I wonder if others have also had these experiences. Should be an interesting day at work tomorrow," she replied.

"Perhaps another glass of wine?" he offered.

"Please."

They continued their visit and James got ready to depart at the end of the evening. "Would you like to stay the night? It's late and I can set you up in the spare room," she offered.

"It's alright I want you to enjoy your new home and have some time without me overstaying my welcome. I had a fantastic evening and will host next time," he said embracing her tightly and giving her a final kiss before leaving.

"Alright, goodnight and make sure you turn on your auto cruise."

"Will do." He said and left.

TWENTY FiVE

Amelatu awoke early the next morning and went into town to have breakfast. On his way to a small eatery he stopped in front of Helios Books and glanced in the store front window. Something there had caught his eye and he proceeded inside. He picked up a virtu book with the Andromeda galaxy on the cover and took it over to the reading area. Once seated he opened it and watched as different sections opened through the vastness of spaced and projected different star systems. Something about what he was watching magnetized his mind and he felt a familiarity with what he was seeing suffuse him. Moving to the final projection a being appeared made of golden oscillating particles and he began to receive a transmission. He relaxed and closed his eyes as a beam of light formed around him and the familiar dissolve of teleportation occurred. Amelatu emerged within a circular space high above ground that had windows on all sides. A golden being stood before him and they moved outside to a large expanse of blue lawn and one bench but otherwise this place was curiously deserted. The being motioned for him to sit and created a holographic collage showing Amelatu the state of affairs here on his original home planet after the people had been disconnected from the Rabum Kataru's collective mind.

A tall female with multicolored skin appeared and approached him; he had never seen anyone like her he thought as intense, metallic eyes held his gaze. "I am Larina," she said in his native tongue. "You are the only surviving member of the Legion and all the colonies that we were able to save are going through re—adjustment similar to what you have experienced. A stable governing body needs to be established that is a marked departure from the ways of the past. Your leadership experience is desired at this time by the Shining Ones to assist in the formation of a planetary council. We have identified others who have great potential as well but we whish to know if you desire to take this task on." She said.

"Yes, I feel this is the right place for me to return to and I would like to see my home flourish," he answered.

"Excellent. There is a program that we have virtually interfaced and tested with the level of consciousness here that will assist your people in stabilization of a progressive society and reconnect them to their spiritual heritage. It involves the dispensation of technologies of mind similar to what you have sampled on Earth. Please experience what I am describing," said Larina and fitted Amelatu with a small device that downloaded the details of the new planetary council, educational platform and social reform. This program is merely to assist the transition and surely you will customize it over time with your people. Once finished and highly impressed with the package that had been created Larina departed and the gold being transported him to the central metropolitan area of his home world. A vast expanse of unusual, curved architecture in deep colors that arced to the heavens with smooth, snakelike, black trim rolled across the miles as far as the eye could see. Fair and medium complexioned people with dark skin and eyes made up the population; this had been one of the main home bases of the Rabum Kataru and would now be a world of influence upon others because of its dense population and heightened interest in the development of technology. Amelatu knew the delicate balance between advancement of this nature and maintaining a level of consciousness that embraced unified freedom of expression without the abuse of power. He felt a surge of anticipation fill him upon his return because of the potential of his home planet to evolve in a new model of mind and spirit that would affect all the other colonies favorably. The Shining Ones had stabilized the planetary grid with uplifting frequencies that helped to open the heart centre and provided information about the period of change to come. Continued input from the new council was needed on an ongoing basis to oversee a smooth transition. Due to the size and importance of this planet's population the Shining Ones would more closely monitor the progress of the transition. All this had been relayed to Amelatu in his earlier orientation.

He walked into the tall building that housed the new planetary council which had been renamed the Council of Shiimti; translating 'House Where the Wind of Life is Breathed In.' He rode a bullet shaped lift with an oval window that allowed one to see the city to the top floor and was escorted by a female assistant into the central chamber. Amelatu walked into a room with a narrowing, cone shaped ceiling and pale, brown walls. Torch lights that formed a solid ring around the room provided ambient light that warmed the complexions of his new fellow council members. A tall woman approached him and led him to the table. "I am Nina and these are the other representatives that have been assembled," she said and introduced each of them to Amelatu. They spent the rest of the day creating adjunct policy to the planetary development guidelines provided by the Shining Ones and then hosted a dinner provided by local suppliers of exotic meat and seafood dishes. That night was the true beginning of Amelatu's life for after the festivities with his council he reunited with his family and settled into his new home.

Atlan walked into the science lab at ten o'clock the next morning and saw John in an animated discussion with two other scientists, Gregory Vance and Tim Reed. Curious as always to see what brain storming his colleagues were up to he approached their table. "What's up?" He asked as he stood sipping his coffee.

They all looked at him with conspiratorial faces and Tim said to the others, "what do you think, should we let him in on it?"

The others smiled and looked Atlan over. "I suppose we can trust him," said John.

"We'll need to take a drive," Gregory said mysteriously.

Atlan could tell they were enjoying their secretive little scenario and agreed to accompany them to the CIV hanger. On the way there his colleagues were strangely silent till Atlan could not stand the obvious 'mystery act' they were perpetuating on his behalf and said, "ok what's going on; we've driven for three miles and you three have not said a word."

Timothy turned from the front seat and said, "its best you sit tight and see for yourself when we arrive."

"Fine," he replied.

They pulled if front of the deserted building that housed the CIV's personal jet and got out of the car. Together the four of them walked into the hanger and walked to the back where a smooth, aerodynamic space craft sat. It was a basic saucer made of a matte silver alloy that was not common to Earth. The design was simple, streamline without much detail and the underneath area produced a phosphorescent light when Gregory turned on. "This is my baby; a project I have been working on all year. I couldn't get it off the ground till yesterday when I took a covert trip around the world. I was of course detected but the speed at which I traveled easily out maneuvered our tracking devices. It is meant to be a surprise so I had to bend a few aviation rules in order to test it," said Gregory.

"My god, I thought we were years away from creating something like this," said Atlan.

"I know, so did we and we didn't believe Gregory at first when he said he had nailed an anti gravity propulsion system that actually worked at such a high level," said Tim.

"Come on board and see the inside," said Gregory.

They boarded the space craft and admired the thorough design that accommodated five aeronauts. The craft was not large but had an adequate observation area and a basic console that looked simple in construct. "I had multiple breakthroughs lately after…"

"Yes we know, Unity Network new programs," said Atlan.

"That's right. The first thing that happened that scrambled my marbles was an alchemical event when I was playing around with alloys; steel to be precise about six months ago. I wanted to find something that was ultra light weight that would compliment the design of this vessel. Upon repeated failed attempts I finally melted steel and played around with it for hours. Not getting anywhere I finally sat bored, observing a boiling cauldron that I had melted down and visualized what I had wanted to find as I stared at it. Lastly before retiring for the night at the insane hour of four am I poured the last batch into molds I had prepared and left the lab. Upon my return the next morning when I lifted the metal out of the molds it to my amazement it weighed about one quarter of its original mass. I was shocked to say the least and had no explanation at the time for what occurred but obviously my persistent nature had affected the steel on a quantum level and altered the subatomic properties. Sure enough upon testing I discovered an alien alloy that is not found anywhere on our planet. Having now created the new atomic structure I was easily able to reproduce more with our current technology. I am calling this new alloy Argatonium. It is as strong and durable as steel but much lighter weight and can be used for the aviation and auto industry."

Atlan touched the alloy of the saucer and marveled at Gregory's creation. "What about the propulsion system of this thing, how did you ever create it so fast?" He asked.

"Well like everyone else interested in anti gravity I messed around with Tessla coils, bulbs etc. till I created my own version of an engine that creates a powerful torsion electromagnetic field with an ambient, ceramic self contained system. The motor is silent and can propel this craft at light speed. One day we will fold space time, I'm sure of it and Diana has experience in that domain. All that would need to occur is a blend of time travel combined with aniti—gravity and I am eager to work with her on progressing space flight."

The three scientists peered at Atlan. He looked at them wondering what the heck was up now. "Are up for a little deviant maneuver?"

He looked at each of them and being the conservative one of the group said cautiously, "what do you have in mind?"

"Just say yes or no," said Gregory.

"Jesus, do I have a choice?"

"Why do you think we're asking?" Said John.

Atlan saw mischief in their middle aged faces that was truly contagious. *I must be loosing my mind,* he thought to himself. Feeling like a schoolboy again he said, "what the heck whatever crazy idea you have in mind I'm definitely in."

"Then fasten your restraints," replied Gregory. Suddenly the music of Wolfgang Amadeus Mozart began to fill the space craft as Gregory powered it up. "hold tight we're about to break aviation policy again," said Gregory as the back hangar door opened and the fine tuned stealth craft lifted off and hit light speed silently gliding along a coordinated projectory straight to CIV headquarters. The flight was unlike anything the three scientists had ever experienced. The quiet power of this craft was truly inspiring in indescribable ways. Gregory landed it in the centre of the orchard at the back of the building.

"Wow," was all Atlan could say.

Gregory could not contain his grin as they left the craft and watched Amit run towards them with the intelligence team and Julio in the rear. "Mamasita," exclaimed Julio. "That is one mother of a mover. We saw something that looked like it was about to hit the building and thought that our end was in sight."

Amit just stared at the craft and automatically protocol over took him and he yelled, "Jesus Christ, do you have any idea what you are doing? My heart almost stopped when I saw this thing approaching!" he exclaimed.

"It's alright Amit, calm down. Gregory wanted to surprise everyone. Look we have space flight accomplished; he did it he has created an interstellar craft that can hit light speed," said Atlan.

"I received reports yesterday from satellite planetary surveillance about an anomalous object traveling at speeds far surpassing the sound barrier that we could not adequately track. I lost sleep over this!"

The four scientists surrounded Amit and led him back into the building. "Copious drinks on us at Abraxas later tonight, we promise, said John."

"Absolutely and for your agents as well," said Tim and Gregory eyeing the serious group of intelligence officers who did not quite know what to make of the situation.

"Fine," said Amit brusquely. "I hope you are here to inform us of your covert activities."

"Yes that's the idea," said Gregory as he put his arm around Amit and they walked together back to the CIV building. "I wanted to wait till this ship was in full operation before I divulged the painstaking work I have been doing after hours for the past year. I apologize for creating a security concern but I wanted to test this craft before I divulged the technology. If I had told you it would have spoiled the surprise."

"God, I do need a drink," said Amit running a hand through his thick, perpetually disheveled hair.

Julio had stayed behind and boarded the craft. His hands ran over the console and he reclined in one of the seats. *I could get used to this,* he thought to himself before exiting and returning to work.

After Gregory's presentation which was broadcast world wide the IM's gathered outside and lovingly examined the craft which they named 'Destiny Blue.' Everyone that night drifted to a sleep filled with visions of explorations deeper than had ever been undertaken by human kind into the vast cosmos that so many races shared.

Morning broke through Julio's window and shone on his face awakening him. He prepared Lisa's lunch and drove her to school. "Daddy I feel so distracted, I watched the broadcast yesterday at nana's after school and could barely sleep. I kept thinking about those children I saw from another world and know I will meet them soon. I don't know how but something so wonderful is happening I am very distracted inside myself," she said.

"I know what you mean I feel excited about all the possibilities too," he said as he kissed her and said goodbye.

It was true Julio had also stayed up late thinking about Destiny Blue and what it would be like to fly the craft. He arrived at the CIV to a group walking on air, literally as they went about their work. He ran into Maya who hugged him so hard she almost knocked the wind out of him. "I am finally *almost* caught up on all the rave feedback about the additions to Unity Network," she said. "I met with James and the increase in people experiencing phenomenon has continued. It seems common people everywhere are experiencing vision into other dimensions all around them. Photographic images have been captured world wide and we have created a global resource where people can share their experiences."

"Amazing, my daughter has been up late seeing all kinds of interesting things outside her bedroom window."

"Children are so in tune, they are usually the first to pick up on change approaching aren't they?"

"I would have to agree with you," said Julio.

In the science lab members of the team worked on various tasks and assembling data. Gregory drank a hot beverage and downed his late breakfast as he studied and mapped coordinates to different star systems in the local universe. This had been a side project he had been compiling information on for the past six months. His fingers slipped as he bit into his muffin and he inadvertently ended up producing a visual of the rose nebula. Mesmerized he watched the gaseous, pink tones move across the hologram. This was not a coordinate he had paid much attention to but the beauty of it was truly stunning. Completely anomalous from the usual galactic data display the hologram began to zoom in and show a select star system within the coordinates he was viewing. The mean distance and projectory appeared mathematically and quickly he entered and saved them. Then the program zoomed in to a select planet and he began to view the topography; it was inhabited by a race of blue skinned beings and was a veritable paradise of lush vegetation, sapphire blue oceans with white sands. A transmission began to somehow flow via Unity Network from the planet; it provided information on landing platforms for visitors and flight path coordinates. Gregory did not quite understand how or why but he had been given the equivalent to an invitation to visit this world that was simply logged as B54232. His hand shook as he printed off a copy of the message and he gathered his colleagues. "Look at this," he said as he shared the information. The other scientists gathered around him and studied the data he had printed.

"Are you sure this isn't a hoax?" Asked Atlan.

"I'm not sure of anything right now but will do what I can to verify this information," replied Gregory.

"If it isn't the implications certainly are interesting to contemplate," said John.

"I agree and personally have a feeling this is authentic. Leave me with it for the day and I will let you know what I find out," replied Gregory.

The team resumed work and Gregory downloaded every space information package he had in order to verify the information that had mysteriously appeared. After working for several hours and finding nothing helpful he resorted to plugging into a brain chip 'cosmic voyage' simulation. He had accessed it briefly before but never participated to its completion. This time he did and found some useful information about the star system that had appeared on his holographic viewer earlier in the day. The planet B54232 was on the program and indeed appeared to be life sustaining. In an unused, quiet office he lay reclined while immersed in his virtual trip. A wormhole appeared and he used all his focus to trance deeply enough that for the first time he rushed through it and felt as if his whole being had dissolved. Suspended in space time he willfully concentrated on the planet of inquiry and began to move swifter than light to the precise location. He appeared on a shore where a child greeted him. "Hello, from whence do you come?" she asked telepathically in a frequency of universal understanding that was beyond words.

"Earth in the Milky Way galaxy, far away from your star system," he answered.

"We have many visitors here," she replied.

"So you welcome those who arrive by craft?" he asked deciding to take a chance.

"Yes, there is a flow of visitors from many places, even other universes. Do you have friends who want to visit us?" She asked.

"A group of us received a message revealing the coordinates to your world and we are new to space flight," he answered.

"Then you will make your journey?"

Gregory smiled. "If all your people are as hospitable as you then chances are yes we will."

The girl smiled, "You will love it here."

Gregory faded back to his body and opened his eyes. He knew he had nothing solid to prove his experience but for him it was enough to take a chance and make the journey. Convincing the CIV was another matter. Likely the council would want to take a vote on the issue but he needed time to contemplate how he would broach the issue.

Julio purchased fried chicken and home cut fries for dinner and picked up Lisa from her nana's house after work. They sat at the kitchen table and ate while she animatedly told him about her day at school. "So many of the kids created virtual pictures of orbs and moving lights that we've seen. We spent half the day sharing experiences and sent them to other schools through the Network. Other kids had also posted stuff," she said.

"I saw some of the phenomenon today that has been appearing; amazing.

"Daddy, I never got a chance to tell you but I had a strange dream last night. I was on a beach with very white sand on a world that has a rose sun and pink sky. There were kids with blue skin playing by the shore and one girl made me a necklace with the prettiest sea shells I have ever seen. I watched the sun set there and in the sky pink swirls with lots of colored stars appeared. I don't know if it was a real place but I have never had a dream like that before. It felt more real than any other I've had."

As she spoke Julio saw in his mind's eye everything that she described. A quickening occurred within his being and he said, "Pumpkin, I have a feeling the dream was real."

"I think so too daddy."

Julio was restless the rest of the night; something was brewing and he could not shake a feeling of anticipation. Of what he did not yet know but he hoped he would find out soon to get a better understanding of his restless anticipation. Little did he know that the answer would arrive sooner than he expected.

Gregory paced through the science lab nervously. "What time is it?" he asked Atlan.

"Half an hour later then the last time you asked. Relax; the results of the vote should be in by later this afternoon."

Earlier in the day he had presented the information about B54232 in the Rose Nebula and Richard had shared the information with the world CIV. Ultimately a space flight to his desired destination was a local sector issue that would have to be decided by the IM's. Most were surprised by Gregory's suggestion to venture so far away from the local galaxy and were hesitant to approve such a mission due to the lack of concrete confirmation of the initial message he had received. Some speculated that the contact had been made by the Shining Ones but without means to reach them they could not verify that theory. Gregory had been adamant that he knew the invitation was authentic. At a point where frustration for Gregory had begun to ensue due to a lack of agreement between IM's Julio had spoken up and shared the dream that his daughter had the previous night. Clearly the world that she had described matched the planet that Gregory had researched and her experience added to the possibility that he was correct in his conclusion about the planet welcoming visitors from Earth. Gregory added that though seemingly far at light speed a crew of five would likely reach their destination within five days. That silenced the IM's and they agreed to weigh the decision and get back to him.

At four o'clock Richard summoned Gregory to his office and announced that the IM's had voted in favor of supporting a journey off planet to the Rose Nebula. Now what remained was the selection of the crew that would accompany him. "You made it by two votes but we decided to go ahead. This is a risky venture since you have barely tested your craft but what maiden voyage of this caliber does not have an element of risk? I don't know who you have in mind to make the flight with you but the CIV has agreed to let you select your crew. You should know however that I was approached by Julio who is avidly interested in accompanying you," he said.

Gregory knew that prior to joining the CIV Julio had years of experience in piloting military craft before the great cataclysms. He had not thought of him at all as a potential crew member but he definitely had some qualifications that would make him a reasonable choice. Truthfully Gregory was so relieved that his mission had been approved that he was more than happy to include Julio at Richard's request. "I will be selecting and orienting my crew over the next few days and as I indicated at the meting we will test Destiny Blue around our solar system prior to final departure to B54232, he answered."

Exalted with his success Gregory left Richard's office and headed back to the lab to deliver the good news to his colleagues.

TWENTY SiX

Preparations for the test flight of Destiny Blue ensued over the course of the next week and Gregory fine tuned the ship's navigation system. It would be calibrated after the flight out of the Earth's atmosphere but he knew that he had designed a superior system and was confident that there would be no problems. A European company had been contracted to design their flight suits which were simple but could maintain a comfortable range in body temperature below zero degrees. Gregory's approved crew consisted of himself, Julio, Tim, Diana and one other astronaut who had piloted space shuttles in the old timeline. There had been no flights since the great cataclysms due to the abandonment of inferior design of the old shuttles. On board conditions of Destiny Blue were designed to be constant and required far less training and adjustment than the technology of the past. Mainly the crew spent time orienting themselves with the navigation system and engine specifications.

When the space suits finally arrived fittings ensued and the crew was outfitted in garments of light weave, elasticity and state of the art temperature modulation. Finally the morning of the test flight arrived and at eight AM with the world watching over Unity Network the crew departed for their maiden flight through the local solar system. As expected the journey was flawless and created relief and excitement about the mission to the Rose

Nebula that would be initiated within three days. Data on the local planets had been gathered over the years with enhanced rover shuttles that were self piloted and instruments collected photos, soil samples etc. that were transmitted via satellite back to Earth. No information had been gathered yet beyond the local solar system so this trip would herald great opportunity to amass data vital to a greater understanding of organic and sentient life elsewhere.

James and Diana had enjoyed an Asian dinner and she sat in her space suit smoking a cigarette. "You definitely look off world in that thing," he said.

"Don't get used to seeing me in it. This thing is supposed to modulate body temperature flawlessly but after two glasses of wine I'm heating up a little."

"Must be my company," he said.

She smiled at him and went into her bedroom to change. She emerged in a pair of shorts and a t—shirt. "God that's better," she said.

"I'm not allowed to smoke on board so I'm enjoying my last cigarette before I leave," she said as she lit another.

James had studied everything he could find about the Rose Nebula and where Diana would be traveling to in the morning. He was truly overjoyed for her but in his gut there was some nervousness because of the great distance that she would be journeying. She had noticed the change in his mood and he finally admitted that he was a bit concerned for her safety.

"Well if you never see me again I've had a fabulous time getting to know you she said holding a glass of wine and putting her arms around him. In fact I think it's time I get to know you a little better," she said pulling him towards the bedroom.

James blushed but could not help but follow. They had dated for a few weeks now and had made a strong friendship bond but in his nature he was so considerate and respectful of women he had not wanted to push himself on her. Getting over Chantal he also wanted to be sure that he had a foundation of compatibility before he launched into anything serious with Diana.

Giddy from wine she pulled him onto the bed and started to laugh as he fell on top of her. He tickled her sides and she squirmed laughing more, her face contorted and flushed. "Stop it! She protested and finally he did and kissed her with surprising sensuality. Once he made up his mind there was no stopping him. That night was an event that Diana would not easily forget and that she thought of often as she peered into space over the days of her ensuing journey.

Julio tucked his daughter into bed and looked into her deep, brown eyes that mirrored his own. "Daddy I am so excited for you," she said. "I had more dreams about the place you are going to visit. I wish you could take me with you."

"Me too and maybe one day you will experience a field trip with your class into space, wouldn't that be something?"

"Yes," she said dreamily and yawned.

He kissed her on the forehead and said, "good night Pumpkin" as he turned off her light and left the room.

Julio checked his supply list and prepared everything he would need for the morning. He would drop Lisa off at her nanas early and she had agreed to take her to school. The flight was scheduled at seven am and he had a feeling that the crew would be up early in anticipation of the journey that they would be making. In the middle of the night Lisa sat up in bed; she had another dream but this time when she visited the children in another world her father was there holding her hand. She lay back in bed and tried to reconcile that he was leaving without her and it had to be that way but something about that felt very wrong. Lisa tossed and turned, finally falling back asleep.

Gregory and his crew assembled at the CIV hangar at six thirty the next morning. Diana arrived after everyone else wearing sunglasses and drinking a large coffee. She had been up till four am with James and then could not sleep in anticipation of her upcoming flight. A recording crew from Unity Network began to set up and record the final moments before the crew departed and briefly interviewed the members as they gathered to depart. In all the preparatory activity no one saw the little girl who snuck around to the back of the hangar and stole on board the space ship. The door had been left open and she climbed inside hiding at the far end of the ship behind the seating area. She wrapped herself in a worn, blue blanket and as her little heart pounded she hoped that she would not be discovered.

Lisa heard footsteps approaching as Gregory and his crew assembled on board the craft. As the camera crew recorded their take off Destiny Blue whizzed out of the hangar and in a flash disappeared out of Earth's orbit. Once the coordinates were set for B54232 the crew relaxed and settled in for the journey. After about seven hours of travel Tim heard a noise coming from behind his seat. "Gregory is there some unsecured cargo back there?" he asked.

"No, not that I'm aware of," he replied.

The sounds continued and finally Tim unfastened his restraint and peered behind his seat. In disbelief he peered into the face of a little girl who looked back at him with some anxiety. "Oh my god!" he exclaimed.

"What?" Said Diana.

"There is a child back here," he said as he lifted her out of her hiding place.

The entire crew looked back and Julio realized that the child Tim held was his daughter. "Oh no," he said. "Lisa what have you done? You are not supposed to be here!"

"I know daddy, I'm sorry but the children on the shore are waiting for me. I dreamed about them again last night," she said through tears that had started to form in the corners of her eyes.

Julio grabbed his daughter and embraced her. "I'm sorry about this everyone. We should turn back."

"No! It's OK I left a note for nana so she wouldn't worry. Please let me go with you. I promise I won't be any trouble. I have my blanket and I can just stay where I was hiding."

"If we turn back now we loose a whole day," said Diana.

"We can't let her stay," said Tim

"Actually the risk to her life is no greater than to her father. I have an extra compact seat that I can unfold for her and that way she will be properly restrained. As long as we don't broadcast her presence to the world we can continue on our journey and she will be safe. There is plenty of food and water in our supply bin," said Gregory. Everyone was surprised at his suggestion but what he said did make some sense and would save them the loss of time and energy in having to turn around. Reluctantly they agreed to allow Lisa to stay and continue the journey. Gregory set up her seat and fastened her in. "You will be much more comfortable now, little miss. Surely you are the youngest cosmonaut ever to fly to another galaxy," he said.

She merely smiled and said, "thank you."

The rest of the journey went smoothly and Lisa was an exceptionally quiet and patient voyager at the age of ten. Mesmerized by the navigation system's display of the various sectors of space they traveled through she slept intermittently and her dreams intensified showing her more of the planet that they would be arriving at soon. To say the least the crew was astounded at the level of detail this little girl provided about the world they would be arriving at shortly and everyone was curious to see if what she relayed to them was accurate.

Finally, they reached the Rose Nebula and slowed the craft to observe the most breathtaking cosmic manifestation that they had ever seen. Passing through deep pink gaseous clouds illuminated by hundreds of stars everyone became quiet and took in the beauty created in this remote place. They approached their destination and circled the planet once then moving towards the landing coordinates. Destiny Blue touched down on a landing platform in at the top of a populated area which exploded with the most exotic natural plant life that proliferated between oblong light colored and bronze building structures. When the crew exited the ship they saw beautiful, blue skinned people with light colored eyes below in what appeared to be a market place. As they descended the steps the locals smiled and looked at them with some curiosity but not total surprise. Clearly they were accustomed to receiving visitors. A woman approached Lisa and placed a scarlet colored flower garland with blue leaves around her head. Lisa smiled at her thinking that she was the most beautiful lady she had ever seen. A rose color sun shone creating a pink atmosphere which reflected off the buildings casting rich warmth over them. Much of what everyone witnessed was as Lisa had described with uncanny accuracy.

"Might as well explore a bit," said Gregory.

They toured the market place and sampled some of the local foods. Diana was given a beautiful shawl made of a colorful fabric resembling silk that she draped around her waist sarong style. Some of the men were approached and given single flowers that were triple the size of anything found on Earth and smelled indescribably heavenly. The women were gorgeous and the crew had to contain themselves not to stare too obviously. After finishing their explorations a man approached Diana and Lisa and squeezed both their hands. "Danata lasitave," he said and led them away from the market.

"Where is he taking you?" Asked Julio.

"Who knows, daddy come and see," said Lisa.

The tall blue skinned man led them down a series of bronze steps coated with a substance that resembled lapis lazuli. At the bottom a spectacular ocean front spanning miles greeted them and Lisa suddenly became animated and said, "this is the place I told you about form my dreams." She let go of the man's hand and ran down the sandy beach and removing her shoes stood in the water. What resembled cabanas with rounded, silken awnings spanned some of the beach front where beverages were sold and places of shade were provided. The crew began to sweat in their suits and retreated to one of the cabanas where they were offered cold drinks. They had no local currency and offered some of their food supplies in return which the locals did not seem very interested in. They merely smiled and served them drinks not concerned about repayment. Lisa ventured a bit further down the beach with her father in tow. He had never seen her so excited.

A few yards away they saw a group of children who had constructed a huge structure from wet sand. A little girl about Lisa's age turned and looked at her. Lisa stopped and her eyes grew wide, she noticed that the girl wore a beautiful necklace made of seashells like in her dream. She approached the other girl and they stood looking at each other. Without a word the child took her hand and led her into the sand enclosure they had built. Julio stood and watched as tears formed in his eyes. He knew that these were the children his daughter had dreamed about many nights and that far on the other side of their universe his child finally met her long distance playmates. He sat and watched them interact till one of the young boys touched him on the shoulder and pointed. Julio looked and saw the air to the side of him coagulate into swirling mist and grow in density. The mist began to part and to his surprise he realized he was looking into CIV headquarters. He called the rest of the crew to join him and they all stared into the manifested connection back to their world. They did not realize at the time that they were transmitting directly to the Unity Network courtesy of the Shining Ones who were aware of their journey. This planet was one of the worlds that were connected through an intergalactic grid to the network of other star systems of enlightened beings. This matrix was the great cosmic mind that one day Earth's technology would become connected to and what the crew was experiencing was a preview of that accomplishment. The IM's waved and saw everything that the crew had experienced thus far transmitted over the network holographically.

As the transmission continued Chantal and Zain appeared through the portal and smiled at Julio and the rest. They also appeared over Unity Network back on Earth and Chantal waved to her friends. Across space time and from far corners of creation hearts and minds merged in a celebratory moment of achievement. Even greater things would evolve for all beings created equal and loved eternally by the mysterious, awesome Source that gives life and inspiration to all who desire it.

Printed in the United States
74019LV00003B/103-186

9 781424 131334